Also by Pauls Toutonghi

Red Weather

Evel Knievel Days

Evel Knievel Days

A NOVEL

Pauls Toutonghi

Crown Publishers
New York

Copyright © 2012 by Pauls Toutonghi

All rights reserved.
Published in the United States by Crown Publishers, an imprint of the Crown Publishing Group, a division of Random House, Inc., New York.
www.crownpublishing.com

CROWN and the Crown colophon are registered trademarks of Random House, Inc.

Library of Congress Cataloging-in-Publication Data

Toutonghi, Pauls.
    Evel Knievel days : a novel / Pauls Toutonghi. — 1st ed.
        p. cm.
    1. Egyptian Americans—Fiction.   I. Title.
    PS3620.O92E94 2012
    813'.6—dc23   2011044748

ISBN 978-0-307-38215-3
eISBN 978-0-307-95572-2

Printed in the United States of America

Text design by Philip Mazzone
Jacket design by Brian Rea
Jacket illustration by Brian Rea

10 9 8 7 6 5 4 3 2 1

First Edition

For Jay Parini and Robert Buckeye

Evel Knievel Days

Prologue

Everyone knows that the Ancient Egyptians mummified their dead. But not everyone knows about the demon god Ammit— the demon god who guarded the Egyptian gateway to paradise. Ammit, the Eater of Hearts. Ammit, the Devourer of Souls. Part crocodile, part lion, part hippopotamus.

If an Egyptian priest mummified your body three thousand years ago, then he carved out your intestines and your lungs and your stomach and your liver. He put each organ in a limestone pot and stacked these pots beside your sarcophagus, beside a copy of your family's *Book of the Dead*—the book of spells and stories and illustrations and recipes that was your inheritance. Then he painted your body with resin, inside and out, as a preservative. Then he wrapped you in linen. But he left your heart in place.

The Egyptians believed that your heart was the repository of your soul. It needed to be preserved intact, so that your soul and your body could transform into *akh*, the part of you that was eternal, that rose up and joined the stars in the night sky. But in order to rise, your heart had to be nearly weightless. And what made your heart heavy? Sin. So when a person came to Ammit, she weighed your heart against a feather. If you'd lived a good life, then your heart would be light—light as a feather.

But if you'd sinned, then Ammit would eat your heart. She would devour it whole and you'd spend eternity there, with her, in torment. Which, of course, brings up the question: How would she season it? The answer, of course, is: Any way she wanted to. And so I have to wonder, what would *my* heart be like on her scale? Would it float up? Or would it sink down and spend eternity in a burning darkness? This is a concern for me. Because let's face it, if Ammit is eating raw human heart flesh—then the catering in her realm is probably subpar.

Part I

If you live long enough with your mother,
you will learn to cook.

—John Hawkes, *The Lime Twig*

per made the fortune of William Andrews Clark, it also made the fortune of this little city in Montana.

While the inhabitants of Butte used to call it "The Richest Hill on Earth," they also called it "The Perch of the Devil." Nitroglycerine, dynamite, pneumatic drilling: The thunder of explosives rolled down from the mine shafts all day long. Arsenic and sulfur and cadmium poured from the mouths of the Anaconda smelters. If cows grazed in Butte, their teeth turned a soft gold color.

At the museum where I worked, I often told tourists about the early settlers near the Anaconda mine. There was so much arsenic in the drinking water that Butte's residents grew dependent on it. Without the arsenic, they'd get headaches and nausea and splintering stomach cramps. Copper made them rich, but it also poisoned them.

That's where my story starts. With an invisible genetic heritage, with a mutation of the ATP7B gene, with an *autosomal recessive genetic disorder* called Wilson's disease. Both of my maternal grandparents were carriers. And so my mother's body could never properly absorb copper. Without medication, copper would build up in her soft tissues, in her liver and her kidneys and her eyes and her brain. She took an army of pastel pharmaceuticals daily; she swallowed a rainbow of cuprimine and cyprine and zinc acetate. Children raised in evangelical households can quote Matthew, Mark, Luke, and John. I know whole sections of *The Merck Manual* by heart.

There were some other aspects of my childhood that were perhaps unusual. Occasionally, my mother would forget a pill and spend a day in bed. Or I'd come home and find her sitting on the roof. "What," I'd yell, "are you doing up there?" She'd answer: "Nothing, darling," her voice as soft and gentle as the coo of a dove. Or: "I'm counting the stars." Or: "I think I can see Idaho from here."

I'd race inside to sort through the medication and determine what she was missing. Then I'd shimmy out onto the roof, carrying a glass of water and a tiny green tablet. Two hours later, she'd be downstairs, cooking or reading a book in front of the fireplace.

The list of foods my mother couldn't eat was a long one: shellfish, mushrooms, nuts, chocolate, dried fruit, dried peas, dried beans, bran, avocados. But her longings, her longings were persistent. "Just one Twix," she'd say, staring at the candy aisle in Safeway. "Please. It won't kill me, I promise." I'd push the cart forward, nine years old and barely tall enough to reach the handle, my mother trailing behind me, begging for a 3 Musketeers.

This did create some problems for a caterer (as you might imagine). Not only was I her custodian, I was also her chief taster—a fact that she reinforced with a frequent and impressive ardor. She'd knock on the doors of friends' houses, or track me down at the park, or appear in the second inning of my Little League baseball games. Once, when I was in eleventh grade, she had me summoned to the principal's office. "We're very sorry, son," Principal Gordon said. "But your great-uncle has passed away. Your mother's outside waiting to take you home." Certainly she was, sitting behind the wheel of our big white Saqr Catering van. I skulked in through the passenger's-side door, staring at the carpet as we made our way off of school grounds and into traffic.

"You're unbelievable," I said. "No one else's mother acts like this."

She looked straight ahead, her face expressionless, her hands on the wheel. For a moment—even though I didn't have a great-uncle—I was worried.

"It's the *shuk shuka*," she finally said. "It's just not right. I can feel it."

I buried my head in my hands. "Jesus," I said. "Nobody's going to notice, Mom. Everybody loves your cooking. You can't just pull me out of school in the middle of the day."

She looked at me earnestly, her face a mixture of regret and anxiety. "I know, sweetheart, I know," she said, and paused. "By God, I know how very much I'm damaging you even as I speak. But listen, darling. Could you just taste it and help me out?"

One fact. One instructive, inelegant fact. My mother's husband, my father, my unknown and distant father, my mockery of that word *father*, of the term, as it's understood by almost everyone—my satellite, my hidden galaxy, my empty suitcase, my vacant motel room—her *husband* deserted us when I was three. He taught her how to cook his country's food, the lamb and beef and chicken and pork dishes of his Coptic Christian parents and grandparents and great-grandparents. And then: vanished, leaving her with his foods and traditions, a hundred thousand dollars in gambling debts, and a three-year-old boy as copper as a penny. He also left her his onions. To be specific: his Egyptian walking onions.

Allium proliferum. Bulbous, sprawling, tentacular plants that filled the yard. Plants with dozens of long tendrils, with fragile purple flowers and clusters of small fruit. He planted them in the months before I was born. After he left us, after he disappeared one morning with the coffee still warm in the coffeepot, after he returned to Egypt on a one-way business-class ticket, my mother was perpetually trying to massacre his plants.

She tried digging. She tried Roundup. She tried garden shears. But Egyptian walking onions are true to their name: They walk, season after season, across your garden. They travel through the air, in seeds, and beneath the ground, in roots. They flourish. They burrow deep. They are tenacious. She never could exterminate them completely. After three or four years, she gave up. Nothing could be done. The onions had won a decisive victory. Like a field general bidding goodbye to a lost battlefield, my mother leaned against the porch and sighed. "Even Braveheart knew when he was beat," she said.

"They eviscerated him in a public square," I said.

She threw her shovel underneath the porch.

"My fault," she said. "Bad example."

So, I was surprised one morning when I heard a polite, persistent knocking on my bedroom door. I rolled over. The doorknob turned, the door swung open, and my mother appeared, holding a small dirt-caked garden trowel.

"Rise and shine," she said.

She looked peculiar, backlit by the light in the hallway. Her cheeks were red and puffy.

"It's so early," I said. I peered at the digital clock on my bedside table. Seven-fifteen A.M. It was Thursday, July 26, 2008.

Now, over two years later, I've come to imagine this moment, this glance at the clock, as the moment when the action of the story, of my story, started to slip out of my grasp—when it stretched and turned and rose out of my cupped palms like smoke, like escaping birdsong. There's an old Egyptian saying: *A birdsong is a prediction.* I could hear the chorus of sparrows through the open window.

"What are you doing?" I asked. It was the mildest form of the question that I could imagine. It was also the most civil. "Have you taken your pills?" I added.

"I have a surprise for you," she said, "in the front yard."

It sounded ominous. She pulled me out of bed. I would help her, of course, but I had a few small tasks I had to complete before I could begin my day. It's not that I had a problem; I was totally normal. It's simply that I needed to arrange the covers of the bed at a certain angle, with just over six inches of white folded back above the top sheet. And then I had to touch all four walls of the room— north, south, east, and west. And then I had to open the door twice, only twice, and look each time into the hallway, while imagining in my head the phrase *all clear.* Then—only then—I could set about the tasks at hand. Some might call this obsessive-compulsive. I'd call it a friendly (gentle) attention to detail. To painstaking detail. Exact detail. Precise and perfect detail.

This was my room. It was my domain, my blessed plot, my provincial kingdom. Rows of books crowded every available shelf. I'd organized them by color. Actually, the system was a little more complicated than that. I'd sorted them by color within discipline, and by alphabetical ranking within discipline. This was my tertiary organizational structure. I had books on biology, chemistry, calculus, engineering. I had encyclopedias and Bibles. I had the Great Books, the classics of world religious thinking, of philosophy and poetry and fiction. I also had an entire section of biographies of Marion Morrison, the man who became John Wayne. I liked to start each day with a Wayne aphorism. For example, this morning I read: *Talk low, talk slow, and don't say too much. Excellent*, I thought. Simply excellent advice.

My mother waited for me to finish my rituals, her countenance cast into a disapproving frown. "Hurry," she said. "It's almost seven-thirty."

"And? What's so important about seven-thirty?"

She frowned more deeply. "It's a minute before seven-thirty-one," she said.

Once I was ready, she ushered me out into the hallway, down the stairs, and through the front door. We stood on the porch, looking out over the garden. We'd never, as long as I could remember, had a yard like anyone else's in Butte. No grass, no gleaming metallic globe on a pedestal, no ceramic creatures of any sort, no cars on blocks. Instead, we had an organic vegetable garden. One that was intertwined by *allium proliferum*, sure, but a vegetable garden nonetheless. Now it looked like a scene of post-apocalyptic devastation. She'd already stripped part of the yard of its vegetation. She was working her way inward, leaving a blasted path of dark black topsoil wherever she went.

"Jesus," I said.

She nodded. "I've been out here since four," she said. "It's time we finished them off."

"Finished what off?" I said.

"Them," she said, gesturing toward the dirt.

"What are you talking about?"

"The onions," she said. "It's time we got rid of these damned Egyptian onions."

My mother hunched down and started hacking at the base of a root. I worried that she was unmedicated, that her liver was rattling to a halt, even as she raised the trowel above her shoulder. I inched toward the subject. "How are you feeling this morning, Mom?"

"Perfect," she said.

"Are you sure you don't need your pills?" I said. "I'll just run and get them."

She turned her face toward mine and stared at me. She seemed on the edge of tears. "It's not my pills," she said. "I've taken them all. Please, just help."

I fell in line beside her. Within minutes, the knees of my jeans bore broad black mud stains—stains that soaked deep into the light blue denim. The smell of dirt and flayed vegetation drifted up and over me. I dug and cleared and labored beneath a hostile sun. I searched my mind for some kind of anniversary, for some comment or news article or scrap of conversation that I'd heard, something that could have initiated this frenzy. Garden care has always seemed to me like useless botanicide. Why remove the weeds when the weeds will just return?

"What about the eggplant?" I said. We'd spent four years growing the eggplant vines, nurturing them from tiny leafy creatures into a sprawling, confident mass. "Shouldn't we save the eggplant?"

"We'll grow a new one," my mother said.

"What about the asparagus?" I said.

"It's curtains for the asparagus," she said. "And don't ask so many questions," she added. "Just get to work. We're going to strip it all. Strip, blast, clear." She straightened her back and wiped sweat from her muddy forehead, inhaling deeply. "Smell that dirt," she said. "That's the odor of success."

I followed the onion roots, working from the surface down deep into the clay. I hacked and hacked with the tip of the shovel. Sweat poured down the sides of my spine. My socks felt like wet tourniquets. By ten o'clock it was ninety-seven blistering degrees.

Thunderclouds build and accumulate gradually; they stack and swell and layer up through the troposphere. Tornadoes form invisibly deep within the storm; the surface is beautiful, but lightning and hail incubate beneath it. That is to say, after nearly two and a half hours of essentially silent work, my mother started to tremble, to tremble slightly and then to shake, to shake, and then, muffling her face with her yellow leather work glove, to cry. She sobbed. She sank down on her knees in a swath of ground that she'd defoliated. I walked over and stood behind her. I rested my hand on her back, unsure what, if anything, I could say. "If you want to tell me what's going on," I said, "I can listen." I bent over and pressed my cheek against hers.

"It's okay," she said.

"I took a psychology course last quarter from the University of Phoenix," I said. "I mean, it was abnormal psych, but still."

My mother smiled. She sighed and blew her nose on her sleeve. After a few minutes the crying subsided. She stood up, unsteady.

"I'll make us lunch," she said, and she walked into the house. I was left there in the yard, poised with the shovel, mud soaking my jeans. I thought of ten different specific things I could have done. But I didn't. I just stood there and let the hot air continue to descend and wrap around me. I let it settle.

See: I think that Tolstoy was wrong. Unhappy families are all alike. They're all alike in this moment—in this pause before something happens, in the pause before someone reacts. And that pause: It can last seconds or minutes or days or months or years.

Though it would be difficult to verify, I do believe that we lived as close as anyone else in America to an EPA Superfund site. One of the largest abandoned open-air strip mines in the world—the Berkeley Pit—was under a mile away. The pit was gigantic. And it was filling with water. It had more arsenic and zinc and cadmium and sulfuric acid than any other body of water in the world. "Who needs a hot tub," my mom used to say, "when you've got a bubbling toxic lake?"

Drive up Park, go right on Wyoming, then left on Mercury. Head for the end of the block, for the last house before the road hits the EPA fencing, a light blue Victorian that's leaning slightly to one side. That was us. Home sweet home. The Loving Shambles, as I liked to call it.

My great-great-grandfather owned most of the hill, but in the early 1920s, production diminished in the mines. The smelters fell silent. He leased out his land, building old-style rooming houses where the ground was most scarred. Finntown sprang up there. On the blasted slope of a blasted hill, on the once-richest slope of the once-richest hill on earth, the Helsinki Bar, St. Urho's Tavern, the Old Finn Hall, the Vike: all of them serving Karhu beer and thin, buttery pancakes with loganberry jam. By the time I was born, in 1985, most of that was gone. By 2008 the only relic of Finntown, as far as I could tell, was the faded blue-and-white stencil of the Finnish flag on the north wall of a nearby warehouse. Every year the stencil dimmed a little more.

Once my mother went inside, I eased up. I worked for another hour. I spent sixty more minutes hacking through the loamy dirt. I could smell garlic sizzling in the kitchen. Tired and aching and sweaty, I took the last of the onions over to the yard waste bin. I looked down at the row of plastic containers. And that's when I found it: a fat yellow envelope mixed in with the recycling, its corrugated edges shining with sticky laminate. I pulled it out and set the envelope on top of the bins.

FOR AMY, it read.

No postage, no address, no other identifying marks. But what I discovered inside was astonishing: a copper bracelet, imbued with a deep and roseate light.

Copper is probably the oldest decorative metal in the world. Ancient Egyptians employed copper to ornament both themselves and their corpses, using it as a bartering tool in this life and the next. The Romans adorned their soldiers with copper flourishes. It is a primitive, powerful, elemental substance. I have to admit: It does make a beautiful, spooky bracelet.

Especially if the bracelet seems to consist of snakes, intertwined snakes, as this one did upon further inspection. Where was the rest of its packaging? I dug through the recycling and then the garbage. I overturned coffee grounds and eggshells and newspapers and empty cans. There were no bigger envelopes, no clues whatsoever to how the bracelet might have arrived at our house. It was a mystery, a talisman from some other time and place. Which time and which place, however, I didn't know.

I walked inside. I headed straight for the kitchen and tossed the bracelet down on the kitchen table. It skittered atop the scarred oak veneer, rolling end over end and coming to rest near the salt and pepper shakers.

"Mom," I said. She was standing at the stove, her back turned to me. "What is this?"

"What is what, darling?" She turned around. She frowned.

"This," I said, pointing at the object on the table. "It was in the trash."

My mother shook her head. "I have no idea what you're talking about," she said.

"The bracelet," I said. I picked it up and walked over and showed it to her. "I found it in an envelope that said, 'For Amy.'"

"Very funny," she said. She brushed a strand of her gray-brown hair out of her face. From her vantage point, she gave the bracelet a cursory inspection. "I've never seen it before in my life," she said, handing it back. "It's ugly."

"No, it's not," I said. "It's beautiful."

"It looks like a prize from a carnival game."

"The curator in me," I said, "thinks it might be worth something."

"Well," my mother said, "this is one instance when the curator in you is wrong. It looks cheap," she added. "It was probably mass-produced in China."

"Nope," I said. "Handmade, without a doubt. And not recently, either. Come on, Mom. Level with me."

"I am level," she said. "Very level. Always level."

She'd turned back to the stove. The soup was simmering and roiling on the stovetop. She'd been in the kitchen for almost an hour now, cooking and listening to a cello sonata.

"Did you make a lot of progress in the yard?" she said.

"As much as I could," I said.

"Good," she said, without elaborating further. "Good."

She relaxed her back. I hadn't noticed how tense, how rigid, it had been before she relaxed it. My mother's posture has always been impeccable. It was strange to see it become momentarily even straighter.

"You seem nervous," I said.

She laughed. "Khosi," she said, "whatever would I have to be nervous about?" She turned off the burner and tapped the spoon on the edge of the pot. She pulled a ladle from the bin on top of the stove. "Here." She filled a bowl. "Eat."

Our emotional lives, I think, thrive in two places, two locations, two imaginaries. One is in the remembrance of things past. The second is in our dreams of the future, in the things we hope for, in the ways we imagine ourselves moving forward through time. Two imaginaries, and my mother skirted these places as best she could. So her emotional life was a mystery to me, except in fragments, in brief illuminations, in roadside flares that gave relief to a figure, or a single afternoon, or an idea from her past. One of these illuminations was cooking. Her chief heroism (and constancy), in fact, was dinner. Every single night, no matter how busy she was—no matter how badly she was coming apart—she cooked a meal. Despite her hatred for my father's onions, my mother could not let go of her love for his food.

Almost everything in the Loving Shambles seemed to break down, to lapse into dirt and disorder and disrepair. But not the cooking. She'd sit there at the table, watching me eat, chewing only on a piece of pita bread, looking at me, saying: "Too much cumin?" Or: "Too little salt?" Or: "The meat is tough? Come on, you can tell me, it's okay. It won't hurt my feelings." Or: "Just be honest. It's too spicy. You can tell me." Or: "The lentils are undercooked, dammit. I knew it. I knew the lentils were undercooked." *Roadside flare:* My mother prepared at least twenty different Egyptian dishes—*sambousek bi lahm, ful medames, omi houriya*—many of which she was really not supposed to eat.

And so—and so—standing there in the kitchen in my dirty clothes, I decided not to bother her anymore about the bracelet, whether or not she seemed to be hiding something. I walked quietly over and peered down into the pot. The viscous green soup continued steaming. The scent of the cooking moved through me. It saturated my tired muscles like a medicinal salve. I put the bracelet in my pocket. *Why not just keep it to myself for now?* I thought. *Why not just keep it like a secret?*

That afternoon I showered and combed my hair and rushed off to work. I kept the copper bracelet in my pocket and emptied my half-eaten bowl of soup into a big plastic thermos. My mother kissed me goodbye at the front door. "I've got an event at six," she said. "You're on your own for dinner." She added cryptically: "Be careful."

I drank more of the *mulukhiyya* and walked through the blossoming heat. I wanted to confer with Natasha Mariner. Natasha was, without doubt, my best friend in Butte. I'd known her since we were three feet tall. She'd gone to elementary and middle school with me. We were both Butte High Bulldogs. That, of course, is the junction where our paths diverged. While she took a scholarship to the University of Montana, in Missoula, where she majored in political science, I stayed home. I read and read and read—but on my own, taking dozens of online classes from ITT Tech and Strayer University and the University of Phoenix, working at the museum thirty hours a week. I was a card-carrying member of MENSA, but the problem was this: I hated leaving Butte. Butte was home. Butte was comfort. Butte was order.

Now Natasha was working part-time in Helena, working as a clerk for Republican State Senator Timothy Crenshaw. I was worried that the job was eroding her excellent liberal sensibilities. Natasha maintained that it was a tool, a means to an end, a line on her résumé. She'd illustrated this point by applying to jobs with liberal think tanks and nonprofits across the country. Just recently, the unthinkable had happened: She'd been offered an entry-level job by the Nature Conservancy—in Washington, D.C. I had a panic attack as soon as I heard the news. To make matters worse, her longtime boyfriend, Calvin Stuckey, had gotten into Georgetown Law in

September. It seemed all but certain, the impending move across the country, three thousand miles from western Montana's most famous half-Egyptian shut-in (me).

It was a nice summer afternoon, despite the heat. Butte isn't a pretty town; it will never make a roster of the most picturesque cities in America. It's stark and dusty and brown, but I still love it, love it for precisely this reason. I headed down Main Street, past Wells Fargo and the old Leggett Hotel. The wind that came in off the eastern plains was warm and dry. A man in a seersucker shirt tipped his Billings Mustangs baseball cap as I passed him on West Granite. I walked past the Berkeley Pit Yacht Club. The Yacht Club—or the Pit Yacht Club, or Berkeley Yacht Club, or Berkeley Yacht Club Manor—was what Natasha and I called Chuck's, the bar closest to my house. It was an honest-to-God dive bar, one with Merle Haggard on the jukebox and a sawdust floor. We once asked the bartender-owner, Chuck Wilson, why he opted for the sawdust. He took a long time to answer, cleaning a series of pint glasses with jets of hot water, wiping their rims with a towel.

"Cheaper than carpet," he finally said. "And it soaks up the blood when there's a bar fight."

Since I'd turned twenty-one, the Yacht Club had become my second home. I now knew every word to "Swinging Doors" and "Tonight the Bottle Let Me Down." There was something comforting in the neon of that jukebox, in the way the cigarette smoke hung in the air, collecting above the pool table, so thick that it was almost creamy. There was something comforting in the order of the bottles of beer, cheap beer like Miller and Michelob and Iron City and Bud, always appearing with the exact same skin of condensation, always arriving cold and identical and crisp. They also had off-track betting, which I'd developed a fondness for. I loved the thrill of watching the races on the monitors located in the bar's back room, a room that always smelled of sweet cigars.

A street scene in downtown Butte? Imagine a ghost town, a Wild West ghost town from a movie with John Wayne, *The Searchers*, say, or *The Cowboys*. Now add eighty years and five stories and a few acres of cement. The streets of downtown have a certain cheerful privacy to them, especially in summer. But whenever I walk anywhere, I expect a tumbleweed to roll through and catch on a stop sign.

The names of the streets themselves tell so much of the story. They can barely be believed: Copper Street, Quartz Street, Granite Street, Mercury Street, Silver Street, Agate Street, Gold Street, Aluminum Street, Platinum Street, Porphyry Street, and my personal favorite, Clear Grit Terrace. What is porphyry? Why, it's a large-grained igneous rock, purple and lovely and common in the Bitterroot Mountains. Only Butte, Montana, would have a street named after it. Butte was a city made by industrialists, by believers in industry. The streets were orderly and straight and wide. When the city's forefathers needed a railroad, they built it right through town. There was no doubt which god the city plan served: the god of commerce, the god of industrial production. I arrived at the Copper King Mansion at 12:31, one minute late. A billboard advertising EVEL KNIEVEL DAYS had been rigged right beside the entrance to the house. I hated being late, even by seconds.

The history of this mansion is something on which, God help me, I could speculate endlessly. I know the names of the masons, many of them summoned from Bavaria for their skill with an awl. I know the names of the Russian hardwoods (Manchurian fir and Mongolian oak and iron birch and red pine) that W. F. Beall & Company imported for the numerous parquet floors. I know where the stained glass for the bay windows was handblown (Turin, Italy) and how many nails were used in the spiral staircase in the kitchen (none, trick question). It took four years and three hundred thousand dollars to construct at a time when the average miner's salary was under a thousand a year.

The layout of the mansion was straightforward. Staterooms on the first floor, bedrooms on the second floor, a grand ballroom (with a full organ) on the third. We had a little gift shop and a front desk for the guides and an employee break room. The exhibits were scattered throughout the house. Piece by piece, they told the history of the state, starting with the thousands of years of indigenous tribal life—the generations upon generations of Assiniboine and Blackfeet and Crow and A'aninin and Kootenai and Salish and Shoshoni and Sioux who called Montana home. A whole wing of the museum was devoted to Lewis and Clark, who entered the Bitterroot Valley on September 4, 1805, and changed its landscape forever.

I darted through the employee entrance and grabbed my name tag from the peg by the door.

KHOSI SAQR

it read.

MUSEUM GUIDE

I stood behind the cashier's desk in the lobby and put on my most winning smile.

I wonder sometimes if my parents chose my name to *provoke* playground teasing. In Arabic, Khosi means *lion*. And Saqr? Saqr means *falcon*. Few kids on the elementary school playground, however, spoke fluent Arabic. So they made fun of both of my names with an impressive and dedicated ardor. They called me "Hozey" and "Cozy" and, when they were a bit older, "Blow Me." But also "Sucker" and "Fucker" and, my personal favorite, "Puker." Sometimes I thought of introducing myself like this at parties: "Blow Me Puker," I'd say upon shaking hands. "So nice to meet you."

This is what it feels like to be half of something: You're never truly anything. You never fit in anywhere. I doubt that I'll ever be quite at ease in America—anywhere other than in my museum. Every time I introduced myself, every class I attended, every time I made a dinner reservation over the phone, I cringed. And so I pretended: "Table for two? Certainly, sir. Under what name?" "Sam Jones," I said, "Sam Jones."

Margaret Vogel, my manager, walked into the room. Margaret Vogel was a matronly old woman who tucked her hair into an imperious gray bun and insisted that all five of her staff members call her Ms. Vogel. She wore her thick bifocals on a practical leather cord. She ate hard-boiled eggs for lunch. She had the strange habit of taking candid Polaroids of her employees. You'd be hard at work, and suddenly, a flash would burst into your peripheral vision. You'd turn toward it and there'd be Ms. Vogel, shaking the photograph vigorously. "Gotcha!" she'd say, and cackle. Rumor had it that she lived with Alice B. Toklas for several months in Paris in the 1960s, and that she'd reserved a plot in the Père Lachaise not far from the final resting place of Gertrude Stein. One of the other guides, Tom Creighton, swore that Ms. Vogel had given him Toklas's secret recipe for hashish crème brûlée. "She made me promise not to show it to anyone," he said, "or I'd be deeply sorry."

Whatever the case, Ms. Vogel kept a watch on a chain in her hip pocket, and presently, she consulted it. She raised an eyebrow. "Seventy-nine seconds late," she said.

"Seventy-two," I said. "Once I'm in the door, I'm on company time."

"You're slipping, Khosi," she said.

I was legendary at the museum for my need for order. Walk through the front door of the Loving Shambles and the reasons behind this need would be immediately obvious. At the mansion, I kept my uniform perfectly ironed and clean, my name tag straight, my workspace free of all debris. In my eight years at the mansion, my register had never been unbalanced at the end of the day.

Ms. Vogel turned and began ascending the main staircase. Her office was on the second floor. It overlooked the entire entryway; its exterior wall was composed of massive wrought-iron French doors. On her way up there, she paused and turned back to me. "Listen," she said, one hand on the red pine banister, "I need you to cover for Carlton tomorrow night. A party for Anaconda Savings Bank. Early evening. Six P.M."

The Copper King Mansion did a significant business as a corporate retreat. We rented out the interior rooms and had our own on-staff cook. Businesses used the grand ballroom to woo their most desirable clients; CEOs rented the home for wedding anniversaries and birthdays and a range of different functions.

"Tomorrow?" I said.

"Yes," Ms. Vogel said. "Do you want the hours or not?"

I did want the hours. They distracted me from my current situation. My voracious online learning had just made me conscious of the ways in which I'd become the *subaltern*. "The history of the American service industry," I could tell anyone who'd listen, "is one of wage slavery and exploitation of the proletariat's labor power." For some reason, not that many people would listen.

But tomorrow was also the second night of Evel Knievel Days— America's only festival entirely devoted to motorcycle daredevils. It was the night of the loudest parade imaginable, an all-purpose, take-all-comers affair that invariably stretched for miles and involved at least one near-catastrophic accident. As far as people-watching opportunities went, Evel Knievel Days was Montana's zenith. I couldn't imagine anything topping this in Wyoming or Idaho or Washington or Oregon, either (California was an entirely different matter). And yet: I did want the hours.

"Sure," I said. "I'm game." Ms. Vogel nodded and disappeared into her office. There were only a few minutes left before the inaugural tour of the day.

Outside, I heard the hydraulic hiss of that first tour bus. Around me rose the precision and order of the mansion, with its broad panels of wallpaper and its tastefully arranged western landscape paintings by William Keith and Charles Russell. The onslaught was about to begin. I could feel the house rattle as the driver downshifted and pulled slowly into the parking space closest to the mansion. The doors at the far end of the museum opened. I heard the sound of the patrons approaching. I prepared my face to meet the faces I would meet.

The first tourist walked through the main doors. He was a large man, and he was wearing a skintight T-shirt that said: DOES THIS SHIRT MAKE MY BASS LOOK FAT? The shirt was emblazoned with a cartoon of a corpulent and happy-looking fish.

"Nice bass," I said to the plus-sized gentleman, dying a little on the inside.

He seemed surprised. "You like it?" he said.

"Yeehaw," I answered.

The sarcasm in my voice was lost in the crush of tourists surging into the lobby. I sighed. Don't get me wrong. I loved my job. I loved the order and taxonomy of the museum, the way it could channel and organize history, give it a flowing narrative. I even loved the shape of museums, in general, and the geometric principle that organized them: the nested rectangle. That's what museums were, box inside of box inside of box. It was tremendously gratifying to think about. When I was twelve years old, my mother and I went to see the Joseph Cornell exhibit at the Seattle Art Museum. It would be my only trip out of Montana in the decade to come. Seattle terrified me. It was big and unruly and often uncontained in space. But Cornell's boxes? They were beautiful and precise and regimented. I was enraptured. Is it strange to say that nothing is as satisfying to me as a series of rectangles, each decreasing in size?

Despite my love of Cornell, I'd never seen his work in person again. I never really traveled after that. The idea of travel was too much to bear. I liked to drive into the hills around the city, but that was always with a return in mind, with a moment of homecoming that I could play out in my head to soothe my fears. Besides, after a lifetime of caring for my mother, could I trust her to be on her own, even for a little while?

Deep breath.

Inhale, exhale.

So: the tourists. The tourists could overwhelm me at first. I remembered my breathing exercises. And I smiled. "Welcome to Butte's Copper King Mansion," I called out in a loud voice. "Built by my great-great-grandfather in 1886." That always got their attention. I tried to project my voice to make it fill the lobby. "My great-great-grandfather William Andrews Clark was a miner. He dug millions of dollars' worth of copper from the hills surrounding Butte. He was a copper king, a second-generation Irish immigrant turned vest-wearing frontier industrialist. By the time he died, his fortune amounted to hundreds of millions of dollars . . ."

Facts, someone once said, are only half an empire. By the end of the day, my anxieties had dulled to a low hum in the background; I would see Natasha soon. It was the evening's last tour. The man in the gray wool overcoat stood at the edge of the crowd.

What destroys order and tidiness and a regimented worldview? In my case, a gray wool overcoat. It was, admittedly, somewhat difficult to miss. I was sweating in my plain cotton button-down. Beneath his coat, I imagined, he was broiling to perfection. He was tremendously handsome in the way that an older man can be handsome. He'd grayed well, with streaks of silver at his temples and a gruff near-white stubble across the planes of his cheeks. His sunglasses were expensive. Small and wiry, they perched on the bridge of his nose like a blackened praying mantis.

As the hour progressed, he eased closer to me. He appeared to be listening intently. He laughed at my bad jokes ("Question: What's the first thing a baby learns to say in Butte? Answer: It's mine!"), and he seemed genuinely moved by my account of the Speculator Mine fire. I spent a significant portion of the tour on the grisly 1917 murder of the labor organizer Frank Little. I told the story in all of its shocking and lurid detail: corrupt cops dragging Little through the streets of Butte behind a Ford truck, then stringing his flayed body from the trestle of a bridge on the outskirts of town.

Everyone had a strategy to get tips.

For me, it was concentrating on the lurid details, on the way the skin peeled off of Little's arms and legs, how vigilantes beat him savagely and castrated him and then hanged him. The deeper the horror, the more the wallets opened. Though guides did make a small hourly wage, most of our salary came from the tourists, the folks whose emotions we sought to arouse.

It had been a long and exhausting day. My feet ached. My voice was hoarse. At the end of the last tour, the stranger had asked an odd question. In a velvety accent of some kind, he'd said: "Are you happy, dear one, with the work you do here?"

Dear one? I thought. I smiled and brushed the question aside, saying yes, I was happy, certainly. "Never let them see you sweat," Tom liked to say. I didn't have the heart to tell him he was quoting a women's deodorant commercial.

When the day ended, when the last patron drifted away and I

had only thirty-two dollars in my pocket, I stumbled to the little break room behind the gift shop and collapsed into one of the over-size padded leather armchairs. It was eight-thirty. There were two of us closing the museum that night—Tom Creighton, Women's Deodorant Peddler, and me. Tom was a tall, skinny kid with a raft of pimples that didn't seem to diminish with the progression of time. He loved tequila. Typically, closing time was when he pulled his flask from his vest pocket and offered me a swig. When I was eighteen, the shot of tequila had seemed dramatic and exciting, an illicit end to a long and challenging day's work. Now it just burned. Today, however, Tom had forgotten the liquor.

"Some creepy dude's hanging around outside," he said.

"What do you mean?" I said.

"When I locked the front door," Tom said, "I saw him sort of scurry away, like he was trying to be inconspicuous."

"Maybe he's a stuntman for Evel Knievel Days?" I suggested. "I've seen a dozen Knievel impersonators walking around town."

"Whatever he is," Tom said, "I think he's a little bizarre."

"Let's call Ms. Vogel?" I said.

"Let's call Ms. Vogel," Tom said.

Ms. Vogel answered her cell phone, as always, on the first ring. Not surprisingly, her advice was cryptic. "You never know to what depths the human heart can sink," she said. And then: "But don't worry about it, it's probably nothing."

Not exactly comforted, we left the break room and headed over to the entrance. We peered through the beveled glass. Sure enough, the stranger was still there. He glanced over his shoulder as he walked away from the mansion. Possibly he was the worst thief in the history of burglary, incompetently casing the museum and arousing the suspicions of 100 percent of the employees. Tom and I watched as the man clambered into a brand-new silver Chevrolet. It gleamed like a shark's tooth in the dim light of the dusk.

He didn't start the engine. He just sat there, gazing into the distance.

"What's wrong with him?" Tom said.

"Maybe he's lonely," I said.

Loneliness—now, that was something I understood. I could identify with any number of lonely symbols. The silver-lit Bitterroot River, the flame of a candle, the solitary moon.

Tom frowned. "Maybe," he said. "Or maybe he's really, really baked. You know what I mean? Like, super-high."

"Your eloquence," I said, "is simply astonishing."

"Whatever, dude," Tom said. And then he mimicked my voice—or a cartoonish version of my voice, high-pitched and overly precise. "Astonishing," he said as he turned and walked toward the employee lounge. "Your eloquence is simply astonishing."

I didn't have the desire to stay at the mansion any longer. Maybe it was the stranger, or the fact that Tom was annoying me, or that my mother had awakened me at dawn to tear apart her garden. I felt the grooves of the bracelet in my pocket, the copper warming my hands.

"You okay closing up?" I said.

"Of course," Tom called from the other room. I heard him sit in the swivel chair and turn on the tiny break-room television.

I gathered up my things, the now-empty thermos, my sunglasses. This was my ritual. It was simple: First I double-checked all the numbers from the till in the gift shop. Then I arranged the pencils on the desktop in descending order according to length, with the shortest pencils closest to the edge of the desk, so they would be used most quickly. Then I sorted and aligned all of the paper clips in the holder, so the morning shift would have quick and easy access to paper-clip-clasping. I returned my name tag to its rightful place. I used a ruler to make sure its ends were straight. Now I had the all-clear. I could head back out into the world. Because of the lurker, I decided to go through the side door, just in case.

Even at nine o'clock, I had to adjust to the heat. It was a blast furnace. I felt my skin lose its tight, air-conditioned dryness. My whole body was abruptly coated in sweat. I inched down the alley and peered around the corner. The sedan was still there, but strangely, it was empty. Where had he gone? I considered running back inside. But I was probably overreacting. I was probably perfectly safe. I reached my hand into my pocket and took out the bracelet. The copper had been polished time and again over the years, and the snakes of the band had the deep, effulgent shine of well-worn metal. Driven by a strange impulse, I slipped it on my wrist. Coolness spread out along my arm and into the rest of my body. I left the mouth of the alley, reversing my course and heading in the other direction. There was, after all, more than one way to get home.

THE ALICE B. TOKLAS HASHISH CRÈME BRÛLÉE

As extracted from Tom Creighton following half a flask of tequila

Serves six

Ingredients

6 grams hashish

1 ½ cups whipping cream

6 large egg yolks

6 tablespoons regular sugar

1 vanilla bean, split lengthwise

6 teaspoons finely granulated sugar

Preparation

For hashish-infused whipping cream: Grind the hashish into a sticky paste. Slowly heat the cream, adding the hashish incrementally, until all the solid matter has dissolved. Do not boil. Remove from heat and cool in refrigerator.

[*Where* you obtain the hashish is none of my business. It's possible, you know, to make your own hashish. There are a few simple tools you need. However: I would like to note that hashish *is* an illegal narcotic. And no one is to blame but yourself if you are arrested while in its possession.]

For the brûlée: Preheat oven to 325°F. Whisk the yolks and regular sugar in a medium bowl. Scrape in the seeds from the vanilla bean.

Gradually whisk the hashish-infused cream into the sugar.

Divide mixture among 6 ramekins. Arrange dishes in a baking pan. Pour enough hot water into the pan to come halfway up the sides of the dishes. Bake for approximately 35–40 minutes until the custard is set. DO NOT OVERBAKE!

Overbaking is the death of brûlée. Simply and truly. The death of brûlée. Did you know brûlée could die? Yes, it can. By over-baking.

Remove the pan from the oven and remove custard cups from the water. Allow custards to cool before placing in the refrigerator. Chill overnight.

Two hours before serving: Preheat broiler. Sprinkle 1 teaspoon finely granulated sugar atop each custard. Place dishes on small baking sheet. Broil until sugar just starts to caramelize, rotating sheet for even browning, about 3 minutes.

Chill until caramelized sugar hardens.

Serve to a family gathering. Presto! The party will get much more interesting, believe me.

Two

The fact that Tom divulged the recipe for the hashish crème brûlée shouldn't be held against him. I'm sure he could sense that, as the son of a caterer, I'd put it to good use someday. I'd do Alice B. Toklas proud. I'd transform an awkward, stuffy family dinner into a beatific trip into the prismatic world of the mind.

God knows I endured enough stodgy family dinners at my grandparents' house when I was a kid. Their antipathy was of the enduring kind; they never forgave me for the circumstances of my birth. An hour after I was born, a nurse handed me to my grandmother.

"Dear God," she said, holding me at arm's length. "He's so brown."

It's true. I was. At birth, my Egyptian blood flared. Over time, I've grown even darker; at birth, I was the color of a paper bag. My broad nose jutted from my oblong face. A brace of black hair crowned my head. I looked, all in all, like a tiny Yasir Arafat.

This complexion made me hate—but also love—my heritage. *Hate* because I stood out, was separate, heterogeneous in a homogeneous state. *Love* because I stood out, was separate, heterogeneous in a homogeneous state. As for my grandmother, it's hard to say if anything improved from that first moment at the hospital bedside. I've often thought of my mother, three months pregnant, sitting on the edge of the newly made bed in Room 511 of Caesar's Palace. My father is downstairs in the lobby, playing roulette. She is also playing roulette, but roulette of a slightly different kind, as she picks up the telephone and dials the 406 area code. The phone rings only once before my grandmother answers. I can imagine the sweat along the grooves of my mother's palms, the white of her knuckles as she clasps the receiver.

By then I was embryonic and soft-shelled, although I already had arms and legs, distinct fingers and toes. It was, in a sense, my debut. It was my first appearance in the news of the world. An impending birth, a marriage in a Las Vegas wedding chapel. My grandfather locked himself in his home office and cried.

I thought about this story almost every time I passed what was my grandparents' opulent Victorian house on Granite Street. Though they both died when I was in middle school, I remembered birthdays and holidays at that home, all of them marked by stiff table linen and even stiffer conversation. The food exquisitely arranged on porcelain plates. A piece of silverware for every course. A butler.

As I walked home, I kept seeing flashes of silver in the corner of my eye, but I'd turn and look and there'd be nothing there, just a lamppost or a gray house or a set of passing headlights. The darkness settled around me. The night sky descended. I glanced from time to time at the stars. Nothing fills me with wonder, said Immanuel Kant, like the star-filled firmament above me and the moral law within me. Stuffy bastard, but—I have to admit—he did have a way with words.

As soon as I turned onto Mercury Street, I saw the porch light was out and the Loving Shambles was dark. Mom never remembered to turn off lights, and the sight of the house—a black shape against a black sky—made me uneasy. I checked the garage. The catering van was gone. I stopped momentarily to look at the garden, which resembled any number of photographs I'd seen of the lunar surface. It was pockmarked and cratered and bare and contributed to my general sense of unease.

"Dammit," I said. I unlocked the front door and tried several light switches before calling Big Sky Power. My mother was notoriously absentminded when it came to bill paying, which was one of the reasons I had to move out. She'd started relying on me to handle things. When I called, I discovered this: The bill was paid, and there were no local outages.

I rummaged through the drawer but couldn't find Mom's pill dispenser. This morning, when she'd insisted we purge the garden of the *allium proliferum*, I'd nearly demanded to count her medication. I'd relented because Mom hated me playing the role of enforcer almost as much as I hated playing it myself. I slammed the drawer shut, feeling uncertain what to do. Tonight she was catering the yearly Evel Knievel banquet/picnic—a picnic populated by some of the most eccentric characters in Butte. Nobody would notice if she acted a little strange. Five years ago I'd found her asleep on the living room floor the morning after the event, a set of Hawaiian leis around her neck, the car parked resolutely in the vegetable garden. Nobody would notice anything amiss with her tonight.

First things first: I needed electricity. I got a flashlight and went down into the basement. The stairs creaked. I illuminated the fuse box with my flashlight's conical glow. Sure enough: Someone had tripped the main breaker. I was about to reach for it when I heard a slow, creaking moan from the floorboards above me.

It is remarkable how quickly your home can go from safe to frightening, how simple darkness can make your imagination flare. The sound seemed to coalesce, to rise and shape itself into footsteps— solid, distinct footsteps. I flicked the switch to the right, and the house surged to life. The sound of it was large and immediate. A half-dozen appliances remembered their duties and their functions. I walked back over to the basement stairs. I ascended them slowly, step by step, straining to hear any sound from the rest of the house.

"Mom?" I called, my voice cracking a little.

"Boo," Natasha Mariner said, leaping out from the hallway.

I yelped and nearly fell backward. "Jesus Christ," I said. "Did you have to do that? I've had the strangest day."

"It just got better," she said. "I brought you beer." She hoisted a six-pack of Miller High Life. Only four of the bottles were intact. One was missing, and one was half-empty and clutched in her other hand. She was, it seemed, a little drunk. Natasha was drunk and I was jumpy. She opened a beer for me, and I launched into a narrative of my day, starting with the walking-onion massacre and continuing through the attentive stranger with the overcoat and the new-model Chevrolet. We eased our way through the house as I talked, heading toward the front porch.

me. It was a partial disclosure, a suggestion of form, an implication of the shape of her arm, the line of her rib cage, the gentle pressure of her breast. I noticed. I imagined. I couldn't help it. And then the chorus of "Heartaches by the Number" swooped out into the night:

Now I've got heartaches by the number,
Troubles by the score . . .

We started singing. We sang as loud as we could. We howled. We yodeled. Natasha practically bayed the last lines. "I love that song," she said, breathing hard.

"I think it's the greatest numerically oriented country-western song about heartbreak," I said.

Natasha laughed. "Don't go out on a limb," she said.

"I am!" I protested. "That's saying a lot. That's saying it's better than 'Lonesome 7-7203' by Hawkshaw Hawkins. And '1-800 Used to Be' by Lorrie Morgan. And 'I'm Gonna Sleep with One Eye Open' by Lester Flatt. And 'Sixteen Tons' by Tennessee Ernie Ford."

"That's not a song about heartbreak," Natasha said.

"Is, too."

"Is not."

"Is, too. It's a song about the heartbreak of laboring for a company store, about the way that capitalism enslaves the working class and yokes them to their own oppression."

"Thank you, Karl Marx," Natasha said. She tipped her beer all the way back, drinking it with alarming speed. With a theatrical flourish, she stood and walked out the door and to the edge of the porch. She pitched the empty bottle up in a shimmering arc through the sky. I heard it shatter on the driveway. This was my first clue that something wasn't right. Natasha wasn't the kind of person who came over to your house and smashed a bottle in your driveway. She was much drunker than I'd thought. She walked back over to me. She grabbed me and pulled me up to standing. The next song was playing, a fast-paced number, and she put her arm around my waist and clasped my right hand with her left. I saw that her nails had been chewed to bloody, ragged half-moons. She pulled my hips tight against hers.

"I can't believe you broke a bottle in my driveway," I said softly.

"Let's dance," Natasha said.

"I don't want to," I said.

"Come on," she said. "I'll lead. I'm a much better dancer than you, anyway."

I turned away from her. "I can't dance," I said. I walked to one end of the porch. In order for me to dance, several things would have to happen in a particular and precise order. I would have to, first of all, take off my shoes. Then I'd have to straighten my socks, pulling them taut against the surface of my legs, until they were precisely 50 percent of the way to my knee. This would give me an ideal surface for dancing, smooth and without wrinkles. Then the shoes would go on again. What a lengthy affair that would be. "I just can't," I added lamely.

"Fine," Natasha said. "Suit yourself." She turned and faced away from me, looking into the darkness of the Butte night. I went inside and retrieved the dustpan and the broom from the hall closet. I returned to the porch.

"Stargazing?" I said over my shoulder, walking toward the glass in the driveway.

"Come on, Khosi," Natasha said. "Let's drive somewhere. Let's go watch the freight trains up above the Berkeley Pit." When I didn't react, she said, "I know: Let's go downtown and—and do something you'll hate."

"Something I'll hate?" I said. I turned around and looked at her. She'd managed to procure the final beer and was in the process of opening it. She looked so beautiful, standing there in silhouette. Shadows gathered across her cheeks, illuminating the whites of her eyes, which shone with a watery intensity. Mosquitoes buzzed around us in a hungry cloud. "You mean," I said, "like break into the mansion and reorganize all the items in the gift shop?"

"No," Natasha said, brandishing her beer like a saber, "that's something you'd *love*. I'm talking about the exact opposite. Let's go to the American Motordrome Wall of Death. I think there's a midnight show."

I must have looked horrified. The American Motordrome Wall of Death was a new attraction at this year's festival. There had been a lot of coverage by the local media. Apparently, it involved gravity-defying motorcycles. It seemed entirely sickening. And letting Natasha loose on the world just now—I didn't know if that was an excellent idea.

"Come on, Khosi," she said. Then she did something that we did all the time. She quoted George Hamilton from *Evel Knievel: The Movie*, in which he played—you guessed it—Evel Knievel. "'I am the last gladiator in the new Rome,'" she exclaimed. "'I go into the

43

arena and I compete against destruction and I win. And next week I go out there and I do it again.'"

I just shook my head. "I don't know," I said. "I'm a little buzzed."

"Well," Natasha said, "Calvin did say he'd go with me tomorrow night."

I considered this. I liked Calvin, but he was sort of an impossible case: the valedictorian of the Class of 2007, a four-year starter on the Grizzlies' lacrosse team, a grin as wide and white as the Bitterroot Mountains. *Ruggedly handsome* would undersell his good looks. It was hard not to be jealous of Calvin Stuckey. He'd graduated a year ahead of her from Montana and had spent much of the past fourteen months building a sustainable agricultural infrastructure in rural Peru. Now law school. His image, his broad grin, popped into my imagination. I nodded. I adjusted my belt around my waist.

"I guess," I said, carefully placing the broom and the dustpan at the edge of the porch, "a little stunt-bike performance might be just what the doctor ordered."

"What doctor?" Natasha said, but already she was smiling and digging through her purse for her car keys; already she'd taken one step ahead of me down the driveway. We got into the Mercedes wagon. First we had a short argument about who should drive. Natasha maintained that she was fine, but then she said, "I'm not as think as you drunk," and it was clear that her argument was not airtight.

I settled in behind the wheel of the Mercedes. Not to sound like a car commercial, but there truly is something elementally magnificent about the Mercedes E350 wagon. This one was twenty years old. But the leather seats were still tense and pillowy, and the cabin cushioned the sound of the world—held you separate from it somehow. The road passed you by, incidental and distant, a soft murmur. The doors were solid. They slammed shut with a noise like the firing of artillery. Its cracked upholstery molded readily to the contour of my back.

This was by no means the first time I'd driven the Mercedes. I reached down into a tear that had been in the driver's seat for as long as I could remember. I worked my fingers into the foamy interior of the cushion. There, where it had been for years, was a tiny silver locket. Inside, in my shaky cursive, I'd written: *The Life and Times of Khosi Saqr, starring Khosi Saqr as himself.* I'd folded the note and snapped shut the locket and stowed it inside the seat when Natasha wasn't looking. It was my secret.

Natasha reached over and took my hand, the one that had been resting on the gearshift. She took it and put it in her lap. She looked down at my fingers, seemed to consider each of them one by one, pressing each of my knuckles between her fingertips. She rubbed my palm, tracing the creases that made their way from one side of it to the other. "It's your lifeline," she said.

"It is," I said. "And if you don't give it back, it will be drastically shortened by a nasty car accident."

We played an old Bill Monroe mix. It was good summer driving music, heavy on the bass and fiddle. Natasha said, "Do you ever think about what we'd be like as a couple?"

"Awful," I said quickly. "Just terrible."

"I disagree," Natasha said.

I conjured a few images of what I imagined would probably be a long and happy relationship.

"We know each other too well," I said. "There'd be no mystery."

"Every relationship's a mystery," Natasha said.

"Now you're sounding like my mother," I said, and Natasha laughed.

Ask anyone in the state to name Montana's most famous resident, dead or alive. They probably won't say William Andrews Clark, my copper magnate forefather, or Jeannette Rankin, the first woman to serve in the United States Congress. They won't choose some governor or actor or successful businessman. They'll invariably say one name: Robert Craig Knievel.

Knievel was born in Butte, and he worked in the Anaconda mine as a teenager. Legend has it that he got fired trying to stunt-jump a bulldozer. He hit the main power line, and Butte was in a blackout for days. Despite this (or maybe because of it), Knievel was Butte's favorite son, so when he got old and seemed to retire from jumping over canyons or rows of buses or through flaming hoops, the city decided to celebrate him with a festival.

And what a festival it had become. It lasted for seventy-two hours on the final weekend in July. It was a circus of motorcycle daredevils and demolition derbies; the cops cordoned off most of downtown and routed the majority of traffic through the suburbs. I'm really not making this up. It seems exaggerated or unlikely or impossible. But nothing galvanized this corner of Montana like stunt jumping and the destruction of machines. Think: a county fair with motor oil and a Hells Angel tattoo. The sound of the festival carried up and into the hills. At a distance, it sounded like muffled thunder. And this was the first festival since Knievel passed away in November. So it was going to be the biggest, loudest, fastest Evel Knievel Days yet.

We parked on Silver Street. Immediately, we saw that the city had been taken over by pirates. Or perhaps not pirates. But a cadre of bandanna-wearing fellows, many of whom had the sort of facial hair that you might associate with lengthy sea voyages. We walked along South Clark Street. There were motorcycles everywhere, an astonishing number of motorcycles. Row upon row of Harleys glistened on the edges of the sidewalks. There was a sense of danger in the air that was lessened somewhat by the massive billboard looming immediately in front of us as we came around the corner and entered Chester Steele Park:

WALL OF DEATH!

it read. Beneath that:

AN AMERICAN ORIGINAL!

The exclamation points only gave the "Wall of Death!" a friendly look, which I didn't imagine was the intended visual goal. We purchased tickets to the next show, the midnight show, the last of the day.

All around us, the detritus of a festival churned through the lamplit darkness. A wildly drunk man was standing on the corner and talking

47

to the stop sign. The ground was littered with Evel Knievel programs and a number of waxed-paper noisemakers. A pack of young men wandered by, all of them equally portly, all of them wearing T-shirts with some combination of red, white, and blue. At the end of the block, the police had set up a traffic barricade. Two officers sat beside it in folding chairs; they looked like sausages stuffed into their uniforms.

I could still feel the crackle of some kind of tension between Natasha and me. But she ran up to the motordrome ahead of me. How to describe the strange thing we saw? One way would be this:

$$|F_h| = m \, |g| \frac{\sin \varnothing}{\cos \varnothing} = m \, |g| \tan \varnothing.$$

That accounts for the centripetal force of the motorcycles. But then the angle of the motordrome would have to be:

$$m \, |g| \tan \varnothing = \frac{m \, |v|^2}{R},$$

or

$$\tan \varnothing = \frac{|v|^2}{|g|/R} \, .$$

There's also this: It looked like a keg of beer—a giant thirty-six-foot-diameter keg of beer. One that was made of wooden boards that had somehow been bent and molded and nailed seamlessly together by the carpenters of a bygone era. I'd never seen such a large circular wooden structure. We took our tickets and filed along a single red velvet rope. The line led us to an alarmingly rickety set of stairs.

"So," I said, searching for something to say. "How's Calvin?"

"Fine," Natasha said. "He wasn't really going to come to this. He hates the idea of it as much as you do."

"You lied to me?" I said.

"I don't know if I'd call it lying, exactly," Natasha said.

"You manipulated my feelings," I said half seriously.

Natasha didn't answer. Instead, she said, "Do you think there's one person out there for you? I mean, my parents have been together for twenty-five years, but is that accidental? Do they love each other because they loved each other so intensely at first, and now they're just comfortable? Couldn't they love someone else just as intensely, I mean, if one of them disappeared?"

We came to the arena. While the motordrome itself was designed by a long-ago New York architect, the stairs were clearly designed by Wal-Mart. They shook as we ascended. We were jammed close together. The slope was precipitous. I couldn't see beyond the person immediately in front of me.

"Doesn't this remind you of a slaughterhouse?" I said, perhaps too loudly. The man ahead of me in line turned slightly and frowned.

"Quiet," Natasha said.

"Moo," I answered.

The motordrome was equipped with a viewing platform at its top. The audience perched there, high above the ground. We looked down the walls of the cylinder. As we settled into our seats, the three riders entered from a hidden door in the wall. Natasha leaned toward me. That perfume, she'd worn that perfume even when she was ten years old. I think she used to steal it from her mom. When we were kids, Natasha would come over to my house almost every day after school. This was the discussion we had again and again: "What do you want to do?" "I don't know. What do you want to do?" "Let's play funeral." "Okay, let's play funeral." We'd orchestrate a grand scene, a cortege and a bier and an imagined assembly of mourners. We'd make the coffin by putting two kitchen chairs together and draping them with a sheet. Who'd died? It depended on the afternoon. Sometimes it was Natasha playing the corpse of her teacher or a famous pop star—one of the Backstreet Boys, for example, or Janet Jackson. Sometimes it was me playing an imaginary dead version of my father. We mourned, we gave eulogies, we acted out scenes of tremendous emotional trauma. I have this memory of Natasha standing above me and wearing a mop as a wig, saying to my assembled imaginary mourners: "He was a beautiful young boy. We will miss him, and it's a shame he had to die like that, squashed by the rolling pumpkins from the pumpkin truck accident on the freeway."

So this is what I thought of at the Evel Knievel Days American Motordrome Wall of Death: a fake funeral playacted by two little kids. I think I was alone in this visualization. As for Natasha's other question, sometimes I did think that I'd only ever been in love with her.

There was certainly a lot of showmanship to the performance: Engines revved, riders stood on the seats of their motorcycles and bowed. Then they started driving in circles. They gradually ascended the walls until they were driving parallel to the floor, spinning dizzily around and around, raising their arms with the triumph of their death-defying feat. If I hadn't been looking directly at it, I wouldn't have believed it was possible.

The audience went crazy. Kids leaned over the railing and handed dollar bills to the riders. I was light-headed from the exhaust. My ears rang, and endorphins began to flood my body. Some part of me couldn't look away from the thing I was watching, and some significant part of me wanted to do nothing more than close my eyes and seal myself off from it. One of the riders was a woman. Two were men. I watched the smallest of them, a lean weasel of a man, a rope with arms and legs and a pitchfork-shaped beard. For the most part he'd smile, beaming at the audience and projecting a wild, carefree aura. But from time to time, a furrowed look of concentration would slip across his face, and it was clear to me that the cheerfulness, the seemingly untroubled demeanor—it was a mask, a falsity for the sake of his job, which was daunting and difficult and required enormous amounts of attentiveness and focus. And that, I thought, was somehow beautiful.

The performance ended. We struggled down the flimsy staircase again and out into the street.

"Amazing!" Natasha yelled as soon as we were clear of the crowd.

"Fresh air," I said, stumbling along, feigning shortness of breath. "Can barely breathe. Must find oxygen."

"Khosi," Natasha said. "Come on! You must have loved that."

"I tolerated it," I said.

She laughed and threw her right arm around my shoulder, and we headed back toward the car. I tried to fold myself away from her touch, to preserve whatever part of me was impervious to the allure of her skin. This was a dangerous situation. We'd be lucky to navigate this evening and make it safely back to our respective homes—to our previous lives—undisturbed.

We walked through the teeming, drunken midnight crowd. My head felt buoyant and stretched, almost like gauze. This was clearly the monoxide. Humor is my crutch, so I told Natasha a non sequitur of a terrible joke ("If at first you don't succeed, skydiving is not for you"). We stood beside the Mercedes while I searched for the keys. I found them, but I fumbled to open the door and propped myself against it. Natasha stood close to me, leaning in a little, wobbling back and forth. And then she reached out and took me in her arms. I was surrounded by the feeling of her, by her corporeal self, by her scent. My head fit neatly beneath her own. She pressed her lips against my hair. It was gentle. We fell together into the front seat of the car.

Natasha's mouth was soft and warm and wet, and her lips tasted like salt. Her legs wrapped around me, her boots heavy against the backs of my thighs, her body beneath mine. We kissed, and I ran the tips of my fingers along the lines of her cheekbones. I kissed her collarbone and unbuttoned her white blouse. She smelled like perfume and sweat and, strangely, firecrackers. I licked the underwire of her bra, winding my tongue slowly underneath the unfriendly, starchy fabric. I fumbled with the clasp of it, feeling the sweat on the tips of my fingers as I struggled with the intricate metalwork. My thoughts skittered madly from destination to destination. Safety had fled. There was only the fact of this moment, the fact of Natasha's body. *Oldest friend*, I thought. The furious surge of desire crested, it expanded to the edges of my body, my newly lost body, my body that felt foreign, foreign and distant.

Natasha grabbed my shoulder blades and pulled me against her, her nails digging into my skin. It was sudden; our clothes were off and we were entangled with each other; I was inside of her; I was inside of her and she gasped and then she was biting, truly biting, the rise of my collarbone. It hurt. I was bleeding, I was sure of it. Was my blood in her mouth? This is what I was thinking of—my blood in Natasha's mouth—as the car shook a little, as the windows clouded with the condensation of our breath, as her body seemed to stretch infinitely long and wide and consume me completely, erase me. We were all erasure, and in the middle of one of the loudest festivals in the country, in the center of its most uproarious night, I could hear nothing but my breathing and Natasha's. There we were in the front seat of the Mercedes station wagon, and it was quiet enough to imagine the ghost of Evel Knievel wrapping itself around the city, enfolding Butte in its infinite vaporous hush.

Growing up, I was drawn to stories about werewolves and lycan-thropes and all manner of shape-changing beasts. I think this was partly my mother's fault. I never knew when I'd come home to find her utterly transformed. My interest in shape-changers, however, had led to an especially mortifying moment in eighth-grade biology class where I'd mentioned *lycanthropy* as if it were a real medical con-dition. The teacher laughed because she thought I was kidding.

"But really," I persisted. "Is there a treatment?"

By lunchtime the whole school had heard the story of Cozy Sucker, the boy who believed in werewolves.

Natasha found me hiding in the PE supply closet, sitting on a pile of playground balls. "I poisoned the Kool-Aid in the lunchroom," she said. "You won't be having any more problems."

"Hope it's slow-acting."

She assured me that it would also be disfiguring. "They'll turn into moose," she said. She always seemed to say the right thing.

In the front seat of the car, I wasn't the only one dislocating from the present moment. Natasha, I noticed, was also somewhere else, her body almost lifeless. We were both naked. My skin stuck to the slightly warm, moist leather, and to make matters worse, I was wedged up against the steering wheel, the knob of the gearshift poking into my side. I looked up at Natasha's face—looked across the flat plane of her stomach and the soft, feathery hair that marked the center of her body. She was staring at the roof of the car.

"Is everything okay?" I said. I kissed her hip bone.

Natasha said nothing. That made me nervous. Then she said, "Khosi," and that made my palms start to sweat. I rested my head on her stomach. I pressed against it with my face; I wanted to burrow. Natasha never used my name in conversation. "There's something I need to tell you," she said. That didn't make things better. I stared up at her: the luxurious sweep of her once-wild red hair, the soft, rich fabric of her unbuttoned blouse crumpled on the seat beside her. There was a touch of East Coast prep school to her clothes these days. There was a whisper of the *real* yacht club about her now—not just the Berkeley Pit Yacht Club, not the yacht club coded with irony.

"Last night," she said, and sighed. "Calvin asked me to marry him."

"Are you kidding me?" I said. "What are you talking about? And—and you said no?" I sat up in the driver's seat. "You said no, otherwise we wouldn't be here. Otherwise we'd be wearing clothes."

Natasha retracted her legs and curled herself into a wedge on the other side of the car. Her voice was soft and distant and ruminative and filled with a certain smoke. "I said yes," she said.

I shook my head. "We just had sex in a station wagon—and you're telling me you're going to marry someone else?"

Natasha reached over and started reassembling her clothes. I looked at the car parked directly in front of us. It was an older car, a 1970s Chevrolet with a big silvery bumper and customized oversize tires. I thought about bumpers and chrome and the invention of vulcanized rubber. I inhaled. I exhaled. The door was still ajar; I opened it all the way, flooding the car with the peppery summer darkness. For some reason, I wanted to laugh. But it wouldn't happen. The diaphragm wouldn't activate. The laughter died in my belly. I got into my clothes, too, and started the engine of the car. Natasha looked at me. "What are you thinking?" she said.

I didn't answer at first. We drove for a while in silence. I looked out at the roadway with its illuminated yellow strips. I turned the situation over in my mind. A wall had been broken. Something had crumbled. I wasn't sure what it was, but I knew it was significant. And I was standing there, in the rubble of it, looking around and trying to reconstitute at least a part of what had been there before.

"You said yes because you love him," I finally said.

I was again aware of Natasha's breathing, which was low and ragged and haltering.

"Of course I love him, Khosi," she said. "But we're twenty-two. Well, he's twenty-three."

I was driving her home. I hadn't known it until that moment, but that's what I was doing. The car was retracing its route from earlier in the evening. I was driving it there. We drove past the Silver Bow County courthouse. The state built the courthouse in 1912 for $482,000, I knew. It towered four imperious stories above the pavement. It was a soft gray-pink color. Marble pillars framed the sides of its main glass dome. I gazed up at it, taking refuge in the facts of its size, its scope, its unshakable intentionality. And then Natasha said, "Wait, stop."

"Stop?" I said.

"There he is, right there. It's Calvin," she said.

Sure enough, walking down the sidewalk, there was Calvin Stuckey. Sometimes, sometimes Butte was too small of a town.

"Speak of the devil and there he is," I said, with perhaps a little too much emphasis.

But as we pulled up beside him, Natasha recoiled as if she'd been burned. "No, never mind," she said. "Don't stop."

"Don't stop?" I said. "He's about to see us. I can't just stare at him and drive by. 'I'm sorry, Calvin, I was just screwing your fiancée a moment ago, so I didn't feel like stopping.'"

"I don't think he wants to see me," she said, sinking lower into the seat. "And I don't know if I want to see him."

"Didn't he just propose to you?" I said, and rolled the car up beside him.

He'd come downtown specifically to find her. He'd left his house after midnight and charted his way through the bedlam of the parade's end. That's what I found out later, anyway: He'd imagined he might find us together downtown. The timing was fortuitous. He spotted our car before we pulled over. We rolled to a halt directly in front of him. He smiled broadly as he walked up to us. His shelf of glistening white teeth illuminated the night like a glacial peak.

"Hey, Khosi," Calvin said. "Hi, Cube."

This was, I knew, his pet name for her. It felt dirty to know their pet names. Or to be the kind of person they shared their pet names with. But there you had it. Cube was simple. Cube as in *sugar. Sugar cube.*

"Congratulations on the engagement, Calvin," I said.

"Thanks," he said. "I went looking for you at the country club."

I put the Mercedes in park and turned off the motor. "Yacht Club," I said.

"Or Yacht Club Manor," Natasha said.

"But I forgot my ascot," Calvin said. "They wouldn't let me in the door."

"That's weird," I said. "Normally, they keep a few behind the counter."

Calvin leaned in, his hand resting on the edge of Natasha's window. She reached over and touched the back of his wrist. She smiled reluctantly at him. "Couldn't sleep?" she said.

Calvin looked over at me. "Can I borrow her for just a minute, Khosi?"

And so I walked home, listening to the sound of my footsteps on the concrete sidewalk. When I turned around to look at them at the end of the block, they were standing there, on the edge of the streetlight's illumination, huddled close together, holding each other despite the heat. My shadow passed underneath me as I walked. A truck downshifted on the interstate. The sound of it carried out across the valley.

As I neared my house, I stopped at the Millers' garden, a garden that I knew to be infested with walking onions. They'd built trellises for the onions, and right now they were blooming—small purple flowers almost invisible in the inky dark. I stood at their fence and felt the roughness of the boards in my hands. I heard something behind the house, rummaging around the trash bins, probably a feral cat or a raccoon. They must have lonely lives, these nocturnal creatures, digging through the remnants of other people's trash, negotiating a darkened world.

The Loving Shambles was dark again, but by now the moon was out and illuminated the front porch. I made my way through the still-unlocked front door. It was just before two A.M. Sure enough, sitting at the dining room table in a circle of illumination, in a spotlight of illumination from a dozen candles, was my mother. She had a cup of tea on the table in front of her. The steam rose into the air, hanging near the chandelier.

"There you are," she said. "I was wondering where you might be, my love."

"Mom," I said. "Are you holding a séance?"

My mother laughed. She stood and walked over and hugged me, wrapping me in her stalklike arms. She was wearing a black pashmina. The fabric of it draped over me and gave off the sweet redolence of mothballs.

"Of course not, Khosi," my mother said. "The ghosts of the dead are all around us. There's no need to summon them with artificial stagecraft."

This was exactly the sort of thing she was prone to saying.

"Did you turn off the power, Mom?"

She took my chin in both of her hands. "I needed peace," she said. "I needed tranquillity."

The Prophet Muhammad (peace and blessings be upon Him) once said: *Never once did I receive a revelation without thinking that my soul had been torn away from me.* My mother's face seemed a little sad. Her forehead folded into a set of horizontal lines.

"Khosi," she said. "Your father's back. Or rather, he was. He just left." And then she pulled me into a fierce, smothering hug. "Tell your mother congratulations," she added. "She is officially divorced."

I often dream that I'm a contestant on *Jeopardy!*

Alex Trebek welcomes and introduces us. Then he turns to the board and says, "These are the categories: Cornish Mining Methods. The Panic of 1907. The Anaconda Mine and Amalgamated Copper. The Western Federation of Miners. And finally, Pinkerton Detectives." He stands back and gestures to us, the contestants. "Khosi," he says, "please make your selection." The camera pulls back, and now it's a montage. I answer everything: $200 and $400 and $600 and $800 and $1,000 questions. I amass a fortune. The other players stand there, silent, flummoxed, dumbfounded, as I surge into the lead. Finally, the board is empty. "Time for Final Jeopardy!" Alex Trebek says, and then he reveals the topic.

I can't quite see the words, but as Alex Trebek reads them—his voice deepening and lengthening each syllable—I'm pitched into a sickening awareness: I've just lost the game. I'm finished. I have no hope. "The Emotional Life of You and Your Family," he says, and I realize that this is not a subject that I know anything about. The game continues without me. My score is forfeit. Zeroes flash in front of my monitor. A comforting young woman in a pantsuit and a headset comes to lead me away. There will be no fortune, not for me.

On that night, I walked to the kitchen and poured myself a Scotch and soda. Then I tried to negotiate the restoration of electricity to the house. "Why don't we just see how peaceful it can be," I suggested, "with one or two lights on in the hallway." I tiptoed down the stairs and threw the breaker once again.

I sat at the table with my mother. The candles remained lit, though they guttered from time to time, sending a broad smoky scent into the air, a scent that mingled with the smell of the warm summer night. I looked at my mother with her cup of steaming tea. She'd brought her pill container downstairs, possibly for my benefit. I scrutinized it as casually as was possible. Today's section was empty. So this wasn't Wilson's disease.

"Divorced?" I said. "What are you talking about?"

"Your father and I," she said. "It's official now. It wasn't official before."

"Good to know that you're being conscientious," I said.

"He came to the house with the paperwork," she said. "And I signed it." She huddled over her mug of tea.

"Dad was here," I said. "Incredible. It's incredible that you didn't think I might want to meet him."

My mother didn't answer. Imagine: blackberry bushes in summer. Imagine: the raw ache of too much time separated from my bed. Imagine: the cool feeling of the tabletop against the palms of my hands. Imagine: the sound of a distant freight train.

Before I could say anything, Mom slumped down and put her head on her arms. "I can't discuss this with you now, obviously," she said.

"How about five minutes from now?" I said.

She didn't answer.

"Officially divorced?" I said. "What do you mean? You were still married?"

She didn't answer.

"When did you know he was coming?" I said.

She didn't answer.

"I can't talk about this now," she said again. And then she said, "No, no, I can. I can. It's fascinating, in a way. You just have no idea. None. You don't know what it's like to wake up every morning missing someone for a month, for a year, for a decade. It's embarrassing."

As my mother talked, I took a few steps over toward the glass of the living room window. I stared up into the darkness. Even though we were in the center of town, I could have counted hundreds, if not thousands, of stars. The night sky in Butte opens up unlike any other sky I've seen. The stars form a canopy, bright and full and overflowing.

I heard the legs of my mother's chair scrape against the floor. "I loved him," she was saying, "but he didn't care about anyone but himself." I heard her walk across the room to where I was standing. I could sense her body, visceral, solid in the room behind me. I turned around. I swiveled, really, right into her open arms. She hugged me then, no, she clutched me—that was the only verb that would adequately describe the strength of her embrace—she clutched me and then held me away from her, looking straight into my eyes.

"You don't know this man," she said. "You think you want to meet him, but you don't. The best day of my life was the day he disappeared."

"I know, Mom," I said. "I know."

Of course I didn't know. Or at least I didn't believe her, not really. She'd said it to me a dozen times, that very sentence, a sentence she'd memorized, that she believed. And then I realized something—I saw the man from the museum again. He reappeared in front of me with the coat and his graying good looks. *My father?* I wondered. *Come to visit?*

"Did he ask to see me?" I said.

I could feel her pull away from me, could feel some part of her reorient, could feel her strain toward some distant magnetic pole. "I told him," she said, "that if he went near you, I'd kill him."

"Okay," I said. "That's friendly."

"I needed to protect you somehow, my dear," she said. "I told him I'd shoot him, or possibly stab him, or—perhaps even poison him. You know: with a dart gun. Like a Russian secret agent."

"And are you going to kill him if *I* do the approaching?"

"Don't be ridiculous," she said. She walked over to the dark mahogany built-in. She reached up and opened the leaded glass of its door. She pulled a pack of Marlboros and a book of matches from a concealed alcove. She lit one. "Don't say a word," she said. "I know they're not good for me. What I really want is a Butterfinger."

"You can't have a Butterfinger," I said almost reflexively. I shook my head. "You've got to know where he's staying."

"He's gone."

"You're lying," I said. "Where is he: Econo Lodge? Holiday Inn? Is he staying with Wada?"

"He left, Khosi," she said. "He got his paperwork and left. He's in the air somewhere, flirting with a stewardess."

I walked over to our big writing desk. I pulled out the Yellow Pages. I dropped it on the leather-padded surface. I looked up *hotels.*

"I'm going to call every single one," I said. "I'll start with *A.* Anaconda Best Western. It has a heated pool."

"You don't understand," my mother said.

"Or here we go," I said. "Anaconda Hampton Inn. They have a continental breakfast and free HBO."

"Your father," my mother said, and here she rubbed the bridge of her nose, pressed in on it, lingering there with her head tilted and the tendons of her neck firing like pistons. "Your father told me he was dying." She looked up and made eye contact. "And that he had to get back to Cairo to see some kind of specialist. I drove him to the airport. I watched him leave myself. He's not here."

"Oh my God." I said. "That's terrible."

"Oh, please," she said. She finished her cigarette. She pulled a second one from the pack. She looked at it, turning over the cylinder in her fingers. I watched the tips of her fingernails negotiate the white seam of the paper. She blew her nose on her sleeve and exhaled. "Damn these sinuses," she said. And then: "Listen, darling. It's just not true. That man is perfectly healthy. He's not dying. I have no idea why he waited twenty years to have me sign the papers, but it's not because he's ill."

I turned away from my mother. I filled my head with as many good things about her as I could imagine. For some reason, I thought of one thing—of playing Yahtzee with her for hours on winter nights, right here at the dining room table, the fireplace hissing and spitting, steady snow falling outside, accumulating on the roads despite the work of the snowplows.

"What," I said, "did he tell you he had?"

"I didn't ask specifics," she said. She lit the second cigarette.

"You could have told me," I said.

"Khosi," she said. "Don't."

"You could have mentioned something: 'Oh, your father's here, by the way, and he says he's dying, maybe you'd like to meet him?'"

"Khosi: He's not dying."

"You can't be sure of that," I said. "You just can't." In a fit of frustration, I turned and went upstairs, leaving my mother to her candles. This is where the important parts of life occur, I think, in the damp interstitial moments, in the transitions that rise from darkness. We could say something, but we don't. Instead, I brushed my teeth aggressively. While I was brushing them, the phone rang. It was Natasha. I decided not to answer. Instead, I turned the phone off completely.

I tried to get some sleep. At three or four in the morning, when the nervous twitching in my neck had subsided somewhat, I did manage to finally close my eyes. There was no *Jeopardy!* dream, no lifelike imitation of Alex Trebek, just darkness and uncomfortable heat and damp covers. I awoke and seemed to see snakes coiling out of the pocket of my jeans, coiling out of the denim and slithering up to hang from the ceiling. They writhed in a luminous and variegated coil. "Khosi," they hissed at me with their sibilant voices. "Khosi, we're waiting for you. We love you. We miss you."

Descartes said that in your dreams you're accustomed to seeing the same things that lunatics see during daylight, and by morning I would've had a hard time arguing with his theory. At six A.M. I got up and padded to the bathroom and took a shower. I stayed in the shower until the water ran cold. Then I got out, my fingers shriveled to tiny prunes.

What's it like to be the child of an immigrant? I know and I don't know, both. I have a family tree somewhere, but I don't know where, and it's probably in Arabic, or possibly French, or possibly both. The past, the history of my family, is a strange and hybrid beast. On the one side: exhaustively documented. I live and work in its midst. But on the other side: nothing. No body, no clothes, no cane, no toupee, no set of dentures, no artifacts whatsoever. Only a vocabulary that vanishes as soon as it's fashioned into language. Only the vocabulary of exile and disappearance.

Three

I GUESS BY NOW IT'S clear that I've been avoiding it. I've been a little distracted, I have to admit, but here it is: *The Life and Times of Akram Saqr and Amy Clark, My One and Only Parents, as Told by Me, My Mother's One and Only Son, Fruit of Her Womb, 100 Percent Maculate Conception, Part One, the Meeting.*

Nineteen seventy-seven was not the best year for fashion. Anyone's family photographs will illustrate this point: pant legs like cone collars on a pet, buttons the size of silver dollars, fabric derived entirely from petroleum. My dad—in the few pictures my mother saved—looks a bit like a carnival clown. White shoes, big sideburns, thick Coke-bottle glasses. It's interesting. My mother didn't keep any of the close-ups. No portraiture, nothing to illustrate the deep character of the man. Only crowd shots, images busy with people, with life going on elsewhere.

But 1977—who remembers the siege of three federal buildings in Washington, D.C., by Hanafi Muslims and the Nation of Islam? The country was riveted as gunmen seized control of a section of the capital and issued a list of demands to the media. Or the contro-versy surrounding the bloody movie *Mohammed, Messenger of God*, the first Hollywood film to be made about the life of Islam's central prophet? Or the Taksim Square massacre in Turkey, one of a dozen mass killings in the Islamic world that year, almost all of which were extensively reported by the national media? Though they didn't lin-ger for decades, all of these stories had a significant impact in their time: Being an Arab in America in 1977 meant that you were a mis-trusted outsider, just like being an Arab in America today, over thirty years later.

When I said that copper was the curse of my family, I only partly meant my mustachioed ancestors and my temperamentally problematic mother. Copper was also my father's skin color, a faded soft copper color, copper cut with a slight blanching agent—he was marked by otherness, by his facial features and his skin and his accent. He looked and sounded like an Arab. There was no escap-ing it.

There was a certain kind of young American—a certain Jimmy Carter–voting, city-living, blues-listening, Woody Allen film–watching demographic—who was drawn to all things Middle East-ern. My young, independently wealthy mother was firmly a part of that demographic. She was intrigued by everything that the main-stream seemed to fear or reject.

My parents met at the apartment of a mutual friend, the woman I now know as Tante Wada. Tante Wada was a chunky, cheerful Egyptian-American woman—one of a new breed of Arab-American women who insisted on taking advantage of the social freedoms offered by late-seventies American culture. Both of her parents had come to Montana in the 1940s, following the war, when she was a little girl. Back then—in 1977—she was getting a master's at Montana Tech, which was where she'd met my father.

When she met him—when my mother met him—Akram Saqr was a short, thin man with a full black beard and those same thick bifocals. He'd come to America to get an MA in engineering administration. He'd ended up at Montana Tech mostly by accident. He liked the name of the state and the fact that it was close to Canada, a country that he associated with skiing and glaciers and massive, marauding polar bears. He liked the idea of winter; he'd never seen snow. All of this information I gathered surreptitiously, piecemeal, over the course of two decades. I listened whenever anyone told stories about my dad, and I tended to write them down in my journal as soon as I got home.

Matchmaking is, I think, every Egyptian's favorite hobby. One night in November 1977, my mother and father found themselves invited to Wada's apartment for *koubeiba*. The three of them cooked the meal together. My father loved to cook Egyptian food; he was in an ebullient mood; he told stories of going to the horse races in Cairo as a boy, of climbing wrought-iron fences to steal mangoes off of giant mango trees, of the city under Nasser, of his early memories of going to the Dar el-Obra el-Masreyya, the Cairo Opera House on Gezira Island.

Thinking of that night they met, I imagined the scent of the sizzling lamb. The rich taste of the pine nuts. I'd eaten that meal fifty times, and yet there was always something so elusive about it, an aftertaste of mystery and pure longing. I imagined my mother making the filling, imagined her hands curling around the long handles of Wada's cast-iron cookware. I imagined the sound of Wada tenderizing the lamb, stripping it off the bone with a carving knife and then pounding it with a square meat mallet, holding it up to the light to see if the membrane of the muscle had become translucent, just like I'd seen her do a hundred times myself. Then I could hear her turning the handle of the meat grinder.

Koubeiba is like a lot of the dishes of the Middle East: claimed by every culture, lauded by every society as the food of its own people, of its own masses, of the Syrian or Egyptian or Algerian street. The Lebanese will tell you that their *koubeiba* is the real *koubeiba*, that Beirut is in fact where the dish originated, and that it should really be called *kibbe*—which is its proper name. Cypriots will educate you about the ancient way to make *koubes*, and will tell you how that dish voyaged from their small island out into the world long before the days of the Mediterranean empires, before the Phoenicians or the Achaemenids or the Greeks or even the Romans. And a Turk? Never ask a Turk who invented *içli köfte*. You are disparaging his honor by even thinking of the question.

My mother did something that was almost unbelievable. Immediately before they made the fritters, she looked at the mixture and smelled it. Then she dipped a finger into the raw ground meat. And she tasted it. And then she turned to my father and Wada and said: "Star anise. Maybe half a teaspoon."

"My heart," Wada said, clutching her chest and staggering backward. "It is broken."

"You've broken her heart," my father echoed, eyes full of mock indignation. "I can see its pieces there, on the floor."

"I cannot breathe," Tante Wada said.

"Breathe, Wada, breathe," my father said. "She may need CPR! Wada? Do you need CPR?"

"I don't know," Wada said. "I see light. I see heaven."

"Wada, how about this: Why not let her change the recipe?" my father suggested. "This is America—anything's possible. This beautiful young lady deserves a chance to add to the recipe, no?"

"My grandmother," Wada said, "is frowning down on us, God rest her soul."

But after dinner, after the perfect *koubeiba*, after the addition (in pencil) of *star anise, 1/4 teaspoon* to the recipe card, after the tiny cups of esophagus-stripping Turkish coffee, the three of them sat in the living room and listened to a record. My father had brought it: Mozart's *Magic Flute*. As the music filled the living room, he explained the entire opera in his luxuriant Egyptian accent, explained it image by image, threading his voice through the open spaces in the score. "*Die Zauberflöte*, in German," he said, and told the story of the Egyptian prince Tamino and his quest to free Pamina, the daughter of the Queen of the Night. He described Papageno, the bird catcher, with his rainbow coat of feathers and his piper's beak, long and elegant as the tendril of a vine. He described the queen's entry, when she soared onto the stage, riding an imperious surge in the music, riding an umbrella of stars and descending from the ceiling. This, then, was a remarkable man. He argued passionately over cooking. He dissected and explained the intricacies of *opera seria*, conjuring images that were strangely beautiful.

Unfortunately, besides his language and his culture, he also brought his addiction to gambling, to casino slots and barroom pull tabs and exorbitant racetrack wagers. But she wouldn't know this for eight years. By then it would be much too late. The story of the night of their meeting I'd gleaned from Tante Wada. The story of the end of their relationship, however, my mother told me herself, especially during lapses in her medication. Honestly, it hurts to think about it in great detail: The restaurant that my parents opened together after he graduated from Montana Tech. The steady acrimony that built between them over his trips to Las Vegas, the threatening phone calls that he eventually couldn't conceal, the letter on the living room mantel after he disappeared, detailing the hundred thousand dollars owed to shady creditors, the tearful conversation at my grandparents' house, the fear for her safety and the safety of her child, the humiliating decision to close the restaurant down altogether. He'd known that her parents would settle his debts for their daughter's sake but that he couldn't stick around if he wanted that to happen.

I guess I've spent a lot of time wondering how my father could have rationalized this choice, how he permitted himself to leave his wife and his son in order to disappear from America entirely, to flee to a country on the other side of the world. I've imagined entire stories for him. I've imagined entire stories, but they lead me to the same emptiness. And the most embarrassing thing? I've always wanted to say *Daddy*, that infantile and diminutive word. I never had the chance to say it, never got to write it on birthday cards or Father's Day cards or letters home from camp.

Also, I have to admit that I always wondered why a woman who lost so much because of an Egyptian man would carry on his culture, continue its customs, continue cooking its food, in such a significant way. All of her recipes came from my father's family—I knew this much for sure. I also knew, from what I'd gathered, that she'd reconstructed many of the recipes alone in our kitchen, Bach sonatas winding their way through the house. So: Why? Why had she done this to herself; why had she trapped herself in a world of nostalgia?

I think the answer has four parts. First, nothing is simple. There aren't always *therefore*s in real life. In real life, there isn't always a chain of cause and effect. In real life, people do things for messy, incomplete reasons. They act without solid motivations, or their motivations are lodged deep beneath the surface of their thoughts in the unconscious mind. Some of my mother's motivations were beyond even her. She awoke before dawn with the garden announcing that it needed to be stripped of its walking onions. And so it simply had to be done.

The second part, I think, had to do with her parents. Though I'd barely known them, I did know that Mr. and Mrs. Clark were about as likely to eat *ful medamas* as a slab of raw tiger. If they had traveled to Asia or Africa, laden with binoculars and rifles and wearing their best safari gear, and if they had witnessed the tiger prowling in the underbrush, and then they'd shot the tiger, conquering it themselves, then they might have sent it home to be stuffed and displayed in their solarium. But that evening, the acrid scent of gunpowder still sticky on their palms, they would have ordered steak and potatoes and washed it down with a sunny California chardonnay. They were just visiting, after all; it was all very lovely, but they weren't planning on staying.

They eschewed my mom's contributions to Thanksgiving dinner. Their idea of Egypt was half Tutankhamen and half Ten Commandments. They'd raised my mother in an austere, moneyed household—and she'd embraced anything that seemed like it might offend their austere, moneyed sensibilities. Hence the commitment to radical politics, the marriage to my father, the unrelenting pursuit of Middle Eastern cuisine.

Third: I think that the meals she cooked reminded her of the beginning of the relationship, of the world that my father had opened for her, of a time when she had so much hope for a shared future. The food was an elemental reminder of that.

Fourth, and perhaps most important, I think it was a challenge. She was not going to fold, to give up, to let a sudden betrayal obliterate the life she'd imagined for herself. Yes, half of that life was missing. But she wasn't going to let herself be destroyed by that. She was just going to revise, to reenvision, to reimagine. She would reorient the narrative with a different center.

Or maybe it was because after she closed the restaurant, the orders never stopped coming in over the phone? The business started slowly, but it grew larger and larger and—I think—took up the vacancy that my father had left behind. And so, I think at least in part because of these things, I found myself every Saturday morning sitting in the passenger seat of Tante Wada's 1973 Ford Maverick, listening to Arabic music on her cheap in-dash CD player and driving to Billings, Montana, where the Islamic Center convened a weekly Arabic Saturday school. My mother insisted I go.

"It'll get you in touch with your broader culture," she said on the first day I accompanied Wada on the three-and-a-half-hour drive, departing at five in the morning. "It will heighten your understanding of the size and scope of the world."

I was six years old.

"I want to connect you to where you came from," she added.

"I came from Butte, Montana," I said.

"I know, sweetie. But it's more complicated than that."

"Why can't you drive me?" I said.

"Mom needs a day off, sweetie," she said.

"From what?" I said.

"That's not important, darling. All you need to know is that Tante Wada is happy to take you there."

I began what would be a ten-year immersion in Middle Eastern politics and religion and the Arabic language. Of course, my father had been a Christian—and not a particularly religious Christian at that. I'd had no religious guidance from any quarter. For her part, Tante Wada had a pragmatic attitude about poaching language lessons for me from the Islamic Center.

"The praying is good for your muscles," she said. "Kneel and stand, kneel and stand. You'll be a better soccer player."

I had a different agenda. "You realize, Wada, that I'm missing Saturday-morning cartoons."

"Be quiet, *habibi*," she said, "and listen to Amr Diab."

When I was a teenager, I'd change our musical selection to Floyd Ming and his Pep Steppers or Uncle Dave Macon or Ernest Phipps and His Holiness Singers. But when I was a kid, Wada translated the lyrics as they pumped through the rattling interior of the little two-door Ford.

Habibi, ya nour el-ain, Diab sang, and Wada translated in a deadpan, tuneless monotone: "Dear one, you are the light in my eyes." *Ya sakin khayali.* "You live in my imagination." *A'ashek bakali sneen o wala ghayrak bibali.* I curled myself in the bucket seat and put my head on my knees and listened to her intone: "I have adored you for years. Oh. There's no one else in my thoughts."

It's a separate book, those Saturdays with Wada and the imam and his more or less devout Islamic brethren. In Islam, the ideal of knowledge is as important as the ideal of prayer. Who knows that here in America? Everyone knows that single word, *jihad.* It's a common part of the American lexicon. Who knows a similar word, *ijtihad,* which means *innovative thinking* and is an Islamic ideal, one encouraged by the Prophet Himself (blessings be upon His name). Who knows that *ijtihad* drove Islamic artisans to perfect cutting-edge techniques in dozens of disciplines, techniques that revolutionized ninth-century art and architecture and mathematics and society? I do, I guess. But that doesn't seem to be helping much.

Tante Wada would wait in the car for me or go shopping in Billings's tiny downtown shopping district. On the way home, I'd be allowed to talk only in Arabic, even when we stopped the car to get gas or use the restroom. Mostly, I'd communicate with hand signals. Occasionally, I'd startle a pimply teenage gas station attendant. *"Aya al hammam?"* I'd demand, standing at the counter at the Arco. *"Al hammam! Al hammam!"* Somehow, almost always, he'd know exactly what I meant.

The next day—Friday, July 27, 2008—all I had to work was the private party in the evening. I always have trouble with empty time off. I never know what to do with myself. That morning I had to fight the urge to go to the museum. I hadn't slept well, so it would be a relief to appear behind the desk and start organizing things, straightening a little bit, making sure that everything was in order. Sorting the pencils in the pencil drawer. Color-coding the keys and arranging them alphabetically. Imagining a dozen new exhibits and writing comprehensive treatments and proposals for each of them. You know, that sort of thing.

It was still early, but I thought about calling one of my high school friends: Jeremy Dean, now studying to be a carpenter in Los Angeles. Or Brandon Baldwin, who'd recently started his first year in a Teach for America program in rural Maine. But all I'd get from calling them was nostalgia and a sense that life had started happening without me, that my friends had all moved away from Montana—to L.A. or New York City or Chicago or the pine woods of Maine—and begun their next adventure.

I checked my messages. Nothing. Not a whisper from Natasha. I turned the phone off.

I decided to drive out into the hills surrounding Butte. I was going stir-crazy in the house. The drive would clear my head, help me put things in order. I threw on some running shorts and a pair of sandals. I padded my way outside. I hit the road and drove north. Debris from Evel Knievel celebrators was scattered everywhere throughout town. Driving through the city, I must have seen three different people in Evel Knievel jumpsuits, some of them even wearing the motorcycle helmet despite the heat. Public trash cans were overflowing. Bottles littered the sides of the road like an outbreak of glass flowers.

This is a big part of what I love about western Montana. Even our cities are surrounded by thousands of acres of forestland. In

Butte, it's a short drive to wilderness. The air conditioner was broken in my old Ford truck, but that was fine. I put in Junior Brown
and drove with all the windows open. The song, "I Bought the
Shoes That Just Walked Out on Me," seemed to be based on an especially piquant cruelty. Within ten minutes, I was surrounded by
nothing but old-growth forest.

For sweeping expanse, for limitless vista and broad unfolding
sky, there was nowhere more striking than Montana, than the states
of the northern plains, with their scrub-brush hillsides and can-
vaslike emptiness. There were no cities. There were a few cattle
ranches. I rolled down the window. Striations of light illuminated
the forest. I took a deep breath of the highway pine. My father had
been here, my own father—here, here in Butte, reappeared, just like
I'd imagined a hundred, a thousand, times. Except he didn't appear
at my elementary school in a white Rolls-Royce, or at my tenth
birthday party in a twirling helicopter. Rather, when he'd come to
see me during my tour at the Copper King Mansion, I'd had no idea
it was him. He'd loomed in the back, inappropriately dressed for the
weather, and I'd been too tired to understand who he was, to match
the face to those few family photographs.

And Natasha.

I thought briefly of the soft pressure of her lips, the feeling of her
skin against mine.

When she and I were children, we were certain of one thing
other than our desire to simulate the funerals of the people around
us. We knew that when we grew up, we'd move to Egypt and become deep-sea divers and search for buried treasure in the wreckage
of Ancient Egyptian cargo ships, in the crystalline currents of the

Red Sea. We devised elaborate plans around this future. We planned itineraries and created professions for ourselves and studied textbooks and made sheaths of drawings. We schemed. We collaborated. We hid suitcases in my attic with changes of clothes and books to read on the road and a copious supply of airmail envelopes for our enigmatic letters home. Oh, how we fantasized about those enigmatic letters home: *Dearest Mother,* we wrote. *Dear Families: We have gone to the Red Sea to become open-water treasure divers. Do not be alarmed. By the time you get this it will be too late to follow.*

Ultimately, I drove back toward the city. There was a limit, after all, to what a single tank of gas could do. I decided to have lunch at Rafiq's Falafel, the only Middle Eastern restaurant in town. Well, the Stop 'n Save did sell an Egyptian chickpea salad, but the only Egyptian thing about it was the picture of the mummy on the container (and possibly the mummified nature of the chickpeas themselves). Rafiq's was real Lebanese food. But whenever I came here, a certain tension simmered beneath the surface of my meal. Farid Rafiq, the owner, was one of my mother's oldest friends. And by *friends*, I mean *competitors*. He longed to buy her business, to fold Saqr Catering into his restaurant and thereby corner the kebab market in our fair city of Butte. So, when I came in, he always hovered nearby, checking to make sure that everything was fine and— perhaps more important—that I wasn't trying to steal his recipes.

Farid Rafiq: He was a big, potbellied man with a penchant for Aqua Velva. You could smell it from twenty yards. He kept a small bottle in his office, and he liked to dab it behind his ears at intervals throughout the day. Whenever he walked by, I couldn't help it: *Aqua Velva,* I'd think. *Cools. Smoothes. Tones.* This afternoon he greeted me with his customary *ahlan wa sahlan. Welcome, welcome!* With a particular gleam in the corner of his eye, he steered me toward the table farthest away from the kitchen.

"We're all out of everything," he said. "Maybe you should try Burger King next door?"

"I don't think their Lebanese food is quite as good as yours," I said. "My mother says hello," I added, which—I have to admit—was more of a threat than a greeting.

"Tell her I'll buy her *mulukhreja* recipe for a thousand dollars," he said.

Even as he poured my water, he continued to insist that the kitchen was closed and that there was nothing on the menu that would even remotely interest me. I was doomed to be unsatisfied. "Why not go get a Whopper?" he suggested. "They are only a dollar ninety-nine. What a tremendous bargain, no? Nearly half a pound of flame-broiled beef!"

"Just think," I said, "of the ecological devastation that occurred for each of those two-dollar burgers."

After Rafiq finally let me order, I spent some time organizing the silverware. It needed to be perfectly aligned—organized, arranged, orchestrated—for the lunch to begin in earnest. Because how—how—could you eat if the tip of your fork and your napkin were out of alignment? It was an impossibility. It would be a travesty.

Somebody once told me: Reasons are the stories that you make up after you act. I understand this, I really do. I wish, I yearn, for the ability to give you my feelings, to simply transfer them to you at this moment, to cut a window into myself and display the substance, the grain and the character, of the images I saw. Because this cut would relieve a pressure. In telling the story, the story would become easier to bear, to hold inside of me, where it is now, private and hidden and completely concealed. What I wanted to do was something spectacular. I wanted to call Natasha, to ask her to join me here, so I could reach over the table and kiss her, so I could press my lips against hers and run my fingers through her hair. She of course was not there. Any version of her would be a hallucination.

When the food came, it was delicious. Rafiq brought it to the table himself, repeating stock phrases about how I was his honored guest and always welcome, *inshallah* (God willing), at his restaurant. I idly wondered if he'd poisoned my meal. But the plates steamed and gave off the thick scent of chickpeas and coriander and saffron rice. He'd just baked the pita on the bread stone in his blazing wood-fired oven. He'd used a massive black-charred paddle. I do agree with M.F.K. Fisher, who said that *the smell of good bread baking is indescribable in its evocation of innocence and delight.*

I took my phone out of my pocket and turned it on again. Off/on, off/on. This time there was one message. I stopped chewing. I punched in my security code. Natasha's voice expanded into the room—hesitant, tired-sounding, tentative. She needed time, she said, to think about everything. She was confused. It was a short, dispiriting message. Of course she was confused. I was confused, too, and hurt as well. But what did I expect? Let's run away together and move to Tahiti? Let's run away and join the circus or start a jug band or drive south to Mexico City? Let's just—perhaps the most thrilling and terrifying of all possible ideas to me—let's run away.

Rafiq lingered too close to the table while I was eating. He made a great show of dusting and straightening and collecting menus. "You like it?" he finally said.

"It's average," I said.

Rafiq smiled. "Thank you," he said. "How *is* your mother, anyway?"

I told him. His casual question turned into a ten-minute narrative of my problems.

"Oh dear," Rafiq said when I'd finished. "You know, I never met your father. But he's a legend in the community."

"Exactly," I said. "Legendary for lying. That's what Mom says now. She says he's not sick. She says there's no way it's true. She says he's healthy as a horse."

Rafiq glanced around the restaurant, perhaps to judge if the few other patrons were listening to us talk. He leaned forward and lowered his voice. "Why would he show up, then?" he said.

"I don't know," I said. "It's strange. Maybe I'll go to Egypt and track him down to ask him."

At that, quite unexpectedly, Rafiq laughed. He laughed and laughed, laughed until tears came to his eyes.

"I could do it," I said.

That only made him laugh more. He snorted. "Khosi Saqr, Butte's best-known hermit."

"I'm really quite social," I said.

"Oh," he said. "I am indeed sorry. It's just so amusing. The thought of you dropping everything and flying around the world to look for your father."

"A number of commercial airlines fly to Cairo," I said.

Rafiq kept laughing. "It's just so impossible," he said. "It would never happen. You, of all people. Your mother, she once told me that as a boy, you sorted your crayons according to their length."

I blushed. "So that I'd know which colors I was using too much. Ease up on the indigo and choose cornflower blue, for example. It's a smart strategy; the crayons last longer."

"Egypt would eat you alive," Rafiq said.

"No, it wouldn't."

I couldn't stop blushing. I could feel the heat of it rising through me. I could feel it filling my cheeks with a steady burn. Embarrassment tumbled through my body, and my senses all felt alive and sharp, despite the lack of air coming into my lungs, and I could hear the clatter of forks and knives and, a few feet away, the single elderly man who slurped at his cup of sweetened mint tea. Behind the wall of the kitchen, Farid Rafiq's sous chef stood poised over a large-mouthed cauldron of soup, a pinch of salt in his left hand, waiting for a moment to add the last bit of flavor to the broth, the broth that had come to a rolling boil, that teemed with heat, its surface tension bursting with pockets of hot expanding air. Beyond that, beyond the exterior wall of this building, and the exterior wall of the next building over, was another room with another set of lives, an insurance agency—depending on the direction you went—or a sporting goods store. And there, sitting at a desk and looking at an actuarial table or standing in an aisle and looking at a price tag or talking softly with someone about things that I could never imagine, were strangers, complete strangers, strangers who lived their lives so close to mine, so close but also utterly separate, and distant, and irredeemably lost to me. If you followed along from house to house, working your way outward through the downtown commercial core, knocking through walls and rendering them invisible, disappearing and reappearing, smoke-floating like a wayward spirit, looking in on people from the city of Butte, and then the country of America, and then outward in an ever expanding geometric intimacy, spanning the whole globe, the entirety of our world, you'd find only a few people who knew me—Khosi Saqr—a handful of people whose recognition of my face would trigger a burst of light in their minds, a brief happy synaptic impulse deep within their memories, the bit of lightning that's prompted by the recognition of someone you know. What a miracle they are, these pictures of us, these evidences of our bodies, carried around in the minds of human beings, human beings who, in my case, were thousands of lonely miles from here—who were encased in the darkness of night even as I sat here and ate lunch by myself on a sunlit summer day. There was an ache in me for them, an ache that was low and dark and alluvial and undid the sheltering sky.

"Rafiq," I said. "Bring me the check."

And so that—that—is how I decided to go to Cairo, Egypt, and track down my erstwhile father. There were a number of intervening steps. There was my teary departure from the mansion, and Ms. Vogel's odd, hurried advice behind the closed door of her office. ("There's a masseuse you should look up if you get to Tangier. He was a friend of Paul Bowles, and he's very discreet and has incredibly strong hands.") There was a hasty doctor's appointment where my family physician, Dr. Scott, told me that it was wrong to leave without at least two months' worth of immunizations. How could I explain the deep and compelling pressure, the urgency, of the trip? I had two weeks, I told him. No more, no less.

"We'll do what we can," he said, his face starched taut and white as a funeral collar. "Are you sure you want to do this? You of all people."

I shook my head. "What does that mean?" I said.

"I'm just pointing out," he said, "that you got a tetanus booster last year because you picked up a rusty wrench."

"Flakes," I said. "Tetanus flakes. They could have penetrated the exterior layer of my skin."

Dr. Scott frowned. "And," he said, "last year you had me remove a freckle."

"It had a slight discoloration," I said.

"It was a freckle," he said.

"It could have been melanoma," I protested.

He turned and reached for the examination room door, still shaking his head. "The nurse will be in with your first doses shortly," he said, and disappeared with a flourish of his lab coat.

There were also a number of startling conversations with my mother.

The first one happened that evening, after I worked the Bitterroot Savings Bank annual shareholders' dinner at the Copper King Mansion. It was a lavish affair for which the catering staff had to wear its nineteenth-century period costumes. Though the Clark Mansion was one of the first in the world to have fully electrical lights—with much of the copper wiring drawn from Clark's own Anaconda Mine—guests who selected the nineteenth-century theme often wanted their evenings to be candlelit. Predictably, the staff hated it. We stumbled everywhere, and the wool of the uniforms itched insatiably.

But the guests seemed to have a good time. Senator Crenshaw was there, as well as former governor Mark Racicot. They were both easy to spot; they both wore Stetson hats. Crenshaw had grown up on a cattle ranch, so he never went to any formal occasion without his Stetson. Somehow this was a guarantee of authenticity in Montana high society. The more formal the dinner, the more likely you were to find a Stetson or two.

I came home exhausted. My collar had chafed a red ring around my neck. My feet ached from the stiff arches of my formal shoes. I found my mother in the kitchen, blender in hand, a suspicious green bottle labeled NUTRITIVE KELP on the counter beside her. "Would you care for a green-algae smoothie?" she said by way of greeting. "They regenerate muscle tissue and help build neural sheathing."

I told her that my neural sheathing was, as far as I could tell, adequate.

"Suit yourself," she said. "It tastes just like the ocean."

Whether or not this was a positive attribute, she didn't say, so we took her kelp smoothie and walked into the living room and sat on the couch. We needed to talk, I told her. She agreed. I guess I illustrated to her how I'd felt about things. As we talked, the conversation seemed inevitable, it seemed like the conclusion of something that had started forty-eight hours ago with the two of us digging through the ruins of our vegetable garden, stripping it of all its vegetation.

I don't know how other people make decisions. From what I understand, not everyone makes decisions like I just had. But it was clear to me then: I needed to find my dad. I needed to track down this missing part of my story, this vanished and fugitive sector of my genealogy, this dim adumbration of my family's lost past.

A quick surprise: When I told her, she surprised me with a gesture. She stood up and walked over to where I was sitting and took me in her arms and hugged me close against her.

I don't remember going up to my room. I was that exhausted. Breakfast felt like a continuation of the previous night with my mother. The bright green smoothie made a reappearance. My mom, however, was a little less comforting. This time she said without any segue: "If you go, you need to know this: Marrying Akram Saqr was the single greatest mistake I ever made."

I paused. "Okay," I said.

"Nothing I have done," she continued, "before or since, has been such an error."

I wanted to point out to her that I knew this, that I knew it as certainly as I knew anything else—that I blamed him, in large part, for the manifestation of the genetic disease that had so characterized my childhood. Anxiety has a physiological effect on the body. My mother had spent years submerged in the anxiety of losing her husband. I wanted to tell her that I did blame him for so many different things, including the currently stripped and vegetationless garden. I wanted to tell her that I harbored no delusions about my father's role in my mother's life. But I couldn't figure out how to say it, not all of it at once.

"I hope I remember to take my pills when you're gone," she said.

"Is that a threat?" I said.

"Oh, Khosi," my mother said. "If you go, you're going to regret it. You will regret this, I promise you."

"When have I ever done anything," I said, "that I regret?"

"This will be first and foremost," she said.

"You can't be sure of that," I said.

"Of course I can," she said. "I lived it."

"I refuse to accept that," I said.

"You can refuse all you want," she said, "but it won't change the incontrovertible fact."

"I have faith in myself," I said.

"Of course you do," she said. "I have faith in you, too."

"Just not now?"

"Not with this man," she said. "You have no idea."

On my last night in Butte, I went to the Yacht Club. I squinted as I walked through the door, adjusting to the lack of light. It was busy. Natasha and I, one night earlier in the summer, had searched the whole bar for a light source other than a neon beer sign. No luck. I suppose it was kind of a rough place. It was also the only place I knew of with off-track betting. I settled in at the bar. A blanket of cigarette smoke enveloped me, rising and tumbling through the air, almost a solid mass. Chuck Wilson removed a rack of pint glasses from the dishwasher. He placed them on the counter in front of him. Before I could say anything, he brought me a double bourbon, neat, and a Miller Lite.

"How'd you know?" I said.

"That's my job."

I took my beer and my bourbon and sat next to the jukebox.

There were country songs on this jukebox, at least fifty country songs that could express the way I was feeling. I'd let Ray Price take control, or Moon Mullican, or Patsy Cline. I fed twenty dollars into the machine. There were at least seven hours, after all, until closing time. I walked over to the OTB monitors. I logged in. I finished my bourbon. I scanned the racing form.

There was a stakes race starting in twenty minutes at Santa Anita. I watched the horses trot out of the paddock and over toward the gate. I chose a green gelding—one with just a few races listed on the form, most of them in smaller tracks. He was a 15–1 long shot, but he had strong numbers in ten furlongs, and that was a good sign. I finished my beer. I was about to place my bet when my phone rang. I glanced at the number. It was Wada.

"Look out," she said. "Incoming."

I took a moment to understand what she meant. "I'm sure she's angry," I said.

"In her fiercest mood."

"She knows I'm at the Yacht Club?" I said.

"*Habibi*," Wada said. "Where else would you be?"

It was a good point. "Thanks," I said, "for the warning."

"No problem. Good luck, my darling boy."

I hung up the phone. When my mother was in this mood—her most fearsome—there was nothing she would refuse to do. The summer I was ten, I hit the lip of the YMCA pool on a dive from the highest board. The sickening sound of bone on concrete shot out across the parents and friends assembled in the stands for the meet. I was lucky, very lucky, to only break an arm. Obviously, I never dove again. But my mother, she was up and running in a fraction of a second. At moments of intense stress, she did this, transformed into someone else, almost, rising to the challenge. She dove into the pool before anyone could stop her. She set some sort of world record for the crawl. She reached me ten seconds before the lifeguards. It was her fierce, steady, confident help that guided me out of the water. I was her baby boy, her tiniest charge. She was surfacing and protecting me. I was hers and hers alone.

I slipped out into the alley behind the bar and ducked around the corner. There she was, sitting in her car, idling the motor, watching me walk toward her.

"Perfect," she said, rolling down the window. "I don't have to go in that place."

"That's not fair," I said. "It's really quite homey."

"Look," she said, "I don't have time for a lot of chitchat. I have to get to tonight's job. I just thought that, you know, some people travel with patron saints and miraculous medals to protect them." She leaned over and pulled something out of the glove box. She handed it to me. I looked down, conscious that I already had the bracelet in my pocket and that I'd adopted *it* as a sort of talisman. But what my mom had handed me was an Evel Knievel Days souvenir program—from 2007. "And so," she concluded, "I got you this."

"Okay," I said, looking down.

"Open it," she said.

Inside was a bookmark—a stylized image of a man riding a red, white, and blue motorcycle. Around his neck was the familiar Evel Knievel cape. Why he chose to wear a cape while riding a motorcycle is something that I will never truly understand. But there, scrawled at the bottom of the bookmark, was a shaky signature. *Keep ridin!* it said. *Evel.*

"This is probably pretty rare," I said.

"I thought it might be his last Evel Knievel Days," she said. "It turned out I was right."

"Thanks, Mom," I said.

"For when you moved out of the house," she said. "I thought that at that point, it would be an appropriate sentiment."

"Keep ridin?" I said.

"Not literally," she said.

"Unless I moved to a ranch," I said.

"It's a bookmark," she said. Her voice rose slightly, leading me toward its desired conclusion. "And so?"

"So there's a book that goes along with it?" I said.

My mother nodded and sighed. She reached between the seats and pulled out a slim white volume. She handed it to me through the open window. *Overcoming Obsessive Thoughts.* My stomach lurched. The ground felt suddenly distant. Momentarily, I flashed back to the hours and hours of mother-son therapy time, to the mental health seminars at the downtown convention center, to the self-help books on tape that lived, a rapacious and accumulating fungus, on the bookshelves of our house.

"Come on," I said. "I don't have a problem."

"Of course not," my mother said. "We all know you're perfectly normal."

"Denial," I said, "ain't just a river in Egypt."

"Very funny," my mother said.

"Look, Mom," I began. I was about to tell her something that she'd told me, countless times: *Your solutions have to be* your *solutions. They can't belong to anyone else.*

"Just read it," she said. "I have to go to work." She frowned. "I mentioned that you're making a terrible mistake."

"Yes," I said.

"Good," she said. She rolled up the window. Then she rolled it down again. "You know," she added, "there's an old Arabic saying: 'Mention the wolf and have your club ready.'"

"There aren't any wolves in Egypt," I said. "I doubt it will come up."

She stared at me.

"What does that even mean?" I said.

"Mention the wolf," she said. "Think about it. Don't go looking for trouble. Just be careful."

She drove away.

I walked home. On my way, I passed the pit. It yawned out into the darkness, dimming away into the body of the hillside. I stopped at the railing of the exterior fence and gazed out at the vast toxic lake. I looked out over the water. An open-pit copper mine is a re-markable thing. Slowly, with shovels and bulldozers and backhoes, miners scoop away the dirt, boring deeper and deeper into the ground. From the sky, they must look like ants, tunneling a geomet-ric shape by the guidance of some invisible principle. They tunnel and blast at the ground with chemicals. They destroy and destroy more deeply and destroy even more deeply still. Once it reaches a certain point, there's nothing that can be done to heal a strip mine. The earth will forever bleed downward, leaking its groundwater through the walls of the mine.

Eventually, the Berkeley Pit will flood. Fifteen years ago, a flock of snow geese landed on its surface. Within hours they were dead. Nobody knew exactly how many had died. Because in the first few hours that those geese floated in the mine, their little goose skins absorbed gallons and gallons of toxic water. Their goose corpses turned orange. Their feathers became inky chemical sponges. They were camouflaged.

I always used to think of the pit as a terrible scar, a pockmark in the skin of the city, of the state, of the country. But as I stood there and replayed my strange last few days in my head, it looked almost beautiful. It was vast and aquatic and it was a contrast to the city that stretched up to its lip. I thought of Wendell Berry, who titled his essay about East Kentucky strip mines "The Landscaping of Hell." Every strip-mining company had learned its trade from my family; I was complicit in this, my blood was corrosive; once upon a time, it broke the crust of the world.

Four

"THE THING YOU NEED TO know about Cairo," my taxi driver
said, "is not the traffic. It's not the pollution. It's not the dust." Here
he extinguished his cigarette, grinding it into his ashtray. "It's the
bread."

He kept glancing at me in his rearview mirror as he drove, a pro-
cedure that I found a little disconcerting. He'd make eye contact
with me for five, ten, fifteen seconds, even as the traffic darted past
us, taillights flaring in angry blossoms of red. I had never, quite
honestly, seen anything like the traffic on the road into Cairo. Even
as we crossed the Sixth of October Bridge and entered the body of
the city, cars moved with an aggressive madness I'd associated only
with a swarm of bees.

"You see," the driver continued, "every revolution in the history
of our country happened because someone raised the price of bread,
ya'ani. And that's why Mubarak is in trouble."

His cell phone rang. He frowned and answered it and instantly
began an animated argument with a man who was, as far as I could

tell, his mortal enemy. With one hand, he held the phone to his ear. With the other hand, he lit a cigarette. I assumed that he was driving with his knees. I searched for my seat belt. Either it had never been installed or it had been removed by sadistic thieves.

His enemy vanquished, the driver snapped the phone shut and looked back at me again. He asked me why I'd come to Egypt.

"I'm here to find my father," I said. "He's Egyptian."

The man nodded but said nothing more. "And what part of America do you come from?" he asked.

"Montana," I said.

"Ah, yes," he said. "It is beautiful." He didn't elaborate on how he'd come to this knowledge. Maybe this was his standard line. ("What part of America do you come from?" "Three Mile Island, Pennsylvania." "Ah, yes. It is beautiful.")

We'd driven down the Al-Orouba Road, and now we were on the Salah Salem. Big white apartment buildings—architecture in a grand modernist style—lined either side of the roadway. I thought about the density of the buildings, arranged row after row after row. And I imagined my father looking at these same buildings, driving this cityscape, having it form the backdrop to his thoughts each day. I saw my dad everywhere. I strained to find him in each person walking along the side of the road. I imagined his face in every billboard, at the wheel of every oncoming car, in the seats of every lumbering, diesel-spewing bus.

"What else should I know about the city?" I said as we pulled up to the Kewayis Cairo Marriott, where I'd gotten a room for the price of an American Motel 6.

The driver thought about this for a moment. "Well," he said, with his hand on the door handle, "people have been living here for seven thousand years."

A porter collected my bags and whisked me through security. The man in front of me in line held a string of prayer beads in his hand. Islam has its own version of a rosary; a *misbaha* has ninety-nine beads on it, one for each of God's names. I'd seen them at the Islamic Center in Billings, but never in the world, never like this. With the *misbaha*, a supplicant will recite all ninety-nine names, repeating them again and again, looping through them with the fingers. The fourteenth name: Al-Mussawir, the Bestower of Form, the Shaper. The nineteenth name of God: Al-Fattah, the Opener. The thirty-eighth name of God: Al-Kabir, the Most Great. The sixty-first: Al-Muhyi, the Giver of Life. Bestowing Form, Opening, the Most Great, the Giver of Life. Cairo, Al-Qahira, the second oldest city on the planet, Mother of the World, an organic beast, a being made by this kind of a divinity, working through the hands of its believers.

Newly landed in Cairo and safely ferried to my room, I slept for nearly sixteen hours, waking only upon the morning call to prayer. The disembodied sound of the muezzin's voice unwound itself around me, even on the tenth floor. It was a call to prayer, sure, but it was also an alarm clock. *Prayer is better than sleep*, he was saying. *The world is beginning to awake.* The call ended. The air conditioner appeared to have stopped working, perhaps out of despair. It had decided to *heat* the room instead. The modern hotel room with its wall of windows was, after all, simply a giant greenhouse.

I stared at the ceiling. I put my legs on the edge of the mattress. But was that the right way to begin the day? Wouldn't I be luckier, safer, faster, happier if I leaped out of bed without coming into contact with the edge of the mattress? I felt the dried sweat on my face, felt its sheen on my upper lip. I was parched. So here I was, in need of two things that were so important to the Prophet (peace and blessings be upon His name): water for the thirsty and knowledge for the ignorant. I sank back into the center of the bed, so very small and alone and puny. I was nothing, I was a fragment of nothing, I was less than a fragment of nothing, I was a fraction of a bit of a sliver of a fragment of nothing. Dust towered over me in its significance. At least dust, with more dust, could make a storm. I could not make a storm.

Honestly, I was afraid of playing private detective. I was afraid of failure, sure. But I was equally afraid of success. I was afraid that I would find my father, and then what? I'd taken those three Xanax and stepped onto the international flight. The softness, the safety, of life at the museum was utterly shattered.

Before leaving, I'd contacted a private investigator who had contacted, in turn, the local police in Egypt. Now I took the two notecards out of my wallet. I looked down at them. My mother had been no help in offering me contact information for my father's family. "I burned it all in a bonfire," she'd said. "When you were six years old." A bonfire of contact information would've been a very small bonfire, but I'd assumed there were other things in the flames. Between the P.I. and Tante Wada, I had a list of eighteen addresses, all of which could contain my father, all of which I'd written on two 3×5 notecards. I'd found five phone numbers, too, but I'd tried them all, and they'd all been disconnected.

I brushed my teeth madly, vigorously, and I wedged myself into my clothes. I'd brought the copper bracelet, too. It had whispered softly to me as I packed, saying: *Bring me, bring me, bring me.* Now, on the brink of leaving the hotel (maybe), I slipped it in my pocket, along with the Evel Knievel bookmark. I needed protection of some kind. This seemed to be a way of getting it. Obsessions and compulsions occur in cycles, and the speed of my cycles, the move from panic to calm to panic once again, seemed to be increasing.

I dashed to the elevators and rocketed down to the lobby. Actually, both of those things probably happened at normal speed, but they felt dangerous to me, they felt like being behind the wheel of a brakeless car. Taking a deep breath—and choosing one of the many addresses on my notecards—I headed out into the maelstrom.

I would not be the first person to compare walking through Cairo to the video game Frogger. The difference being that if I were flattened by a truck (or a taxi or a private sedan or a military Humvee or a pedicab or a motorcycle or a rickshaw or a donkey pulling a wooden cart full of melons, all of which sped by with a certain wild grandeur) (except for the donkey, the donkey was slow and sweet), I would not regenerate a new life at the bottom of the screen.

One hundred and twenty degrees. A dusty hot wind. I'm a sucker for cities, but Cairo wasn't easy. It didn't open itself to me immediately. I wasn't prepared for it, not really. I mean, I knew a lot about the place from textbooks, from hours and hours in the little Saturday school in Billings. Tante Wada had supplemented my studies with a series of videos, videos that she'd often show me as soon as we got back to her house, videos with names like *Yemen Today!* and *Oh My, Oman!* These had been aggressively cheerful instructional films with cheap production values and direct sponsorship from the Ministries of Tourism. They didn't get me knowledge of the street in the Arab world, of the textures of daily life. Somehow I wasn't prepared for the visual image of the poverty, for the pollution, for the rows of informal settlement houses that sagged into each other, that seemed to be reaching for the street, leaning toward it and opening their hands in supplication. I thought of Dickens's Coketown, with its black ladders appended to the outsides of tenement buildings, black ladders used exclusively by undertakers to lift out coffins where the stairs were too narrow.

I found myself avoiding the asphalt where possible, because it was melting. The asphalt was melting and I saw children playing with it, scooping handfuls of it from the margins of the roadway, scooping it up and flinging it at each other like mud. I sweated through my new shirt, the fabric sticking to my chest and my back. My feet chafed against my new loafers, which turned out to be a little too big. Blisters bloomed on both of my ankles, big wet blisters that sent tendrils of pain up the backs of my calves with each step.

It wasn't all grim. One of the things that worked in my favor was that anyone I talked to thought my accent was hilarious. A few people laughed at me outright as soon as I began to speak. I couldn't blame them. Imagine someone asking you for directions in proper Victorian English: *Kind sir, perchance you could direct me to the nearest purveyor of fine comestibles?* I took the subway (surprisingly pleasant) to the other side of downtown. I walked and sweltered but finally made it to the first address.

2 Omar Ibn El Khattab. Big apartment building, ground-floor apartment, two pigs in the courtyard in a jolly-looking, trash-filled

sty. The pigs sniffed me as I walked past, raising their snouts in unison and smelling the air. I found Apartment 2 and knocked on the door, using the sizable brass knocker, its metal scorching hot in my palm. I knocked three times, long ponderous knocks, knocks that could certainly be heard in the interior of the house. I heard shuffling in the apartment. Someone was opening a series of locks. What would Natasha think of me now? My heart clattered in my chest. Sure, this wasn't jumping over the Grand Canyon, like Robert Craig Knievel, but for me—for me it was close.

The door swung open, revealing a wiry little man in a powder-blue Adidas tracksuit.

"*Sabaah el-kheir,*" he said. *Good afternoon.*

"Good afternoon," I repeated. So: This wasn't my father. Not that I'd expected to find him immediately, but it would have been nice, I have to admit. Standing there in the doorway, I panicked. My words blurred together, my accent was all wrong. I was using my stiffest formal Arabic.

"I'm from America," I said in a rush. "My father deserted me when I was three, and I lived with my mother for my entire life, and now I've tracked him down to here, to Cairo—he's Egyptian—and I really think he might be living here, his name is Akram Saqr, and he is kind of short, like, like, like a circus bear." That's exactly what I said, word for word, with the exception of *circus bear*. In my panic I couldn't remember the Arabic word for *circus*, so I said instead "bear on a chain that wears a hat."

It was not one of my linguistic high points.

The man in the tracksuit just smiled at me. "America?" he said. "Will you be voting for Barack Obama?"

"Of course," I said. "Who else?"

The man grinned. "My name is Ahmes. Please come in."

Inside the house, I met a half dozen of Ahmes's relatives. No one had ever heard of my father.

"You would like perhaps some rice with chicken livers?" Ahmes's mother asked me. She was a tiny, wrinkled postage stamp of a woman. I knew the drill, in part from years of living with my mother. The answer was yes, even if the answer was no. I ate the livers, scooping them up with my fingers. They were tender and greasy and salty and delicious.

Ahmes made a phone call to an elderly relative in Alexandria who'd lived in the house as a child. She'd heard of a Saqr in the neighborhood, but he'd been a translator of old French novels. The relative hadn't heard his name in nearly fifty years. Then Ahmes's son, Gabir, pulled out his Toshiba laptop. He connected to their cousin in Dubai via Skype. Gabir introduced me to this stranger and prompted me to tell my entire story from the beginning. This stranger then called his mother in Damascus, whom he thought knew of a Saqr. She did, it turned out, but not one named Akram. And so my image spanned the Middle East, beamed around the globe by satellite, living however briefly in the air, in a language as brief as a single breath.

I should have known that nothing good could happen to me once my hands smelled like chicken livers. I looked at my map for directions to the second address: 8 Al-Gamaliya Street. As I headed there, the boulevards narrowed. This was the older part of the city. Over centuries, Cairo had layered its roads higher and higher, the stones and asphalt and concrete accumulating like the layers of a cake. Houses now looked like they were sinking into the earth. First-floor windows no longer let in any light.

There were fewer pedestrians. Phone lines and cable television lines and electrical lines looped overhead. Air conditioners dripped coolant—steadily, gradually—onto the pavement around me. A store window offered an array of dried fish, all of them hanging from ropes affixed to the ceiling. I paused in front of this shop, staring at the dead, dry eyes of the perch and the catfish and the trout. I felt like I was underwater, standing on the bottom of a lake.

8 Al-Gamaliya had a doorbell. I rang it.

Egyptians are known for their hospitality. The streets of Egypt were full of cheerful, friendly strangers. This was not a house full of cheerful, friendly strangers. No one answered the door. I should have taken that as a sign. But the door did seem to be slightly ajar, and when I pushed on it, it gave way. In fact, it swung open.

"Hello?" I called. I poked my head around the corner of the doorway.

There was nothing in the front hall—no furniture, no rugs, no evidence of human presence. There was a single ladder just to the left of the entrance. The whole interior, actually, seemed to be a construction site. A big room that was visible from the doorway had been sealed off with sheets of hanging plastic.

To this day, I'm not sure why I decided to go farther into the building. It must have been part of my compulsive thinking: *I've made it this far*, I must have thought, *so I have to see the thing through to the end.* Too bad that it almost turned out to be *my* end. The hallway led toward a room at the back of the building. Its illumination flooded out toward me, beckoning me. I walked through a doorway.

The room I entered may once have been a kitchen. Now it had been stripped of all of its appliances. All that remained was a single round table around which sat three men in sport jackets, playing cards. It took them a moment or two to see me. When they did, they stood up immediately and began shouting at me in a language I didn't understand.

"I'm an American," I said, inching back out of the room.

The men exchanged looks. One of them walked over to the wall and reached for a single black button. A buzzer sounded somewhere in the depths of the house. I heard rapid footsteps, and then three more men came running from an alleyway veranda, surging through the rusted French doors and into the room. The six men had a hurried exchange. Then a man who must have been the leader of the group started walking toward me. He was smiling in a way that seemed vaguely predatory. He was still speaking the language that I didn't understand.

Instinctively, I backed away. I backed all the way down the hall, just far enough to determine that: 1) Yes, he was chasing me. 2) No, it wasn't so he could give me a proper, welcoming embrace. I fled. With a dexterity that surprised me, I used one hand to topple the ladder that stood near the aperture of the door, and the other hand to slam the door, itself. A double impediment. Perhaps it would not have impressed a jaded action-movie fan. It sure impressed the hell out of me.

I was running then, running down the street I'd just traversed in the opposite direction. Blockading the door had given me a half-minute head start. In my panic, I ducked into the medina, into the Khan el-Kalili, hoping to get lost in the crowds. Clouds of propane and cumin opened before me as I ran. I was gasping for breath. The hot, dry Cairo air seemed to scorch my lungs.

The streets of the medina were a confounding maze. It had once been a walled city, after all, built like a rabbit warren to defend itself against invasion. As I fled, I saw a number of people above me, leaping from rooftop to rooftop. Who were they? I couldn't tell. All I knew was that I'd turn a corner and see one of the men who'd chased me. Then I'd dash back the way I came and, two turns later, see the same man. I couldn't lose them, no matter how hard I tried. I was too easy to spot in my American clothes.

I was heading north through the medina when I passed a sign for something I remembered from my guidebooks: El-Habb, an ancient Coptic Christian church that dated from the fourth century. I followed the arrows and dashed up the exterior stairs, and sure enough, there was a massive group of foreigners poised outside of the basilica entrance.

It was a strange reversal. To save myself, I became the very kind of person I'd spent so many years subtly dreading at the Copper King Mansion: a tourist. I sidled into the group and bluffed my way through the main gate. I got in for free, at least; that was a plus.

I scanned the interior for any sort of hiding place. Sure, I blended into this group of tourists, but would it be enough? The walls of the church were covered in icons. These were the Coptic saints—and they were enmeshed in scenes of martyrdom. They were small iconic images painted to fit the smallish wall panels. The saints looked out and over me into the infinite distance. "We come from a time of great suffering," their mournful eyes seemed to say. "Also a time when people were much shorter than they are today."

I loitered near the back of the nave. I glanced out of the double doors before they closed. In the little courtyard outside of El-Habb, I immediately spotted one of the men who'd followed me. What—exactly what—had I blundered into? I stood out, I was easy to spot, a blundering American in loud American clothes.

I had an idea. At one end of the church was a man sitting at a table selling holy postcards. He was about my size. I rushed over to him and shoved another customer out of the way.

"How much," I said in Arabic, "for your clothes?"

"Please, sir," the man said, evidently thinking I was trying to rob him. "I have very little. I have nothing you'd want."

I looked over my shoulder. "No, no," I said. "You misunderstand. I will give you my clothes and money. Lots of money," I added. "Maybe two hundred pounds?"

"For my shirt?" he said, his mouth agape.

"And your pants," I said.

"My pants?"

"And your shoes," I said.

Egyptians love to haggle. The man raised both palms in the air. "The shoes are extra," he said. "They are well worn."

"Excellent," I said. I stuffed a number of notes into his open palm.

The man looked at them. "It's been a pleasure doing business with you," he said, and smiled.

Five minutes later, after a hurried wardrobe change in an unused confessional, I took my place among the parishioners in the pews.

I hung my head low, placing it on my hands, kneeling in the posture of a deeply penitent man. My heart was thudding in my chest. I sat there with my head down, and slowly, slowly, my breathing returned to normal. With nothing else to do, I listened to the babble of the various languages—the pattern of the foreign voices that seemed to follow roughly the same script, the tour guides pausing in the same places, pointing out the same holy relics. I closed my eyes. And then I did pray. I prayed for guidance, for safety, for some kind of divine protection.

After half an hour or so, I noticed that everything had grown quiet, that even the tour guides had ceased their bubbling explication. I cautiously straightened up and lifted my head. My neck burned from being in the same position for all that time. I looked around. My pursuers were nowhere to be seen. There were only tourists in here. And then, from the space behind me, from the little balcony at the back of the church, a singing rose up, a number of voices intertwining and cutting through the air. It was a hymn. I turned and saw a black-robed choir, all of them wearing threaded gold belts. One of the men had a censer and shook the white smoke of incense into the room. Everyone thinks of Islam when they think of Egypt. They forget that the country has been, for nearly two thousand years, the seat of the Coptic Christian church.

Sitting there in the pew, that's when I realized: *The notecards.* The notecards with the addresses. In my haste to change into these new clothes, I'd lost track of them. I thought I'd tucked them under the waist of my new linen pants, but now that I looked, I could find only one. The singing ended, and in a strange moment for the interior of a church, the audience broke into applause. I used this cover to scramble back over to the confessionals. I searched the one I'd used as a changing booth. Nothing.

I leaned against the little screen. I closed my eyes. This had gone badly, badly wrong. And then—then the strangest thing happened. There's no other way to say it: Resting momentarily in the confessional, exhausted and hot and sweating, I looked up and saw a ghost. Or rather, I didn't see a ghost, exactly. Something a little different than that. Actually, I heard a ghost.

"What are your sins, pardner?" said a deep voice with a western twang to it. It took me a moment to realize that the voice had spoken English and that—given my current circumstances—English was inappropriate. "Go ahead and tell me," the voice added from the other side of the confessional wall. "I won't bite."

"I'm sorry?" I said, frowning in the half dark.

"I said: Let 'er rip. I'm all ears. Yes, sir. All ears."

"How did you know I spoke English?" I whispered.

"I know all sorts of things, Khosi," the voice said.

My name? I panicked and reached for the door.

It's embarrassing—embarrassing to admit to a hallucination, and not just any kind of hallucination but a ghost, and not a ghostly figure, not an insubstantial blur at the edge of your vision, not a glowing orb in some shoe-boxed black-and-white photograph, but a fully developed bodily apparition, a ghost with arms and legs and a substantial, solid essence—not to mention the wardrobe of an Old West cowboy and a broom-sized mustache. That's exactly what I saw, what was suddenly wedged on the seat beside me in the confessional, the confessional which was truly not big enough for two full-sized adults. My hand fell back to my side.

"Scoot over, son," the man said. "It's tighter than a well-digger's lunch-bucket in here."

I squinted through the darkness. "You look," I said, "just like a photograph from the place I used to work."

The figure nodded and tipped its hat. "William Andrews Clark," he said. "Damn glad to meet you."

The William Andrews Clark I knew about became a U.S. senator. He circulated in Washington and died in his mansion on Fifth Avenue. This version of him, however, was more rough-and-tumble. This version looked like an extra from a Hollywood western.

"Well, you really fouled that one up, pardner," he said.

"What are you?" I whispered. "I mean: Are you what I think you are?"

"Indeed, Khosi," he said. "I was—"

"The original copper king. Anaconda Willie. Clark the Shark."

"Ah," he said. "My reputation precedes me. In that case: Maybe you've got a match for me to light my cigar?"

The Ghost of William Andrews Clark took out a silver monogrammed cigar case and popped it open. He selected a single thin cylinder.

"You can't smoke in here," I said. "Oh my God, I'm hallucinating. I'm hallucinating my great-great-grandfather in an Egyptian confessional."

"Would you also like a cigar?" he said. "I could possibly spare a Nicaraguan. They're a hundred years old."

"Jesus Christ," I said.

"Please don't take the Lord's name in vain," he said. "That's burro milk."

"Burro milk?"

"Bunk. Hogswaddle. Claptrap." He cleared his throat. "Inappropriate."

Suddenly, he was puffing on the cigar, smoke billowing into the air.

"How'd you do that?" I said.

"It's a little trick Saint Sebastian taught me," said the Ghost of William Andrews Clark.

"Oh my God," I said. "My tenuous grasp on sanity has been utterly destroyed."

This only seemed to amuse the ghost. He laughed. "Nonsense," he said. "I'm just here to warn you."

"To warn me?" I said.

"Watch yourself today," he said.

"What are you talking about?" I said.

"I'm telling you, Khosi: Sometimes life's got a sting like bumble-bee whiskey."

"Am I going to be attacked by a swarm of bees?"

The Ghost of William Andrews Clark chuckled. "Of course not, son," he said. "But remember this: Know what I do when I ride into trouble?"

He paused.

He waited.

Finally, I said, "What?"

"Just keep ridin."

"Are you really giving me advice?" I said. "A ghost is giving me advice?"

"Absolutely," he said.

"Why are you sharing this lovely advice with me?" I asked.

"Well," he said, "you've given me a lot."

"I have?" I said.

"Sure," he said. "My memory. You've helped preserve my memory in the minds and hearts of the masses. And for that, I'm grateful." He leaned forward. His voice was low and confidential. "You know, that goes a long way up there." He pointed upward. "It keeps you in the forefront of the Boss's mind."

"Ms. Vogel?" I said.

"Very funny," said the Ghost of William Andrews Clark. "Although I will admit, they do share certain characteristics."

"I've got to get out of here," I said.

I opened the confessional door. And for the second time that day, I ran. My legs churned forward, I stumbled in my haste to get away from the church. I had clearly gotten out on the wrong side of the bed. I considered going back to my hotel. No, I decided, that was too reserved. I needed to take more extreme action. I needed to get a taxi back to the airport. I needed to find a yellow taxi (only a yellow taxi would do) and use my credit cards to buy myself a one-way ticket home. I needed to get to Montana. And fast.

We are full of molecules and enzymes and cells, tens of thousands of enzymes inside of each cell, binding to different molecular bodies and processing them to make the compounds of life. Molecular recognition, I learned in my online biology class, is the fundamental mechanism of living matter. Something was misfiring in my brain, something was being misrecognized and broken down in the wrong way and filed in the wrong filing cabinet. Metaphorical filing cabinets, of course, but filing cabinets nonetheless.

The ghost was relentless. He followed me. He appeared beside me on the street; his spurs jingled with every step. "Boo," he said.

"I thought I left you back there," I said. I put my hand to my ear. At least this way, people might think I was having a phone conversation. Or that I was an agent of the secret police. There were a lot of them, after all, on the Egyptian streets.

"I'm a ghost, Khosi. I can be everywhere at once and anywhere I want."

"Anywhere?" I said. "Then what is Natasha doing right now?"

"Brushing her teeth," he said. He cleared his throat again.

"Sure," I said. I was inching along the wall of the building. Not far from me was a little park. The buildings separated, and a tiny lush garden appeared, with a single bench in the midst of a dozen palm trees. The bench was unoccupied. I sat down. I rested my head in my hands. I didn't need to look to know that the Ghost of William Andrews Clark had settled in beside me. "Sure—brushing her teeth. I obviously can't verify or disprove your statement." I glanced over at the apparition. "You realize this means I should be committed," I added.

"Nonsense, pardner. You know, Khosi, my first night in Butte, I had to pitch a tent. I was—really and truly—a pioneer. The mud was knee-deep. I didn't dry off until the sun rose the next day." He took one last drag on his cigar, then stubbed the cigar out on the heel of his boot. "I'm here to tell you, son: If you're a pioneer, you've got to work harder. This ain't easy, what you're trying to do."

"No," I said. "But I'm not a pioneer." I paused. "I can't possibly do this."

"Unacceptable," he said.

"Why?" I said. "I lost one of my notecards. That's half of my addresses."

"You can't get down, son, because of these little disasters."

"Little disasters?" I said. "There were men screaming at me and chasing me and I had to buy a stranger's clothes off his back."

"Don't worry," said the Ghost of William Andrews Clark. "There will be more of that."

"More?" I said. "No, thank you. This was poorly conceived. By me. I came here for the wrong reasons."

"Son," he said, "you lost one of your address cards? That's what's got you down? Here, let me see the other one."

"Why?" I said.

"Just let me see it."

I handed over the single most important piece of paper I possessed in the world—handed it over to a spectral image. I'm not sure what I expected might happen. Perhaps I thought that the notecard would fall dramatically to the ground, that I'd glance down at it and see it in the dirt and then I'd look up and be free of the hallucination. Instead, I felt a chill move through my hand as it neared the hand of the Ghost of William Andrews Clark. I felt a coldness spread up through my arm and into the center of my chest. The ghost clutched the card and held it aloft for just a moment.

"This is what I like to call," he said, "the Subterranean Switcheroo."

"Subterranean?" I said. Before I could say anything more, the notecard sparked and flared and exploded in flames. "No!" I called, but it burned and burned and then rose like a rice-paper lantern, a tiny flame pulled into the air by the desiccated wind. "What have you done?" I said.

The Ghost of William Andrews Clark just leaned back and smiled. "Do you trust me?" he said.

"Hell, no, I don't trust you," I said.

"You can trust me, Khosi," he said, "because this is the only address you're going to need."

The same bony, faded, chalk-colored hand reached out and, from nothing, from nowhere, produced a replica of the card I'd just seen rise into the sky. I looked down, and there, written in my handwriting, in a perfect replica of my careful numerals, was a single centered address: 20 ABDEL REHIM SABRI STREET. I tried to understand, to make quick sense of what had happened, but before I could, I heard a rustle nearby and felt the faintest puff of air, the faintest breath of camphor, and then the clatter of receding horse hooves. I looked up. The Ghost of William Andrews Clark had disappeared. After some time, I realized he wasn't coming back.

"Nice talking to you," I said quietly to the empty street.

I wandered a bit, walking the streets of that part of the city. My knees were shaking. Once, in high school, I'd sat up with Natasha all night while she came down from an acid trip. I'd kept reassuring her that the floor of my bedroom was indeed the floor of my bedroom, that the carpet was indeed just the carpet, that nothing was bending or floating or melting away. That was the closest I'd ever come to any sort of hallucinogen. What had he said? *Keep ridin?* And then I realized: He'd been quoting Evel Knievel.

As I walked, I saw a giant billboard painted onto the side of a brick building, its size comparable to the billboards in Times Square. A man in a business suit was smiling into the camera and holding his cell phone aloft in triumph. He had perfect luminous teeth. His Oxford shirt was starched and white, and he'd been carefully manicured. The text behind him said:

GET PRAYER TIMES FOR MILLIONS OF CITIES WORLDWIDE!
AUTOMATIC LOCATION DETECTOR GPS!
GOOGLE MAPS!
PRINTABLE MONTHLY PRAYER CALENDAR WITH
GREGORIAN AND HIJRI DATES!
SUHOOR AND IFTAR TIMES FOR RAMADAN COMPLIANCE!
BLESSED BY CLERICS! TRUSTED! RELIABLE!

The word *Google* was transliterated. Arabic characters spelled it out phonetically. As I stood there staring at the sign, a mosquito landed on my arm and, before I could even feel it, drank its fill. I looked down and saw the beginning of an itchy welt.

Maybe the ghost was the answer to my prayers? Or maybe the answer was this: *The Life and Times of Akram Saqr and Amy Clark, My One and Only Parents, as Told by Me, My Mother's One and Only Son, Fruit of Her Womb, 100 Percent Maculate Conception, Part Two.* It was an image that I couldn't shake, an image from the end of my parents' marriage. It had to be a lie. It wasn't possible that I remembered this. Except that I did. I was three years old when my father left. But still,

I had this memory: the memory of him standing above my bed in the dim light of a morning, his hand reaching down to brush the hair back from my forehead.

His face, in my memory, is missing. It's a blur, a smear, an indistinct set of features above me. It is, more than anything else, a feeling. His face is a feeling. In my version of that memory, I tell him not to leave. I stand on the mattress, unsteady, stubby-legged, wearing pajamas. I tell him not to leave, and he sits down at my bedside. Please, please forgive me this embarrassing, imagined memory; in this embarrassing, imagined memory, my father starts singing. It is a lullaby. It's not a song in English or in Arabic. Instead, it's a French lullaby about the nativity myth: *"Il Est Né, le Divine Enfant."* My father finishes, and he gets up and kisses my forehead again. And then he starts to leave. I tell him: "Please don't leave me." And he says: "I have to leave." And I tell him again: "Please don't leave us." And he says: "I'm leaving." And I can't tell if he's angry or sad or if he even hears me.

Tante Wada once told me something about the night of their wedding: Later that night my mother joined my father at the blackjack table, and together, they won five hundred dollars. Then they went to the bar attached to the casino and bought everyone a round of drinks. And there, at three A.M. in Caesar's Palace, my father leaped up on the bar in his bright white tuxedo and white leather shoes. "For my beautiful new wife," he called, and a discordant cheer rose up from the inebriated patrons. When he tried to climb down off the bar, he spilled a shrimp cocktail on my mother's off-the-rack, ill-fitting gown.

None of this changed what I had in my hand, what I hadn't put down since the ghost had given it to me: 20 Abdel Rehim Sabri. Every time I crossed a street, I was sure to step precisely onto each sidewalk. I kept glancing over my shoulder, making sure nothing was going to materialize in midair. If my foot landed in precisely the right place on the street, if it had the properly geometric ninety-degree angle to the chaos and disorder of the pavement, then I'd be fine. I'd be safe.

Only occasionally was the sidewalk in disrepair, necessitating some kind of emergency action on my part. Once I had to turn around and recross the street twice, east to west. Once my way was blocked by a vendor with a cage of chickens on her head. I waited patiently beside her as she concluded a transaction, pulling a protesting chicken from its last home with her strangulating grip. Feathers fluttered through the air. The other chickens, momentarily spared, resumed their clucking. I stood on the edge of the street and saw scraps of ghost in every peripheral movement, heard them in every honk of a car horn. Finally, the vendor moved along. I stepped on the exact square of sidewalk she'd been inhabiting. Relief flooded over me. Momentary relief.

My legs kept moving. Alleyway led to boulevard led to alleyway. I found Abdel Rehim Sabri and made my way toward Number 20. The apartment I wanted was on the second floor. I climbed the tiled staircase. There was graffiti in Arabic on the walls. *Such messy handwriting*, I noted. I rang the bell. A thin young woman answered the door. Her hair was shaggy and cut in a way that accentuated her rich olive eyes. She wore an eye shadow that seemed to contain faint gold glitter. Wrapped around her upper body—but not her head—was a silvery silken shawl. Its ends bore small glass beads.

"*Masa'aa el-kheir*," she said. *Good evening.*

In Arabic, the word for love, *hawa*, is almost indistinguishable from the word for air, *haawa*. The only difference is a slight aspiration, a breath inward, a minor doubled inflection. Now, standing in the sudden breeze created by the opening doorway, I felt the connection between the two words: In July, in Cairo, any burst of air was a burst of love, a brief freedom from the stultifying heat.

"Hello," I said in Arabic. "I'm looking for someone—perhaps you can help me? I am looking for a man named Akram Saqr."

She paused for quite a long time, turning the hem of that shawl over in her long, elegant nails. There was the smallest clatter, the smallest noise of lacquered nail brushing against beads. It's funny that I heard this sound so distinctly.

"Why are you looking for him?" she finally said.

An unexpected question—or rather, a simple question with a complicated answer. Not to mention the fact that this probably meant the ghost had been right; this was the only address I needed. I wiped the sweat off my face.

"So you know him?" I asked.

"Very well," she said. She paused. "He's my fiancé."

Five

FIANCÉ: A FRENCH WORD, I immediately thought, derived from the word for *to promise*. This took only a fraction of a second as the dictionary page floated up and in front of me. It wasn't a photographic memory, exactly, that I had, but more a disquieting pattern of obsessive thought. I photographed the things I saw for later. This time it was the page of a dictionary.

"Are you feeling ill?" the woman asked. She switched to English: "Can I get you something to drink?"

"One moment," I said, also in English.

I paced away from the door, afraid to look back, afraid to see the look of concern and care, the look that would astonish me once again. Engaged? I should have known. I should have known that marriages, like illnesses, cluster together—entering your life in multiples, in twins, or triplets, even. My father was engaged again. That was why he'd traveled to the United States to get my mother's official signature on a divorce decree; he'd needed it legally. And should I pinch this woman to make sure she wasn't a ghost?

I scanned the street for some kind of refuge, some place where I might be safe. Nothing. It was a foreign street, broad and thick with traffic. The sun was relentless in the pale blue, slightly smoggy sky. Great. I wasn't exactly the most resilient fellow in the world. This was something of a challenge. I turned back and walked over to the woman. She had inched back into the house, and I noticed that she was now holding the door so that she could easily slam it shut, if necessary. Possibly, possibly, there was an undercurrent of fear beneath her look of concern?

"Can I come in?" I asked. "I've traveled a long way with a very important message for him, and I'm feeling quite tired."

The woman seemed to hesitate. She glanced over her shoulder into the hall of the building. She looked back at me. "One moment," she said. "Ibrahim," she called.

Ibrahim appeared in five seconds—a big, burly man wearing a formal housecoat. "Yes, madam?"

"Would you show this man inside?" she said. She smiled at me. "Come in," she added. "Sit down."

Can I describe for you the fact of a door frame? It towered above me as I passed through it. It felt like an aperture, a conveyance, a means of conduit from one life into another. For the first time in years, I didn't pause on the threshold, I didn't perform any ablutions or touch anything or think of some image that might protect me.

The apartment was a modernist marvel. It was a calming interior space, a space entirely devoid of clutter. Clean white marble was everywhere: the floors, the tables, the buffet, all of them hewn from the milk-veined, silver-flecked rock. There was a single tall iron lamp in the center of the main living room. It shed soft illumination over the interior, giving it a calcium glow.

"This is beautiful," I said.

"Thank you. Won't you have a seat?"

My father's fiancée asked Ibrahim for two cups of tea. He'd been standing nearby, at attention while we sat down. He appeared to hesitate and then disappeared wordlessly.

"I'm sorry," I said. "You astonished me just then, at the door."

"I could tell. I need to introduce myself. It's very rude of me, otherwise. My name is Agnes Mouri."

"It's very nice to meet you, Ms. Mouri." I paused. "Where did you meet my—your fiancé?"

Agnes Mouri looked down. "We met through mutual friends," she said.

Sweat stood out on the sides of my forehead. I felt my throat constrict. I tried to guess her age. Twenty-seven? Twenty-nine? She was young, in any case, at least twenty years younger than my father. And then I realized that I had to do it: I had to be honest. It wasn't easy for me. It was, in fact, the last thing that I wanted to do. When you grow up in a household with an unpredictable parent, with the constant duty of shepherding her emotions from condition to condition, the last thing you want to do is provoke a confrontation. Ever. Of any kind. But here I was. "My name is Khosi Saqr," I said, and waited for her reaction. She smiled broadly.

"Saqr?" she exclaimed. "Why, then you are a relative of Akram's."

This wasn't the reaction I'd expected. "Do you know who I am?" I said.

She frowned. "Not exactly. But are you one of Banafrit's children? Or Fatima's?" A look of puzzlement skittered across her face. "Khosi? But I thought I would have met you by now." The look of puzzlement expanded. "Wait a minute. Are you named after Akram's son? The one who died?"

It was strange, the sensation of my heart dropping into my stomach and my legs turning leaden, all while my head felt so unnaturally light that I thought I might float away.

"No," I said. "Not that I know of. But I am his son. And I'm very much alive."

"His son?" she said. "You mean his nephew."

"His son," I said.

Ibrahim arrived with the lime-flower tea. The idea of a servant made me nervous. I would have been just as happy getting my own drink from the kitchen. The tea had the smell of fresh citrus. There were also six small madeleines on a flowery porcelain plate. I looked at the soft arches of the cookies. I imagined—briefly, powerfully, comprehensively—diving into the safe luxury of those cookies, surrounded by the soft, buttery sponge cake, an escape.

"His son?" Agnes Mouri said again. "There must be some mistake. His son drowned, along with his first wife. She was an American. Like you, I'm assuming?"

I nodded slowly. "Yes. From Montana," I said.

"Montana, yes," she said, furrowing her brow. "But Akram's son drowned. It was a terrible tragedy. It completely changed the course of his life."

"Really?" I said.

That was when it came together for me. The escape back to his country, the disgrace of his abrupt arrival, his apparent lack of luggage, the lie that solved everything. The total cut from the previous life, the words that must have felt stunning and foreign and outrageous in the way that they aroused sympathy, in the way that they drew the family around him, the undeserving man, the fugitive, the deserter. The image of my father shifted, his countenance darkened in the imaginary portrait I'd rendered of him: An undercurrent of sorrow rose beneath the cheerful gambler's face. He was a liar, lying was a deep grain in him, a pattern that marked him with depth and constancy.

Agnes Mouri's tea cooled on its tray. It went from steaming warm to still and cold. At first she said: "But that's impossible." Later, she said: "I cannot believe this." And then, as I continued talking, continued detailing my father's life in Montana as I understood it, explicating the end of my parents' relationship, an end that did not, as far as I knew, contain any drowning whatsoever, she said: "*Khalas, khalas, khalas.*" Which means, in the Egyptian dialect of Arabic, *Enough, enough, enough.* Finally, we sat there in silence for quite some time.

"I'm sorry," she said. "As you can imagine, this is not how I expected to spend my Saturday."

"It's Saturday?" I said.

She just stared at the blank white wall, the white wall with its single stripe of charcoal paint running vertically from floor to ceiling. "I just don't believe you," she said. "I'm sorry."

"Why would I be lying to you?" I said.

"I don't know," she said. "Revenge? Revenge against me. Against my father. He was a wealthy and powerful man. Akram wouldn't lie to me like this."

"It must seem true to him," I said, scrambling. "After all these years."

"It's not that," she said. "It's much more complicated than that."

I wondered what she meant, but before I could ask her anything, she pulled a cell phone out of the drawer in the end table. "I'm going to call him."

"Please don't do that," I said.

"Why not?" she said. "If you were really his son, wouldn't you want me to call? Don't you think he should be honest with me? His fiancée, of all people?"

I didn't want this—I was already so far from home, so enveloped in a different culture, in a different world. I was wearing another man's clothes. I was speaking a foreign language. I felt like half a person. I felt like the kind of person who could imagine that William Andrews Clark was a gun-toting Wild West cowboy, a specter who'd decided to depart from his eternal rest and directly intervene in my earthly affairs. To calm myself, I started counting the tiles that formed a glistening mosaic in the floor. I began to sweat again, despite the gentle cool breeze that came from the air conditioners in the hallway.

"Of course," I said. "But maybe he was working his way up to it."

"That's ridiculous," she said. "He should come over here and explain himself to me. To us."

"Yes, he should. But that's not how I've imagined it. And the visualization—it's important to me. You have to trust me. My father is who he says he is." I paused. "Except when he's not."

"Exactly," she said. "Imagine how I feel. Can you even imagine how I feel?"

That was true. I couldn't. I stood up and walked over to the far wall of the apartment, where there was a bank of windows. The windows had a view of the tops of mango trees—leafy mango trees with their bright yellow-green crowns. Beneath the windows was the street, with its snarl of traffic. There was a painting just behind her, an oil canvas in the style of a muted Rothko. It bore primarily gray and light blue sections. I was staring at the painting as I walked back to her. She followed my gaze.

"It's an original," she said. "I bought it in Paris."

"Listen," I said. "We started off badly. All wrong. I don't know anything about you. Or—that sounds wrong, too. Forgive me, my Arabic isn't as good as my English. I lose subtlety in Arabic."

She smiled. "And I lose subtlety in English," she said in English. "But I thought Americans didn't learn other languages."

"We're too busy bombing weddings?"

Agnes Mouri stirred her tea. "It just seems," she said, "that the Americans I meet only speak one."

"With each language," I said, "you add another person to your-self."

"Then I am five people," she said. "But why is it so difficult to get anything accomplished?"

I looked at her. The cell phone was still lurking there, poised in her hand. "For work?"

"Or in any part of my life."

"What do you do?"

Agnes Mouri straightened her back. She gathered together a few renegade strands of her thick reddish-black hair and tucked them behind her ears. It was an endearing gesture. She lifted her chin slightly. She adjusted the loose shawl, tossing it farther over her shoulder. "I'm an antiquities dealer," she said.

I'd never met an antiquities dealer before. I told her this. She wasn't surprised. It was an industry that centered around the Mediterranean, at least in part because of the extreme age of the human settlements in this part of the world. I glanced around the sitting area of her apartment. I was astonished by the lack of anything ancient, of even the smallest trace of the pharaohs or the pyramids or, say, the Sphinx.

"You have to understand," Agnes Mouri said, "that I can't just ignore what you've told me."

"Of course," I said.

"I can't ignore the fact that my fiancé might have a twenty-year-old child."

"Twenty-three," I said.

She frowned. "And an ex-wife." She shook her head. "A living ex-wife."

I stared at her. She really was quite beautiful; she was about to become my stepmother.

"When did you meet my father?" I said.

"Eleven months ago. I met him at the Gezira Sporting Club. At the bar there, after a polo match. He rode in the polo match."

It was my turn to be astonished. "I didn't know he played polo," I said.

"He was terrible," Agnes Mouri said, laughing a little. "He fell off his horse."

"For some reason," I said, "that doesn't surprise me."

"And then," she continued, "when I asked him why he'd fallen, he told me he'd never played polo before. Never. He'd just watched. But someone had fallen ill. And there was a visiting team from Argentina. Egypt doesn't have a lot of polo players, believe me. And so he volunteered." Agnes Mouri smiled. "He told them he'd been a star player at his American university." She shook her head. "It really was quite dangerous."

"He lied," I said.

She looked at me sharply. "He lied," she said.

"It seems like a theme," I said.

That was the wrong thing to say. If there's one thing I've learned, it's this: The citadel of the self is built on tremulous supports. Much more tremulous than we might imagine. Pressure, even the smallest pressure, can cause something drastic to happen. And we are fragile, all of us, so damn fragile. The organism, the body and mind and spirit, are quite poorly designed. Emotions can break us, too. They can come from nowhere and suddenly we are destroyed. Agnes Mouri began to cry. Not dramatically, not with sobbing and hysteria. But slowly and steadily.

"Please," I said. "Please don't cry."

Why had the ghost sent me here, of all places? Damn ghost. Never trust an undead copper baron.

"Forgive me," I said. "I shouldn't have come. I think there's been a mistake. I must have the wrong Akram."

Agnes Mouri dried her eyes with the back of her wrist. "The wrong Akram Saqr," she said. "It's not exactly a common name."

"Well," I said, "there were several names it could have been. I think the man I'm looking for is much older than your fiancé."

"We *should* call him," she said. "To clear this all up right now."

I stood. "I've taken up too much of your time already," I said. I wanted to leave before she started dialing the phone. "I'll just show myself out," I said.

"But you haven't finished your tea," she said.

"You've been very kind to invite me in," I said, moving toward the front door. "I should have done more research. I shouldn't have upset you. Please don't be upset."

"Wait a moment," she said.

I was backing out of the room. "Congratulations on your engagement," I said. "Sorry about the misunderstanding."

I left my soon-to-be-stepmother behind, left her in her clean-lined, marble-filled apartment, left her to her cooled tea and her interrupted Saturday. The door closed behind me with a solid thud. The street opened in front of me, newly gigantic and foreign and torched by the evening sun.

As soon as I was in the street, I heard the next call of the muezzin—the fourth call of the day. A number of men knelt on prayer mats in stalls and in little alcoves here and there. I closed my eyes and listened to the amplified sound of the prayer call. From my hotel room, it had seemed serene and distant. Down here on the street, things were different. There seemed to be a number of muezzin in this neighborhood. Their amplifiers cut through the day, layering one on top of another, creating a cacophony of dueling prayer calls. There was a little bread cart just to my left, a man selling big, slightly sweet pretzels and *fiteer*, the ubiquitous Egyptian pancakes. The owner was evidently a Christian. He was holding his hands over his ears. "Is it always this loud?" I asked him in Arabic. He leaned in toward me, a questioning look animating the features of his face.

"Is it always this loud?" I repeated.

He furrowed his forehead and nodded. *"Allah akbar,"* he said, and smiled. *God is great.*

It was late evening. The sun was beginning to slip toward the horizon. The air pollution did two things. It made the sunset more gradual. The day wasn't as bright as it could have been without the intervening haze of breathable carbon. But the sunset was also brighter, more pink and orange and yellow. It lit up the margins of the firmament. It made the sky worthy of that word, *firmament.*

My stomach churned. I'd seen a ghost after all, a flesh-and-blood version of a man who'd been dead for a century. How could I trust anything? How could I believe my encounter with Agnes Mouri? Had *she* really existed? Was I actually in Cairo? The streets threatened to dissolve. I almost expected them to lift like a movie set, to reveal, perhaps, the padded walls of some Pacific Northwest asylum.

The hotel was a welcome relief. I burrowed under the familiar sheets and lay propped on my elbow, looking out through the window, looking out as the evening gave way to night, and the night gave way to deeper night, and the deeper night gave way to a fragile morning.

I spent the next day, Sunday, being a tourist. It was the happiest, calmest day I'd had in weeks. I walked up and down the length of the Nile. I visited the Egyptian Museum with its funerary vases and elaborately illustrated Books of the Dead. I stared for nearly half an hour at Tutankhamen's famous death mask, twenty-five pounds of jewel-inlaid solid gold. He'd been small—a boy-king—and he'd led a life full of pain, suffering from malaria and bone necrosis and a clubfoot. After leaving the museum, I wandered through the city, feeling anonymous. I ate more street food. I went back to my room early and watched a Lebanese soap opera about a family of brothers who betray one another in business deals. I slept. A sticky, heavy, cocooned sleep.

At seven-thirty the next morning the phone rang.

"Mr. Saqr," said the desk clerk. "You have a visitor in the lobby."

"Who is it?"

"One moment, sir." The phone line went quiet. After a few moments, the clerk returned. "I'm sorry, sir, but I cannot obtain that information."

"Well, why don't you just ask him?"

"I'm sorry, sir." He paused. "But that's impossible."

Fifteen minutes later, I stepped out of the elevator, half expecting to come face-to-face with the Ghost of William Andrews Clark. I went to the front desk and asked the clerk to direct me further. He nodded and extended his arm to his left and pointed. I turned around, and I will never forget that moment—never forget what I saw.

What I saw was the man from the museum—my father—standing there in the flesh and the sinew and the ligament and the bone and the blood and the soul, *yes*, perhaps even the soul, hovering in front of me, too shocked to do anything but stare. We recognized each other. He was wearing the same heavy overcoat. There was no figurative language to describe that moment. It was stripped, bleached of color and content and bare of secondary life. I thought: *What if I sneeze? Will that ruin the moment?* I thought: *I wonder if it's still a hundred and twenty degrees outside?* I thought: *Evel Knievel has nothing on this.* I thought: *Alfred Nobel's recipe for dynamite: three parts nitroglycerin, one part diatomaceous earth, one small admixture of sodium carbonate.*

We met halfway between the café and the front desk. He spoke first. "You've caused a lot of problems for me, Khosi," he said.

My eyes widened. I looked at him, afraid to say anything.

"My fiancée is locked in her bedroom," he added. "She's calling off the wedding."

"I see," I whispered.

He nodded and frowned.

"I didn't have your address," I said.

"Well," he said, "I guess it's not completely your fault, then."

"Not at all," I said. "And it was luck that led me to your fiancée. Luck and a ghost." I hesitated. "It was a ghost of a chance," I corrected, "that I'd find her."

His frown deepened. "Khosi, listen," he said in English. "Do you play backgammon?"

"I speak Arabic, you know," I said in Arabic.

He said, "You *do* speak Arabic. That was very nice indeed. But let's stick to English. And: Do you play backgammon?"

There was something strange about my dad's demeanor. His posture reminded me of the porters at the hotel. He looked completely healthy.

"Yes," I said, "I know how to play backgammon."

"Let's get out of here, then," he said, "so we can talk properly."

We ventured back out into the city. As we walked, I noticed the small backgammon box poking out of one of the pockets of the gray coat.

Cairo has a café culture. You hear that about the cities of Europe, but in the Middle East, it's even more true. Men congregate in the cafés. They congregate on the margins of the cafés. They sit against the walls of the buildings beside the cafés. They spill into the streets surrounding the cafés. Two things are ubiquitous in Egypt's capital city: televised news and sweet mint tea. It seems to be more vital to the life of Cairo than the oil that runs its industries. A lot of the cafés are built downward from the street to preserve some amount of the coolness of the soil and to avoid the blistering heat of the day. We passed two crowded establishments, but my father shook his head. I followed him to Abn al-Shryn, a small place tucked in an alley ten blocks from the Kewayis Cairo Marriott.

Within minutes we were seated at one of the tables on the cusp of the café, half in and half out, the streetlights just beginning to turn on at the ends of the block. He'd procured a water pipe, which he filled with apricot-flavored tobacco. "When I was a teenager," he told me as we sat down, "I used to fill these with hashish. I'd mix hashish in with the tobacco." He sighed and shook his head. "It was so delicious, you couldn't even imagine." He'd also ordered us coffee and bottles of mineral water. The waiter had called him by name. Now he began to arrange the backgammon board between us.

"I'm sorry," I said. "I have to take a moment, here."

"Light or dark?" my father said.

"Dark," I said. I glanced over at him. "How can you wear that coat in this heat?"

He chuckled. "This? This isn't heat. It's only—how do you say—one hundred Fahrenheit degrees. When it's warm like this, it's best to wear thick clothes and drink hot tea. Here, have a little tobacco. It calms the blood. I may smoke a cigarette as well."

"You shouldn't be smoking," I said.

He concentrated on the gesture of taking a pack of cigarettes out of his coat pocket. "Dunhill?" he said, and extended them to me. The writing on the pack, I saw, was in Arabic.

"No, thanks," I said. "I'll stick to one kind of tobacco."

He nodded. "Fair enough," he said. "I like to smoke cigarettes when I'm nervous. You—you're nervous, but you don't like to smoke cigarettes. Everybody's nervous. Probably the waiter is nervous, too. I'll answer your question in a second. But first, because we are all so nervous, can I tell you a story?"

I nodded. My father was sitting across from me, telling me a story as if he were an old friend—someone who'd popped into the hotel for a drink—and to accentuate the strangeness of everything, he looked a little like Cary Grant. A Middle Eastern Cary Grant, sure, but Cary Grant nonetheless.

"When I was six years old in Cairo," he said. "I went to see *Lawrence of Arabia* at the cinema. Have you seen it, *Lawrence of Arabia*?"

I shook my head. My father's eyebrows shot upward into an arc. He was still holding the Dunhill in his hand, and he waved it through the air, almost like a conductor waves a baton.

"Ah!" he said. "How is that possible? A pity! That is such a pity! And a travesty. *Une bêtise.* I will buy you the DVD tomorrow, downtown." He cleared his throat and took a sip of his drink. "I went to see it so many times, you know, in 1962. We'd pay one piaster and we'd hang on the railing in the balcony—ten of us, all of my friends.

We learned the words. Or the sound of the words, anyway, what we thought the words sounded like, because we didn't speak English. We all wanted to be Omar Sharif. Every one of us. Many of them still do, I think, the friends of mine who are alive. And I met him not long ago, Sharif, because he still lives in Cairo, in his family's house. He used to smoke, too, you know—they say two and a half packs a day. But then he had triple-bypass surgery and quit, *habibi*.

"Anyway, we'd learn the lines, you know. And we would say them as they happened. Think of it, what a thing: a line of boys hanging like monkeys on the railing of the balcony and saying the lines of the movie as they happened. But I'm going on and on. You're wondering, perhaps, when I will cease talking?"

I blinked several times, wide-eyed. Without meaning to, I shook my head.

"We wanted to be just like Sharif, all of us. One of my friends would have a cigarette—one cigarette—and he'd light it right when Sharif lit a cigarette on-screen. We'd pass it down the row of boys, you know. I was six years old. And that's how I started smoking."

He inhaled deeply from the Dunhill and then exhaled through his nostrils. I blinked some more. "Be like Omar Sharif," he said. "Smoke Lucky Strikes. It's toasted. It wasn't until I came to America that I realized that the cigarette companies bought those scenes in the movies. And—as for your mother," he concluded, "don't believe a word she says about me."

"You can see how that would be a challenge," I said. "Her having raised me and everything."

"*Habibi*," he said, "that sounded wrong. I didn't mean it like that.

What I meant is that she needed it. When I left, Khosi, in 1988, you see, we were still very much in love."

"She says she hates you," I said.

"Of course," my father said. "But you don't hate people whom you do not care about." He used the word *whom*, slipped it easily into the conversation, as if he were saying *coffee* or *mango*. He rummaged in a pocket and took out the pack of cigarettes again.

"What greater gift can you give your ex-wife," my father said, "than the gift of your own death?" Here he laughed, a loud, off-kilter laugh, one that I didn't share. And when I didn't share it, he said, "Look, why did you come today? You could have come at any time. You knew I was Egyptian. You knew where I lived. More or less. Why not come when you were sixteen?"

"I was a minor," I said.

"Then why not when you were twenty?"

"I was in college," I said.

"See: You are more like me than you believe, *habibi*. The margin between action and inaction is quite small." He held up his thumb and his forefinger, held them an inch apart, illustrating the margin. "Just like the margin between the truth and a lie." My father ran a hand through his thick silvery hair. "I knew you'd come," he continued, "after that day in the museum. I knew you would. But what a thing: Right here, in front of me, Khosi, my own darling boy." And then he did something that I had in no way anticipated. He stood up and walked around the table and knelt beside me, almost knocking over the water pipe with its smoldering ball of condensed tobacco. He knelt beside me and he took me in his arms and held me against his chest, he smothered me in that coat, really. I could smell the citrine odor of his aftershave and the lingering odor of the Dunhill.

I cleared my throat and pushed him away slightly, straightening my shirt, which had wrinkled from the combination of my own body heat and the fierce pressure of my father's embrace. "What about backgammon?" I said.

He nodded and sat back down. "Backgammon," he said, his voice deepening in register.

We played the first moves in silence. There was only the small clatter of our dice and the burbling of the water pipe. A few conversations ebbed and flowed around us, and I caught the occasional word. It was tough to understand the Egyptian dialect. The pronunciation, first of all, was entirely different from what I was used to. Every *j* sound became a *g* sound.

I rolled a six and a five. Eleven moves. I have to admit that I love board games. I love their codified rules, with their careful delineation of what's right and what's wrong. By far my favorite kind of game is the simple mathematical kind, the kind that involves a basic grid and pieces that were probably once rocks. Backgammon is a perfect example. And it is such an enduring mystery, the very fact of its existence. It is nearly five thousand years old. It's directly related to the ancient Egyptian game of *senet*, which was unearthed from the sarcophagi of the pharaohs.

"Do you want to bet?" my father said. "A small gentleman's wager?"

I stared at him. "Isn't that what caused your problems in the first place?" I said. "Isn't that what caused *my* problems in the first place?"

He shook his head and raised his palms in a suppliant gesture. "No bet, then," he said. "It's okay."

"Can you tell me one thing, at least?" I said. "Since you seem to be so bad at answering questions."

"Of course," he said.

"Why didn't you ever write to me?"

My father frowned. "Of course I wrote to you, *el hamdillah*," he said. "At least, I don't know, ten times. But I'm sure your mother guarded the mail. She probably burned the letters. Or threw them away, anyhow, somewhere you couldn't find them."

Ten times, I thought. I thought again: *Ten times?* At first that seemed like a big number. Then it seemed like a tiny number. I did the math. "So you're not dying," I said, "and you wrote me one letter every two years."

"I never received any letters in return," he said.

"But you haven't been living in the Sahara Desert," I said. "You've had a phone, I'm sure."

My father poked at the smoldering ball of tobacco in our water pipe, a ball that by now was surrounded by a corona of ashes. "How good is your Arabic?" he said finally, in Arabic.

"It's all classical," I said. "It's kind of a shame because people have been laughing at me." It was true. They'd laughed at me and then tried to imitate my way of speaking, using formal address and formal diction and carefully pronounced verbs and nouns and adjectives. I imagined it was particularly ironic here in Cairo, where everything seemed to be dominated by such informality: informal traffic, informal settlements, informal systems of payment in nearly every store.

"That's okay," my father said. "We can teach you the real thing."

I couldn't help but notice that this was a promise of a mutual future. It also made me angry. "Tell me why you lied to her," I said. "Or at least apologize. To me, to Mom, to somebody."

My father picked up the dice. He rolled them. "Doubles!" he exclaimed. When he handed the dice to me, he made eye contact. "I have something for you," he said.

He reached into his pocket and took out a small stack of what looked at first like money. *A bribe?* I thought. But then I saw that the stack was much too thick for banknotes. It was a stack of photographs. Polaroids. Unmistakably, they were Polaroids of me, me working at the Copper King Mansion, standing at the till, guiding a tour, carrying out the trash to the big Dumpsters behind the house. I remembered that photograph distinctly. The flash had surprised me, and I'd tripped and stumbled and fallen on top of one of the bags, its composted refuse leaking all over my clothes. I conjured the image of Ms. Vogel, snapping her pictures and surprising me almost every time. As a result, I looked a little startled in each photograph. I sat there and flipped through almost eight years of my life, watching my acne bloom from an isolated condition to a furious storm and back to an isolated condition.

"Pictures of you," he said.

"No kidding," I said in English. "That's not what I meant. What I meant is: How did you get them?"

"It's not important how I got them. What's important, *ya'ani*, is that I kept them. I kept them."

This—this, then, was madness. I was utterly mad. I hadn't thought this through, not thoroughly enough. My heart rattled the bones of my chest. My breath tightened in my throat. I could not breathe. This was where my story would end, at an outdoor café in Cairo, poised on the edge of a backgammon move. I would die of a panic attack right there.

But then I experienced a visitation. Perhaps in response to my prayers? I visualized Ms. Vogel. I imagined her standing in El-Habb. She was standing on the altar with her hair in a bun, a clipboard in her hand, doing a safety check of the exhibit. She inspected the statue of Jesus on the cross, wiggling Him slightly to ensure that He was mounted in place. "There's no substitute for awareness," she'd said to me time and time again. "I first learned about awareness on the Riviera in 1962. It was a different time. Your lessons will be less complex." I pictured her straightening the papers on the clipboard, tightening the bun, and nodding in approval. She was in control. Then she took a Polaroid of the icon. "Gotcha!" she exclaimed.

I wiped the sweat off my forehead, wiped the stinging sweat out of my eyes. I looked at my father. He was sitting there, holding the dice, turning them over and over in his hands as if trying to rub off their spots. He tucked the Polaroids back into their place of concealment. Then he said: "Do you want to come to the house tomorrow morning and meet the family?"

"Yes," I said. "Yes, I would love that."

"Excellent," he said, leaning back. "But first I would like to ask of you one small favor."

The small favor, it turned out, was actually a large favor. Maybe the largeness of it was why my father had switched to Arabic. Maybe he knew that he could better control me there, in that language, since our vocabularies were so unequal.

"I'm sorry?" I said.

"Can you," he said again, "pretend to be someone else? Someone other than who you are? Perhaps you can be Wael, the son of my friend Malik?"

"Wael?" I said. "The son of your friend Malik?"

"Exactly," he said.

"Do you even have a friend Malik?" I said.

"Not exactly," he said.

"But I'm his son?" I said.

"Exactly," he said.

"Aren't parents supposed to encourage their children to tell the truth?" I said. "No. No, I won't do it."

"Come on, Khosi," my father said. "What's a small lie between two gentlemen?"

"No," I said. "I deserve better."

We finished the game in silence. Techno music hung in the air like gauze, filtering in and out of hearing, just barely audible, rising from some sub rosa dance club.

"Let's go," my father said.

"Wait," I said. "Aren't you forgetting something?"

"What?" he said.

"Payment?" I said.

He laughed. "Oh no," he said. "There is no need. I never pay here. They know who I am."

As if to illustrate the point, he waved to the waiters as we walked away. The waiters nodded and waved back. We walked for a while in silence.

"I'm sorry," I said at last. "I just can't pretend to be someone I'm not."

"It's only for a little while, until they get used to you. Then I will tell them the truth. This is better, trust me. I know my family. It's the Saqr way."

The Saqr way? I thought. *What are we—a car rental company?* I wanted to object further, but then I realized: It didn't matter what I did tomorrow. Agreeing to the deception was the price of admission. Once I was inside, I could act however I wanted to act. I didn't have to play a role. I didn't have to be anyone other than myself, someone who'd traveled across an ocean to reclaim a part of his birthright.

"Fine," I said. "I'll be the gentleman son of your gentleman friend Malik."

"Excellent," my father said. "I'll write the address down for you."

"No!" I exclaimed, but then when I noticed his look of puzzlement, I realized that I'd overreacted. "Just tell me."

He watched me suspiciously. "37 Talaat Harb," he said. *"Bukra inshallah,"* he added. *Tomorrow, God willing.*

"God willing," I said.

"Goodbye, Khosi."

My father leaned down and kissed my cheeks sequentially. The skin of his face was rough with stubble, and it scraped against my skin. I stood there and watched him disappear into the crowds of the daytime city. He didn't turn around. He didn't look back.

Why has our country, writes the Egyptian novelist Mohamed El-Bisatie, *endured long years of colonization—and the worst sorts of colonization: Turkish, French, English?* The answer is, in part, cotton. Egyptian cotton sheets, with their luxurious high thread count—they have a legacy of suffering, too. Everybody knows what cotton did to the United States. But who knows the story of Egypt's plantations, which brought about the downfall of a well-planned civil society—and caused the country to spiral into bankruptcy and British rule?

In 1860, during the American Civil War, the blockade stopped the South from exporting crops. So British textile mills turned to the Nile Delta for raw materials; Egyptian farmers had grown cotton there since 4000 B.C.E. For five years, British demand was massive. The Egyptian ruler, Ismail the Magnificent, took out loan after loan from European banks to finance the construction of the country's infrastructure. The upper tiers of Egyptian society grew unbelievably wealthy. But then in 1865 America started exporting once again. As quickly as they'd arrived, the British merchants disappeared, taking their contracts with them. This bankrupted the country, allowing for its takeover just fifteen years later.

When I first learned this, I inescapably thought of my father. He was a colonist in this exact sense of the word.

That night I couldn't sleep. I lay awake in my hotel room, staring at the ceiling, imagining Ms. Vogel snapping those photos of me for my father, surreptitiously mailing them across an ocean. Sleep wouldn't come. Or at least I thought it wouldn't. As I lay there, I was floating up and out across the city into a shadowy nightmare version of Cairo where the traffic was even more aggressive, and the dust thicker in the air, and the heat utterly merciless. I floated over the tourist boats gliding up and down the Nile and landed gently on a dock, a dock with a view of the entire nightlit city. I watched as American tourist after American tourist stepped into the Nile, stepped off the end of the dock and into its waters. Or was it the Bitterroot River, just outside of Butte? I couldn't tell for sure anymore. There was just the dark, flowing water—and the bodies. They were drowning. But there was nothing I could do to help. And then Agnes Mouri stood beside me, and she held me in her arms to comfort me, telling me that this was just the way it had to be, it was the way it had always been, and I could smell the ginger of her perfume and feel the soft press of her arms around me, and I realized with a sickening surge of fear that despite what we were witnessing together, here on the shores of this river—despite our shared and communal burden—she and I were complete and total strangers.

Part II

When the Nile—that river with seven mouths—
eases its flood and returns from the wet fields
to its alluvial bed,
the peasants turn the soil
and find strange, unknown creatures:
Some just born, some only beginning
to take form,
imperfect,
changeable. And so—
in a single body—one part
might be alive, and another
might be a formless scrap
of soil.

—from Ovid's *Metamorphoses,*
   Book One

Six

THE NEXT MORNING I JETTISONED the Egyptian clothes, choosing instead a second sweatshirt and a second pair of jeans. I had a
coffee-and-pastry breakfast and made my way out into the street,
through the security gauntlet and through the subsequent gauntlet
of vendors. Though it was punishingly hot, I walked all the way to
37 Talaat Harb. I didn't know how I'd handle the lie, but I knew that
I'd be faithful to my own interests.

A few minutes from the address, I stopped to buy a bottle of
mineral water from a street vendor. The vendor opened the ice-cold
bottle for me, and when I turned back toward the street, I saw a familiar sight: cowboy boots and the cuffs of a charcoal, pin-striped
business suit.

"Howdy, Junior," said the Ghost of William Andrews Clark. "I
thought you'd never summon me again."

"I didn't," I said. I was whispering. I looked back at the vendor.
"Shouldn't you be more discreet?"

"Don't worry," he said. "Only the dogs can see me. Well, techni-cally, almost any animal. And the pathologically insane."

"That's comforting," I said.

"It's been a while, Khosi," he said.

"It's been three days," I said. "And I'm furious. My father's fiancée?"

"Ah," said the Ghost of William Andrews Clark. "I thought that would be a rough one."

"I need you to leave me alone," I said. "To disappear." I started walking. The hand-to-ear, yes-I-am-talking-on-a-cell-phone trick was starting to annoy me.

"Aren't you at all interested in what I can do?" he said.

"You've got to realize," I said, "that I've been having a rough time of it recently."

"Just watch this, pardner," said the Ghost of William Andrews Clark. He picked up a handful of dirt and threw it into the air. The dirt blazed momentarily—golden, shimmering and golden—hanging in the air, refusing to fall, suspended and gleaming in a beam of sun-light. Then the Ghost of William Andrews Clark moved his hands as though conducting an orchestra. The flecks followed, moving to the left and the right, swooping like a bird, enveloping a passing pedestrian, and then falling to the ground. It was a wondrous sight. I watched it happen right there in front of me.

"Magic," the ghost said, "plain and simple."

"I need some whiskey," I said.

"Me, too, padre!" he exclaimed. "But I'm in a rush. And I've got another message for you. This'll be quicker than greased lightning, then it's back to the compound."

"Wait," I said. "The compound? Where do ghosts live, anyway, when they're not haunting the earth?"

The Ghost of William Andrews Clark shook his head. "You know, I'm not sure," he said. "It's sort of like if I asked you where you live. You live where you live, and that's all. It's reality. We live in our own reality." He paused. "Are you ready for the warning?"

"As ready as I'll ever be," I said.

"Things aren't good in Montana," he said.

"Things aren't good in Montana?" I repeated. "When *have* they been good? Now, *that* would have been a surprise: 'Things are great in Montana!'"

"No need to get cheeky, pardner," he said.

"I'm not getting cheeky," I said. "When you said you had a warning for me, my heart started pounding. I mean, I thought you were going to warn me about my father."

"I was," said the Ghost of William Andrews Clark. "But I changed my mind."

I stopped walking. "What about him?" I said.

"Take your pick," he said. "There's any number of warnings I could give you. But Montana's more pressing. A bit of a calamity."

"That sounds awful," I said.

"Don't get discouraged," he said. "Keep your head up, hoss. Remember that I love you."

A gust of wind blew along the street, throwing dust in the air and momentarily blinding me. By the time I opened my eyes again, I was alone. There was only the crush of pedestrian traffic on the scoured Cairo street.

"You love me?" I said. "Wait. Is everybody healthy? Is it my mom? Or Natasha? Or the Copper King Mansion? Did the mansion burn down? Is something wrong with Ms. Vogel? Hello?"

There was no response, just silence. A few folks edged away from me but continued on toward their destinations. The city closed ranks around me. I was devoured.

37 Talaat Harb was close to the center of Cairo, a nice neighborhood not far from the Nile. Though it wasn't as stately and elegant as Zemalek, it wasn't the informal settlement district, either, with its courtyard pigs and decrepit overcrowding. And it was nothing like the medina. The building was built in the regal French style, with every crenellation softened by ornamental beauty. Ornamental beauty. Broad mouths of windows one floor above the street, rising out toward decorated cornices. None of the apartments was accessible from the main street, from Talaat Harb. So I had to loop around to a long trash-strewn alley and go through a wrought-iron gate that had rusted permanently ajar. The space between the gate and the crumbling stucco of the wall wasn't big. Flakes of rust stained the fabric of my new white shirt.

Halfway down the alley, I heard the sound of running water. By the time I got to the courtyard that housed the entry staircase, I could no longer hear the sounds of the city; there was only the gentle bubbling of the little fountain, in the center of which was a beautiful stone leaf, a curved stone leaf that had been overrun by moss and had crumbled slightly around the edges. The water came from a single tarnished copper pipe. Despite the fact that it was a trickle, the sound of it somehow expanded to fill the entire alcove. It rose up along the four stories of the apartment building, the four stories with their inward-facing balconies.

These are the adjectives that come to mind when I think about that building: velvety, threadbare, sooty, crumbling, cracked, expansive, lush, mango-colored, lacquered, formal. At some point, one of the inhabitants had painted the walls of the courtyard a bright mango color. That had faded over the years, and now the paint was blanched and chipping, irregular in its concealment of the stucco walls.

I rang the bell. After a few moments, a pillowy middle-aged woman answered. She was wearing acid-washed Levi's and a mustard-colored blouse. She looked me up and down, trying to decipher exactly what type of individual I was. Then, suddenly, she spat on the ground between us.

"Ha!" she said. And that was all.

The spitting was unusual. *That's a dangerous habit*, I considered telling her, *one responsible for the spread of communicable disease.*

"Akram!" she called. "He's here."

Almost immediately, I heard my father's baritone voice saying in English: "Coming! Coming! One moment." As soon as I heard him, all memory of the ghostly warning evaporated. I heard an accompanying female voice saying in Arabic, "You let him sleep at a hotel? What kind of man are you? I knew you were rotten, but this—this is terrible, even by your standards."

The old woman pushed the door open a little farther and stood aside. I saw two people making their way down the hallway toward me: my father and a crowlike woman with a black muslin scarf wrapped loosely around her head. They walked together but apart;

149

my father was grimacing and his posture seemed harried and harassed.

"I told you to wait in the kitchen," he said. He turned to me and opened his hands in supplication. "Wael happens to love his hotel," he said. "It's the best in the city." He paused and sighed. "This is my sister Fatima," he said.

"*Eldest* sister," Fatima said, bowing at the waist as soon as my father made the introduction. "And you must be Wael," she said, looking directly into my eyes. "The son of my brother's friend Malik. My brother has told me all about you."

"He has?" I said.

"Yes," Fatima said. "How you are traveling to our country to discover the roots of your father, Malik. I think it is a beautiful story— and you can't stay in a hotel, no matter how much you like it."

My father reached for me and took me in his arms. He grabbed both of my shoulders. "No, no," he said. "See how rested he looks."

"I do?" I said, genuinely surprised. Then I had an idea. "You know," I said, "I *could* use a nice, comfortable bed in a nice, comfortable house."

"See?" Fatima said. "He'd love to stay. What a scoundrel you are, Akram Saqr."

My father went pale. "I think that's not a good idea," he said, scrambling. "Because of his search for his roots."

"Nonsense!" another female voice boomed. "He can stay with us! There's room in our part of the house." Then there were five people in the hallway, which was starting to feel a little crowded.

"My younger sister Banafrit," my father said, rubbing his forehead as if he had a headache.

"*Youngest* sister," my aunt Banafrit said. She was not wearing a head scarf of any kind. "*Enchanté*," she said, extending the back of her hand for me to kiss.

They stood next to each other then, my two aunts. Fatima looked so much like a crow that I almost expected her to have feathery wings tucked somewhere, perhaps beneath her *hijab*. Her nose had glossy, clean, scrubbed skin—skin like the coating of a beak—and her eyes had a mischievous avian glimmer. Would she shake your hand? Or would she peck it?

Banafrit didn't look like a bird. Banafrit looked like a plate of mashed potatoes. She was large and exuberant and perfumed and lathered with every kind of buttery makeup imaginable. She wore cords of gold jewelry. They draped around her neck by the dozens. My two aunts were opposites in nearly every physical characteristic. And yet both of them had the same nose, the nose that also graced my father's countenance—and my own. When I looked at them, I saw myself. Did they see themselves in me?

Each aunt protested that I should stay with her. They fought over me for at least five minutes. I fueled the conflict, enjoying the coloration of my father's cheeks, which progressed from ashen to yellowy ashen to greenish ashen to pure sea-foam green. Even though I was enjoying myself, I longed for my desk with its carefully aligned pencils, with its artfully sharpened graphite tips and scrupulously clean erasers. I longed for Natasha and her conspiratorial presence; she would help me make my father squirm.

The hotel issue was not settled, but all at once my father was waving me deeper into the house and the big double doors were clicking shut behind me and he was saying, "Welcome, welcome! *Ahlan wa sahlan.*"

Somehow my father was holding a lit cigarette. I didn't even see him light it. It just appeared in his hand, trailing a plume of smoke like the tail of a rooster.

"Nervous?" I said.

My aunts swept ahead of us and into the main living room.

"God has guided you here," my father whispered, "and now we will pick up the pieces."

As I progressed through the house, I named the things I passed, silently ticking off their Arabic designations in my head as if they were my college dorm room flashcards: *bab*, doorway. *Kitabi*, books. My father flicked on the light switch. *Noor*, I thought, and stepped into the illuminated living room. It, too, had a parquet floor. I thought of the Copper King Mansion, where the floor had been lovingly maintained and waxed and scrubbed with Murphy's Oil Soap once a week. This floor had not been maintained at all. The inlaid woods were chipped and cracked and, in some cases, entirely missing. I could see the bare stonework beneath the thin layer of the parquet.

It looked like the kind of thing I imagined from one of the art districts of East Berlin, the home of an ideologically successful East German playwright, perhaps, room after room overflowing with shabby antique furniture and books. There appeared to be two levels to the apartment. The main floor had a big empty ballroom that we presently walked through, my dad smoking a Dunhill and narrating a tour in Arabic.

If my aunts thought it was strange for my father to narrate a tour of the family home, neither of them said a thing. They walked on ahead into the kitchen.

"Here is the rosary of my great-uncle Michael," he said in Arabic, but retaining the French word for uncle, *oncle*, with its deep *o* and resounding flourish at the end. Indeed, his Arabic was peppered with French and English phrases. The object to which he was pointing, however, was one that didn't need translation. It was a massive set of beads with a silvery replica of the crucifix at its end. Each bead was the size of a chickpea.

"Coptic archbishop," my father said. "The higher the rank, the bigger the beads."

"Is that true?" I said.

"I don't really know," he said.

"How's Agnes?" I whispered to him as we walked along.

My father sighed. "It's truly terrible," he said. "Even my *newest* lies aren't working."

"Have you considered the truth?" I said. Wait. "Why am I giving *you* life lessons?"

"I do appreciate it," he said. That was all he said on the topic. We continued walking in silence. Finally, he stopped in front of a large framed black-and-white photograph of a cheerful-looking old man. "And here, here is my father," he said softly to me, "God rest his soul."

"My grandfather," I whispered.

I stared at the photograph. It was most remarkable for my grandfather's soft eyes. He had gentle eyes—eyes that looked slightly amused, as if they were in on a secret joke.

Every doorway seemed to be framed with flaking paint. The panels of wallpaper, once opulent and floral, were now stained and patchy; in several places, they'd drooped to the floor, where they lay, curled and wilted. Beyond the ballroom were a living room and a kitchen. Off of one side of the living room was a balcony big enough for roller skating. And this was not an idle comparison. Presently, a twelve-year-old boy skated in off the veranda, an iPod tucked under his belt. He waved. Then he disappeared down a hallway into the recesses of the apartment.

"That's my youngest son, Victor," Banafrit said. "He loves the American film *Rollerball*."

I indicated that I did not know the American film *Rollerball*.

"It is terrible," Banafrit said. "But he wants to be the main character, the one who is played by the actor James Caan."

It was funny to hear the sentence in Arabic, and then the English name, James Caan. But then I lost track of Banafrit, and Fatima, and the old woman, and my father. I lost track of everyone else in the room, because I was standing in front of a framed piece of art, a great branching tree that reached from near the floor to near the ceiling, at least two meters tall. Above the tree, which was drawn in slightly faded black ink, were two easily recognizable words: "'Saqr Family,'" I read aloud. This was *naskh* calligraphy, a looping formal Arabic script.

I looked around. Everyone had left except my father, who was standing in the doorway to the kitchen, watching me. A litany of facts tumbled through my mind like clattering dice, my Arabic calligraphy class at the Billings Islamic Center springing back into memory: *Invented by Ibn Muqlah in the tenth century*, naskh *was the most common script for the Holy Koran, written with a wide- and chisel-nosed pen*. I looked at the short stems of the letters, at the deep curves, at the decorative flourishes near the tree's margins. The script coiled and arched and shaped itself into a series of bright black leaves. There was a sentence, written at eye level, in ink that was fresh and new.

"'In the Name of Allah,'" I read, translating hesitatingly, slowly, one word at a time. "'The Most Benevolent, the Most Merciful. Not a leaf falls but He knows it.'"

"Fatima added it," my father said. "Since she converted, she's been unstoppable. She even changed her name."

"I meant to ask," I said, "about the head scarf."

"The hijab?" my father said. "Almost all the women wear them these days, even if they aren't Muslim. Except Banafrit. She's not afraid of anything."

I nodded and then read the rest of the text aloud. "'Saqr Family. The family tree of the late Saleem ibn Shahallah ibn Elias ibn Nasrallah ibn Nameh ibn Saqr. Born in Allepo around 1705, married 1740.'" And then, on the branch that was cut off: "'The older brother, Georges, became a monk and was titled Khouri Assayeh, the General Director of the Monastery of St. Michael, at Zunia.'"

"A holy fool," my father said.

I stood there looking up at this artist's rendering of my genealogy. The body buried in the soil, the roots rising from the rib cage, the generations of the past giving nourishment to the generations of the future.

"Where am I on here?" I asked.

Fatima poked her head around the corner. "Are you going to stand there all day talking and talking," she called, "or are you going to come in here and have some food?"

"But look," I said, pointing up to the wall. "The family tree."

"And?" Fatima said.

"It's amazing?" I said. "It's beautiful?"

"Isn't that adorable," Fatima said. "He's such an American. Now come in here and have something to eat."

My father shrugged. And so I reluctantly left the family tree behind. As I walked into the kitchen with its long wooden dining table and stacks of chipped earthenware dishes, with its hanging dried bunches of peppers and cool tile floor, Banafrit rushed me over to an unoccupied chair. She installed me at the head of the table.

"How can you not be in awe of that painting?" I said. Actually, I didn't say *painting*. I couldn't remember the word for painting, for some reason, so I said, "Plant behind glass." This was a problem with negotiating a foreign language; occasionally, it went badly wrong. They all seemed amused, but my father was the one to respond. "It's nothing special," he said.

"He'll take a coffee," Banafrit said.

"Why not tea?" Fatima said. She was standing at the stove and holding a big pot of boiling water.

"He'd like coffee," Banafrit said. "I can tell."

"I'll ask him if he'll have tea," Fatima said. She turned to me. "Will you have coffee or tea?"

All three of them peered at me. I felt like the mouse scrutinized by the owl family in the rafters. "Both?" I said hesitantly.

"Excellent choice," Banafrit said, nodding.

"He's very smart," Fatima said approvingly.

"Don't flatter him," Banafrit said.

"You're the one who put him at the head of the table," Fatima said.

"I put him there because it makes him look dignified," Banafrit said.

"I don't care," Fatima said, "as long as he helps us prepare lunch."

If the first object that told the story of my father was that document, the ghostly tree to which the rest of the family seemed to be indifferent, then here was the second part of the story of my father: An onion. Or a bowl of onions. Because the bowl of onions landed in the center of the table, a big red earthenware bowl, overflowing with small bulbous shapes. They were pungent and purple, and sure enough, Egyptian walking onions, not out of place here in Egypt. Probably quite common, actually. Fatima handed each of us a knife.

I held the knife in my right hand. I hoisted it theatrically into the air. I traced small circles with its tip in a gesture that I thought was a little menacing—but also perhaps festive?

"Attention, everyone," I said in Arabic. "I have an announcement."

"No, no," my father said. "No announcements."

"Announcements are enjoyable," I said.

"Not while cooking," he said.

"I would like an announcement," Banafrit said.

"Me, too," Fatima said. "An announcement could be nice."

"Absolutely no announcements," my father said. "I forbid announcements while I am preparing a dish."

I cleared my throat. "I would like to say—" I began.

"—that he is tremendously grateful for your hospitality," my father said. "And that he doesn't know how to repay you."

"Except by staying here at the house," I said. I smiled broadly.

"No, no," my father said, "that is unfortunately impossible."

"It is *necessary*," Banafrit said. "He will stay with me."

"No, he will stay with me," Fatima said.

Someone once said to me: *Life is like an onion. You peel away the layers, and what is at the center?* I'm not sure even what that means, exactly, since there are so many different kinds of emptiness. But the phrase is memorable. *Life is like an onion.* I do agree, though, that our lives reside in objects, that we live in them, through them—that we give them grace.

"Stop your endless bickering," said the old woman who'd met me at the door, walking into the kitchen holding a stack of table linens that reached several feet above her head.

"Wael," my father said. "This is Kebi Merit, our cook."

With an enormous sigh, Kebi Merit nodded to me and dropped the linens on the kitchen table. Then she collapsed into a chair beside them. She sighed again and began reciting some kind of prayer. She said it softly to herself while she started folding napkins and tablecloths.

Kebi Merit's presence seemed to halt the argument between the sisters. There was a long silence in which the only sound was the steady clicking of my father's knife through onion flesh. Tears came to my eyes. No one else seemed to notice.

"So, Wael," Fatima finally said. "Tell us about your father, Malik?"

I coughed. "Why doesn't Akram tell you," I said. I turned to him. "My father tells me that you are old, old friends."

"The oldest," my father said.

"You know," Kebi Merit said. "It's strange. But I've just been thinking. And I don't remember anyone named Malik from when you were a boy, Akram."

"You're old and losing your memory," my father said.

"No. I remember everything," Kebi Merit said. "Why can't I remember Wael's father, Malik?"

"He and I were inseparable when we were children," my father said. "Like two halves of the same person. Then he moved to Europe before I went to Montana for graduate school."

"Like two halves of the same person?" I said.

"He went to Switzerland," my father said, talking over me. "To the Swiss Alps."

It was almost chilling to hear my father quickly fabricate my life story, complete with an education at the Sorbonne, in Paris, and extensive travels around the world. No matter where I went, apparently, I missed my family home—this neighborhood in Cairo—where my ancestry stretched for hundreds, if not thousands, of years. That was how I'd come back here, to the family of his father's oldest childhood friend, to learn the truth about my Egyptian heritage. It was, in some ways, a fictionalization of my own life. It struck me as a strange and particularly brutal gesture. I decided to strike back.

"My mother was a prostitute," I said, pointing at my father. "You left that out."

His eyes opened wide. Momentarily, he was speechless. Then he said, "I felt awkward revealing that information."

"And you introduced her to my father, Malik," I added, "because you tried to save her from the streets. You didn't tell your sisters that?"

"Now, Wael," my father said.

I looked intently at him. "He's very well known in the family," I said, "for his charity work."

"Akram," Banafrit said, "why haven't you spoken of this before?"

"Well," my father said, shrugging, "I did only what was necessary. I'm no hero."

"Then you must not have told them how she died," I said.

"How she died?" he said.

"Go on," I said. I looked at Banafrit and Fatima. "It's very tragic."

"She was struck by a car," my father said.

"That you were driving," I said.

Banafrit gasped and dropped her knife and made the sign of the cross. She stood and walked over and enveloped me in her ample embrace. "You poor, poor boy," she said. "You poor, poor boy." I had the momentary sensation of drowning as the flesh over her biceps settled around my mouth like a muffler.

Fatima reached out and placed her hand on her brother's shoulder. "This is a sad story," she said. "You should have trusted us with it before."

It was a sad story indeed—the tale of a prostitute accidentally run over by the very man who was trying to save her from the streets. It had taken an unexpected turn and provoked sympathy for my father. This was resolutely not what I'd had in mind. Although, to be honest, I hadn't had much in mind at all. I'd just wanted to punish him, to make him uncomfortable. But now I'd failed at even that.

I pulled out of Banafrit's embace. "I have to make a phone call," I said. "I'll just step outside for a moment."

"Fine, fine," my father said without looking at me. "Go right ahead." Clearly, he was thinking: *Good riddance.* As I walked away, I heard him making apologies on my behalf. The truth was, I needed a moment to calm down. I ducked into a bathroom, closing the door behind me. There was a mirror, and I looked in it, stared at my wide-set eyes and my bony nose. I ran the water and daubed it on my forehead.

When I was a teenager, I read *The Road to Wigan Pier*. It was an act of self-loathing. I wanted to see what it was that my family had helped create, helped actualize in the world. The book was indelible. There's a line in it I've never been able to forget: *When a miner comes up from the pit, his face is so pale that it is noticeable even through the mask of coal dust.* There's no air deep beneath the ground, or at least not the oxygen-rich air that we breathe up on the surface. I learned about black lung and boot rot and the many ways that miners could be crushed by collapsing rock or plummeting thousand-pound extraction equipment. *No wonder Dad left*, I remembered thinking. *He didn't want to be implicated.* Ridiculous, but still—years later— the thought lingered as I ran the cool water and wiped my face clean.

A miner surfacing from a pit, I thought.

Familial love is invisible. I'd come all the way around the world to find an invisible thing.

The lining of your arteries, the very blood you have circulating in you, pumping madly through your body, is .00001 percent copper. Why do you think your blood tastes like pennies? I turned off the faucet, conscious of the fact that I was wasting water. Cairo was growing by a million people a year. Ninety-five percent of Egypt is a desert. I took a few deep breaths. I dried my skin with a small hand towel. I turned and slowly opened the door and stepped back out into the apartment.

Kebi Merit was standing there, wrinkled and hunched over. She glared at me. "I know," she said in a voice that was even and measured. "I know your secret."

I stared at Kebi Merit. Her face was tight, pulled tight against itself, and she squinted at me, squinted relentlessly. At certain times in life, anything can have the magnificence of a symbol; as Kebi Merit leaned in toward me, the light in the hallway chose that moment to flicker and fail. Why do lightbulbs die? Many reasons: an air leak in the glass, a surge in electrical voltage. Most common is evaporation. Tungsten vapor evaporates off the surface of the filament, solidifies as smoke, and settles on the surface of the bulb. Eventually, this makes the filament too brittle. It can't sustain the current. It fractures.

"I'm sorry?" I said.

"I know who you are," she said. "Both of your aunts suspect it, too. They'd never admit it. But they know. When you came to the door, it was confirmed."

I paused. "The truth is a powerful thing," I said. "It is very liberating."

At this, Kebi Merit smiled. "Or dangerous," she said. "Sometimes it is very dangerous."

I was about to confess. I was about to appeal to her maternal side and tell her who I was, and to ask for her assistance in knowing—truly knowing—the person my father was, the people who were my family, here on this side of the world. But then I got scared. Instead of answering, I fled from her. I fled from her and scurried back into the kitchen.

"Khosi," my father said as soon as I was back in the room. "I need to talk to you for a moment in private."

Kitchen, hallway. Kitchen, hallway. Kebi Merit had disappeared. Where she'd gone, I didn't know.

"What were you doing in there?" he said, leaning toward me. "You were torturing me—and enjoying it."

What could I say? "Yes," I said. "I was enjoying it."

"I'll take care of everything," he said. *Oh, no,* I thought. *Now what?* With that, he turned on his heel and charged into the kitchen, a soldier dashing back into a battle from which he'd emerged only briefly.

I stayed out there. I walked down along the corridor and took a closer look at the place. Every doorway had elaborate crown moldings with ornamented flourishes that had been carved by hand probably close to a hundred years ago. Cobwebs draped the tops of these moldings, hanging there like celebratory ribbons. I knew a bit about grand interior spaces. Five years earlier, when I'd started at the Copper King Mansion, there had been a wing of the house that the new owners hadn't yet restored. I liked to loiter in the shabby grandeur of it, in the big dusty rooms with their ceilings that I couldn't leap and touch. Occasionally, I'd find some detail—a single screw, or a strip of flooring, or a patch of wallpaper—that was perfectly intact, that had survived the decades with its full original appearance. These were tiny relics of the past to me, a direct connection between my time and the long-ago carpenter.

The Copper King Mansion: It was such a part of my psyche, my self, my sense of who I was. The encyclopedic way I'd learned its statistics. Anything you know, that you know well, becomes an intimacy. The knowledge of it is private. It is something that you take with you wherever you go. What happens to it when you're gone—now, that's a different mystery. But while I looked at the peeling wallpaper of my father's home in Cairo, I remembered every detail of my former workplace, comparing its elements to the elements of the house at 37 Talaat Harb.

A commotion from the direction of the kitchen disturbed this reflection. My father appeared at the end of the hallway. He was being trailed by Kebi Merit and Aunt Banafrit and Aunt Fatima, still holding her onion-chopping knife. It was disconcerting to watch her wave the nine-inch blade to illustrate her points.

My father was protesting loudly. "It's just a change of plans," he called out in Arabic. "It's nothing."

"You hate our cooking," Fatima said. She pointed to me with the knife. "He hates our cooking, that's why he's leaving."

"Don't be ridiculous," my father said. "He's never tasted your cooking."

"He hates the idea of our cooking," Fatima insisted.

"At least let us give you a little something," Banafrit said, "to take with you. Maybe half a chicken. You shared that beautiful story with us, Wael, about your mother, and we feel like we need to at least feed you."

They'd all gathered around me in the corridor. My dad inched us toward the front door. "We'll buy food on the street," he said. "You all have a lot of work to do. We're just getting in your way."

"But I want to stay," I said.

"Yes, yes," Kebi Merit said. "Stay. Stay a while. Just think, Akram: He has so much to tell us."

My dad shook his head. "Say goodbye to my sisters," he said, "and we'll go on a tour of the city."

My aunts said their desultory goodbyes. "Go with the grace of God," Fatima said, and then we were back on the street and the dust was kicking up around our feet.

"That was close," my father said as soon as we were alone. "I told you: Follow my lead." He paused. "You know, you seem to be constantly making the most terrible errors in judgment."

"That's hilarious," I said, "coming from you."

"I'm not the one who's traveling around the world," he said, "wrecking marriages."

"You're not?" I said.

"No," he said. "I'm traveling around the world and resolving failed marriages in order to start new ones." He cleared his throat. "Obviously, you can tell there's a difference."

I was about to deny this, but just then a car swerved toward us. It missed my father by inches and let out a vociferous blast of its horn.

Honking and cats.

These were the most prominent features of the Cairene street, and I noticed both as soon as we stepped out of the alleyway behind Talaat Harb. It happened fast: We took our leave of Aunt Fatima and Aunt Banafrit and Kebi Merit. There were a number of stray cats hanging around the end to the alley. Lanky and inscrutable, they took ballerina steps through the grime. And a chorus of honking accompanied our arrival at the main thoroughfare. Drivers in Cairo, it seemed, honked to warn you that you were in their way, they honked to tell you that they were merging, they honked as a means of greeting, they honked to express their feelings toward the world, they honked when they were bored. I think they also honked to announce the rain or the sunset; like an inky swath of geese scattered across an inverted sky, they filled the air with the sound of their life. They honked to affirm themselves.

Out in that horn-filled, cat-filled street, we'd walked fifteen or twenty feet before I said, "Where are we going?"

"I have an errand to do," he said. "You can help your father get something accomplished."

I didn't like the sound of that, but it was a bright, hot day, hotter than the last. At close to noon, it must have been well over a hundred degrees. We were in the center of the city. The buildings around us seemed to be sorted into two broad categories: 1) hulks of abandoned concrete buildings that had been stripped of everything and had not been demolished; 2) renovated nineteenth-century apartment houses with ornamented facades and shops at street level. There seemed to be no pattern to this method of urban preservation. And sometimes, sometimes people were living in the abandoned, unfinished, crumbling towers, lots of people, enough people that you could see their colorful plastic tents blooming there like moss on the bones of a skeleton.

"We need to talk," I said.

"Oh, no," my father said. "Let's not stop here. It's too hot. Let's at least have this argument in the shade."

"I'm not on the family tree," I said.

"There you go," he said. "Just like I thought. I knew it was a mistake. One thing always leads to another." He switched to English. "Let you into the house, and soon you'll be living there."

"Is that an Egyptian proverb?" I said.

"No," he said. "It's the truth."

"I'm your son," I said. "I should live in your house at least once in my life."

"Khosi, my love, my dearest. The sun is burning a hole in my head. I can feel it cutting through my hair and down into my brain. It is cooking my brain."

"You're on the tree," I said. "I saw an Akram."

"Sure, sure," he said. "I'm on there. It just hasn't been updated in a few years."

"No," I said, a sick feeling rising out of my stomach. "That boy on roller skates, Banafrit's son Victor. I looked for him. He was there. The newest ink."

My father walked away from me. He walked away and leaned against a building, beneath the shade of another building. He adjusted his spectacles and wiped the sweat out of his eyes. He shrugged. "A tragic omission," he said. "But really—your grandfather's fault."

"God rest his soul?" I said.

"Precisely," he said.

"You never told them a thing about us," I said.

He put his glasses back on. He frowned. "*Habibi*, calm down. Stop yelling."

"I'm not yelling," I yelled.

"Hush," he said. "Or we'll attract the attention of the police."

It was true. There were unusual numbers of police everywhere. They wore bright white uniforms, uniforms that were the brightest thing for miles. The amount of starch that the Egyptian police had to use, it was dizzying to think about. Their chalk-colored uniforms came with rakish black berets and matching obsidian leather belts.

I lowered my voice a little. "It's pathological," I said. "You abandoned your wife—and your son."

"First of all," my father said. "I didn't abandon you. And second: I had to leave. I had no choice. The people I'd borrowed money from—they would have hurt you both without hesitation. They were criminals. They were thugs." He sighed and took out his packet of cigarettes. Again he offered me one. Again I declined. "I put you both in danger. It took me years to understand that, *habibi*." He inhaled deeply, then exhaled through his nostrils. "You don't understand how hard it is for me to say that. I've made big mistakes in my life. Huge errors. But that's changing. Can you understand that?"

"I guess I can't," I said.

"Khosi, listen. The omission was intentional. Amy—your mother—and I, we wanted to be gradual about it. If you think her family was bad, imagine mine. Their only son marrying an American. This was Egypt in the early eighties, just years after the 1973 war. In my father's mind, if she was an American, then she was a Zionist."

"Oh, dear God in heaven," I said, my voice wry and sardonic. "Please, anything but that."

They say that living a day in Cairo is like smoking a pack and a half of cigarettes. The smog hangs over the city, a dense blanket of smog, one that dissipates only part of the way into the desert or across either sea. How many cigarettes a day was my father smoking? Presently, he lit another.

"Can you smoke in the subway?" I said.

"No," he said, "not at all." He sprang into action anyway, leading me down the steps and into the subterranean depths of the metro. At the guard booth, he slipped a bill to the attendant along with a couple of cigarettes. He did it so fast that I had to watch him carefully to see it. The guard nodded and, without making eye contact, waved us both through.

"That," my father said, "is a lesson for life."

"Bribe anyone you can?" I said. "So you can get emphysema?"

He scowled at me and exhaled a cloud of smoke. "You can get what you desire," he said, "if you simply apply yourself."

"Is *that* an Egyptian proverb?" I said.

"No," he said. "But it should be."

We made our way into the metro.

As I got down there, I wondered what people saw when they scrutinized me, when I passed before their eyes. Was I a momentary apparition, a face in the station of the metro, there and then not there, like a petal on a wet black bough? I noticed that only the men seemed to watch me. The women, for the most part, didn't pay me any attention. Though the center cars of the subway were reserved for women, there was mixing on the platforms and in the hallways of the station. That was when I really noticed the head scarves. It was true. Nearly every woman wore one. What must it be like to wrap your head in cloth every time you go outside? To never feel the sensation of wind against the skin of your neck?

"Where are we going?" I said. "I just realized I have no idea."

"This is a tour of the city," my father said. "I'm taking you on a tour of the place that means the most to me in Cairo."

"Maybe I don't want to go on a tour," I said.

The train station filled with the usual sound of the arriving and departing trains. The tunnels were lit with strange orange lights that gave everything the vague look of a jack-o'-lantern. I listened to the roar of train wheels along steel tracks. I felt the quick whoosh of air when a subway line arrived at the station. I felt the vibration of it all in my body, felt it viscerally in the bones of my legs, which seemed to rattle at the knees.

"Of course you want to go on a tour," he said. "I love you, Khosi," he added. "I'm your father, and I'm here now."

Where were we going? The Gezira Sporting Club. Looking back on it now, I realize I should have sensed that something was wrong. I should have sensed that nothing good was going to come of this trip.

We rode the train two stops. Not far, considering the world we emerged into, a world so unlike the rest of Cairo. Suddenly, instead of crowds, there were broad, sedate, palm-lined streets, streets with big palatial houses behind wrought-iron fences. And strangely pruned Popsicle trees. Everywhere, the bright green Popsicle trees, looking like something cut from the pages of *Alice in Wonderland*. Cairo was covered in a miasma of taupe dust. To be free of it seemed almost like teleportation.

It's strange that on an island in the center of the city, in the center of the Nile, in the midst of this seventeen-million-person sprawl, is a bucolic garden paradise of large estates and lush, verdant vegetation. And this is tropical vegetation. Acacia trees, jasmine bushes, eucalyptus, cypress, salt cedar. Grass of every shade of green, each lawn slightly different from the next, most of them groomed exhaustively. Gezira shares an island with the neighborhood of Zemalek, the most exclusive neighborhood in Cairo. The club rises from the southern part of the island, offering its acres of gardens and sports fields and outdoor spaces, outdoor spaces utterly lacking in honking or cats. And: a racetrack.

"I play polo here," my dad said. "Have you ever seen a polo match?"

I said no, I'd never seen a polo match. But I had seen the American Motordrome Wall of Death—and he could see it, too, if he decided to accompany me back to the United States next June for Evel Knievel Days.

He didn't seem overly impressed. "There is a festival named after whom?" he said.

"You really weren't meant to stay in Montana," I said. "Evel Knievel was a famous motorcycle daredevil."

My father looked imperious and haughty. "Evel Knievel is nothing compared to Guillermo Gracida," he said.

"Never heard of him," I said.

"Don't be proud of that," my father said. "Guillermo Gracida is the most famous polo player of the twentieth century. Sixteen U.S. Open wins. Twenty-one years as a ten-goal forward."

"It's just polo," I said.

"The sport of kings," my father objected. "It is the fastest sport you can watch. Well, the fastest sport that's legal."

"Is there a lot of polo in Egypt?" I said. I hesitated, armed with my secret knowledge. "Do you play?"

"Not really," my father said. "I mean, first of all, you need grass. You can play on clay, on a dirt floor, but it's not the same. There's something about the scent of a grass field—it defies all description."

If he wanted to let me further into his life, this was his opportunity. It hurt a little that he didn't say anything. Not that I expected much. But still—that was his chance.

We'd surfaced in the center of a garden, in the shadow of a big white complex. It was the Opera House, the Opera House at the Opera subway stop. The building itself sprawled over an acre of land—a series of domes, broad flat domes that seemed to rise up, up into the bright horizon, as if they were about to take wing. It was a new building, built a few decades ago, and its white soapstone glistened with an inlaid grain. It was pristine and almost terribly beautiful. It combined the four main structures of Islamic architecture: the mosque, the palace, the tomb, and the fort. It seemed to be all of these at once. I stared. As often happened to me when I was confronted by a pretty thing, I thought of a song by Willie Nelson. This was a liability of listening to country and western. For some reason, the chorus of "My Heroes Have Always Been Cowboys" started playing in the jukebox of my mind.

Though I'd come from a world of privilege, that privilege had always been a generation removed. It lived in the past, buried beneath a tombstone or framed behind a piece of glass. It wasn't the kind of privilege that rode polo ponies and offered to show me Gezira and Zemalek. Here in broader Cairo, it was drastically at odds with the surroundings, which were, almost without exception, poor. Now we passed through security, through a gate that was manned by three armed police officers, all of them wearing the same white uniform. Strangely, we didn't have to stop at the checkpoint. The officers simply opened the gate for my father, scurrying into motion as soon as he approached. "Akram!" one of them exclaimed.

My dad smiled and nodded and waved and made his way through the opened checkpoint.

"Jamil," he called, "how's your wife?"

"Good, sir, *el hamdillah*. Thank you for asking, sir. Have a nice day, sir."

I was fascinated by the guards' deference to my father. He pulled me behind him like debris in the wake of a fast-moving ship. His stride seemed to lengthen as he walked onto the grounds of the Gezira Sporting Club.

"I have to tell you something important," my father said as we headed deeper into the club.

"Fine," I said. "I'm all ears."

"What?" he said.

"It's a colloquial expression," I said.

"I see," he said. He paused. "This is hard to say. Or rather, the words—I don't know the right words."

"Go on," I said. "It's fine. I'm interested in anything you want to tell me."

"You are made of ears?" he said.

"Many," I said.

"Well," my father said, "you see, Khosi, my life had become unmanageable. Unimaginably unmanageable." He stopped speaking. He was evidently struggling. Then he seemed to change tactics. I wish he'd continued with the first approach, because then maybe, just possibly, things would have turned out differently. But he didn't. "No, *habibi*," he said, "let me tell you a story instead. You'll like this story, since you like to make up stories about people getting hit by cars."

We'd walked out onto a grassy playing field. It was long, longer than a football field, and covered with markings in phosphorescent white chalk. I bent down and pinched some of it between two fingers. It was wet, and it rolled into little clumps like sloughed skin. The sun had less power here, for some reason, in the midst of the grass. But my father was talking:

"Ford Motor Company," he said, "Ford Motor Company. They came to Egypt in 1926. That's when they started selling the first Fords in our country. And what were they selling? The Model T. It was the last year they made them. You understand?" He said it as if it were possible that I didn't understand. I wondered what part I might not have understood. The Model T? The Ford Motor Company? Nineteen twenty-six?

"Anyway," he continued, "your grandfather, my father, he was the first person in Egypt to buy one. He bought the first black Model T Ford, right out of the showroom in downtown Cairo. He was twenty-two years old and something of a playboy. There were other cars around, sure, but his was the first Ford. So he hired a driver, and he toured around the country with his friends. To Alexandria. To Siwa. To the Red Sea. You know: for a picnic.

"And then one day he was outside the city in the car, and the driver came up over a hill, and there was a cow in the middle of the road. And he hit the cow. Right in the middle. It split like a cake."

"Dear God," I said. "Poor thing."

"I agree," my father said. "Horrific, too. The creature, it had just wandered into the road. On the roads back then, nothing moved faster than a jackal or a hyena. The cow didn't know what hit it. My father barely survived." We'd walked all the way across the field and were entering a long wooden structure. The smell of it rose and surrounded me. It was a smell I recognized from the state fair in Silver Bow County. It was the smell of a stable. Sure enough, there were two dozen horses, many of them in their stalls, hiding from the brutal midday heat.

"Horses," I said. I couldn't think of what else to say.

"Yes," my father said. And then, in Arabic: "*Remal al-sahra.*" This meant *desert sand.* Since he was leaning into the stall of a sand-colored roan, since he was reaching across the metal bar and patting a horse on the side of its long, sloping nose, I assumed it was the horse's name.

"He's the fastest horse on the African continent," my father continued. He sighed and looked at me and said, "I didn't finish the story. You see, they didn't know what to do. The cow was dead. It couldn't be restored. Clearly, there was someone at fault. But it was the beginning of the automobile in Egypt. There weren't that many of them around. And so: The authorities put the car in jail."

"Thank God," I said. "Keeping the public safe."

"They took it and chained it in the main lot of the jail, chained it to a radiator, and they kept it there for a month. Finally, my grandfather showed up. He posted its bail. But he never drove it again. He was afraid to ever drive it. That's the story of how he started breeding horses. He still rode horses, rode them through the city of Cairo, until he died last year."

I was flooded with a peculiar drowning feeling, a feeling like I was trying to float but failing, like the water was rising over my shoulders and pulling me toward the bottom of something, the bottom of some invisible lake.

My father shook his head. "But that story—the one I just told you—isn't true."

I stared at him.

"You see, that's the way I always tell it. With the cow. But it's not true. It's a lie. In fact, it was a boy—a village boy. The car hit a boy and killed him. The first automotive fatality in the history of the country caused by a Ford. My father's fault, at least indirectly. So he never drove again. But when I tell that story the real way, the way it actually happened, it gets an entirely different reaction."

That was all that he said for a long while. He lit another Dunhill. We left Remal al-sahra and wandered down toward the paddock. I could hear my feet shuffle across the baked clay of the exercise yard.

"Listen," my father said. "I've had two lives. Two lives in full. This is a strange experience, believe me. Who has two entire separate lives? It is, how do you say: bewildering. The first one started here, a mile from here, in Zemalek, in 1956. The second one started when I met your mother in 1977, when I was just twenty-one. It lasted eight years, and then this life started again."

We walked into another stall. My father stood in front of a row of saddles. He stood there beside them, framed against them, an unlikely image. Since I turned twenty-one, I'd been drawn to off-track betting at the Yacht Club, sure. But until now I'd never considered that it might be a genetic affliction.

My father fished beneath the saddle for something. He took out a black padded neoprene laptop case. It was heavy and appeared to be stuffed with a number of small rectangular objects. He handed it to me. "Take this to the office behind the stables," he said. "Look inside—if you're curious."

I unzipped the pouch. Inside it I found banknotes—stacks and stacks of banknotes—euros, actually, twenty-euro notes, little clumps of them, bound with rubber bands. I blinked. "That's a lot of money," I said.

"It certainly is," he said. "Take it to the office—to Room Nine. There will be a man in there. His name is not important. Just be sure it's Room Nine. Tell him Akram sent you. Give him the case." He paused. "Easy. It will take you five minutes. Then we can go back to the house. And you can make any kind of trouble you want."

I looked up at him. "You mean we'll tell your sisters the truth?" I said.

"Sure, sure," my father said. "And then we can go to dinner. A nice dinner, maybe in a cruise boat on the Nile."

"It'll take me five minutes?" I said.

"More or less," my father said.

"Why do you owe them this money?" I said.

"Ah," my father said. "Club dues." He cleared his throat. "You said you wanted to see authentic Egyptian life. Here is your opportunity."

And what an opportunity it was. I zipped the case back up. "I think I'll just take this and leave the country," I said.

"Khosi," he said, "you're a lot of things, but one of them is not dishonest. Even I can tell you that."

I turned and started to move out into the sunlight.

"Five minutes," my father said. "I'll meet you back here."

His voice lessened and dimmed into the distance. I tucked the case under my arm and walked away.

Seven

FOR SUCH AN EXPANSIVE FACILITY in the center of the capital of Africa's largest country, the Gezira Sporting Club had dingy offices. Or at least the ones behind the stables. They were located in a small cinder-block add-on, a tiny building that smelled of hay and old turf and horse manure. It was not an intoxicating cocktail.

I walked through the front door to find the place deserted. There was a little unstaffed reception area. It abutted a long hallway with a linoleum floor; small rooms opened out on either side of it, evenly spaced. They were clearly numbered, the numerals centered on the surface of the doors. I walked down to Room 9. I knocked. Immediately, I heard the shuffle of someone moving around inside.

"*Allo, meen?*" said a deep male voice.

I tried the doorknob. The door swung quickly open. I stepped in. The door swung quickly closed. It must have been on a spring.

A burly man in a business suit and sunglasses sat at a desk. The desk, I saw, had some papers on it, but it was mostly bare. A computer monitor illuminated the corner of the room. My gaze careened from left to right to left again. I noticed the man's tie: It was thin and bright crimson, the color of fresh blood. And that was when I noticed the gun.

It was a pistol of some kind, and it was placed carefully on the desk, beside the telephone, facing the door. Facing me. The man looked up and then down at the pistol, then up at me again.

"Hello," I said in loud precise English, too shocked to remember any words in Arabic.

"Do you maybe have wrong room?" he said, his accent thick but understandable. I wondered briefly about this question. Indeed, what was behind the other doors, one through eight? Different men with different-colored ties and perhaps different weapons? A mace, a knife, a spear, a dagger, a grenade, a land mine, an ax? A set of brass knuckles?

"Room Nine," I said, sticking to English.

The man looked a little more concerned. He also looked a little more burly, but that could have been a trick of the lighting.

"Yes," he said. "Room Nine."

"I have something for you," I said. I put the parcel on the desk, inches away from the gun. "It's from Akram Saqr."

At my father's name, the man became animated. He stood up immediately. He reached across the desk and picked up the pistol, which he tucked into a holster on the side of his belt. In literature, the gun has to go off if it appears in the first act. But this was life. I was sincerely hoping that I'd at least reached the second act.

"When you see him?" the man said, coming around the desk to stand in front of me. "When he give this to you? You speak Arabic?"

I decided, based on his heightened interest, that *Yes, I speak fluent*

Arabic and *I just saw him five minutes ago* were not the most prudent answers. I merely shook my head. "I'll be going now," I said, backing up and putting my hand on the doorknob.

"You stay," the man said. That didn't seem like an invitation. He indicated the only other chair in the room. "Sit," he said. "Wait." He left the room.

I sat and waited. I sat and waited for much longer than five minutes. Twenty-five minutes, actually. At fifteen minutes, I stood up and tried to leave. The door was locked. I hadn't heard him lock it on the way out, but locked it was. And the room was hot. It kept getting hotter and hotter. There were no windows for me to escape through, just solid cinder-block paneling. Finally, I heard footsteps. Two sets of footsteps.

The Burly Man was accompanied by an Even Burlier Man, who loomed over me like a nightclub bouncer. Each of his biceps was the size of a Christmas ham.

"You are a messenger for Akram Saqr?" he said.

I nodded. This might be a bad time, I figured, to mention that I was his son.

"And you brought his payment for us," he said.

I nodded again.

The Even Burlier Man reached into his pocket and took out a very large, very wicked-looking knife. A knife with a glinting curved tip. A tip that was almost definitely intended to yank out internal organs. The knife was conscious of its wicked nature. *Hello, my young victim*, it was saying. *I am ready to disembowel you.*

"This is late," said the Even Burlier Man, waving the neoprene pouch in the air. "Maybe I should take an interest charge." He put the tip of the knife against my neck. "Maybe I should take some flesh as well, to pay me for my time."

"Please don't," I said.

Thinking back on it, I wish I'd said something witty, something full of cinematic bravado, something like *Go ahead and try.* Or *I eat thugs like you for breakfast.* Both of these could have gotten me killed. Maybe I would have run into another problem with my formal Arabic: *For me, a morning meal, the large man of your stature.* Sometimes, sometimes when I'm telling the story after a few drinks, this can be exactly what I said.

The Even Burlier Man spat on the ground. He cursed in a dialect of Arabic that I didn't understand. Then he swung open the spring-loaded door. "Run," he suggested.

I ran. For the second time in three days, I ran for my life. I was getting some excellent cardiovascular conditioning.

It wasn't more than half a mile to the stables, where I found my father still waiting, half concealed in an empty horse stall. He seemed happy to see me. I wanted to hit him, to swing at him, to slug him, to swipe at him. I felt my muscles clench. I felt my fingers draw together, curl into fists. If this feeling, this surge of emotion, had been missing before—MIA, uncataloged, absent, omitted, gone, lacking, ghostly, vaporous, vanishing—all I can say is: Of course. Of course it had.

"Ah," he said, noticing my condition. "You had some trouble in there."

"Those weren't club dues," I said.

"No," he said. "Did they threaten you?"

"Did they threaten me?" I said. "You asshole. You just made me risk my life for you."

"Khosi, please," he said. "That's an exaggeration. And I'm your father. You can't call me names like that."

"Asshole," I said. I looked over my shoulder. "You fucking asshole."

"Take a deep breath," he said. "It couldn't have been that bad."

"I'm leaving right now," I said. "There's no way I'm letting those goons follow me. And the minute I leave, I'm never talking to you, ever again."

"Calm down," he said. "I had no idea they'd be so angry."

"I was nearly killed," I said. I sighed and wiped the sweat off my forehead. "You're not any different than you ever were."

He stiffened. "Of course I am," he said. "That's all I am: different. Nothing like I used to be."

"You said you got in trouble with the mob in Montana."

My father nodded.

"Who were those men, then?" I said. "The Heliopolis Schoolteachers' Auxiliary? The Association of Egyptian Librarians? The Rotary Club, Cairo Branch?"

"Khosi."

"Those men were criminals," I said.

"Please," he said. "I can explain."

I was on the edge of tears. "His knife wanted to eat me," I said.

When I made the decision to leave, it was easy; it was quick; I turned in place and walked out through the stables, retracing our path along the chalked playing fields. "Khosi!" my father called from the space behind me, his voice somehow both insistent and hushed. "Khosi, wait! Where are you going? Khosi!" I didn't turn around or explain myself or tell him what I was doing. I disappeared. I tried to hurt him like he'd hurt me.

If you go to Cairo, you'll regret it, my mom had said, and now I thought I understood why. I wandered back through the streets of the metropolis. My head ached. It was just before dusk, and the lights of the Kewayis Marriott seemed artificial and jarring. The mess with my father could be ignored for now, for tonight, when I was this exhausted. I closed my eyes in the mirrored elevator to my floor, not willing to look at my reflection or the reflections of others. I opened the door to my room with a sigh, sliding the key in the lock and preparing to take a shower. Maybe I would burrow into my room, refusing to come out. Maybe I'd just ignore the family of Nasrallah Saqr. Maybe I'd spend the remainder of my time here watching *MTV Lebanon.*

I closed the door behind me. Immediately, I noticed that something was wrong. I smelled the scent of roasted garlic and cumin and baked pastry. I walked around the corner and encountered a luxuriant spread of food: pita bread and small dishes of hummus and tightly rolled, stuffed grape leaves, all of it arranged on the bed. And there, sitting beside the food, was my mother—neatly dressed, wearing her blue rhinestone-rimmed eyeglasses. She smiled broadly. "Oh, thank God," she said, beaming at me from her overstuffed chair. "I was starting to think I had the wrong room."

"Mom," I said. "What are you doing here?"

"Hi, darling," she said. She stood and walked over to me. "Inabi?" she added, offering me a stuffed grape leaf from one of the little rectangular containers. "I brought the lamb in an ice chest."

"I can't believe it," I said.

"I know: I got through security without a hitch. The lamb kept for the entire trip. And you can't imagine how nice the desk clerk was once I explained my situation to him. He loves my cooking." She frowned. "He asked me to become one of his wives. I think he was only joking, though." She began to peel off the lids of the flotilla of little Tupperware containers.

"This is crazy," I said.

My mother came over and put her hand on my shoulder. "Taste this—I'm not sure it's right. You know, I went by Rafiq's the day you left, but he was at Burger King getting a Whopper. I stole his falafel recipe while he was out."

I walked over and collapsed into one of the chairs beside her. "You just wouldn't believe what I've been through," I said. I looked over at my mother. She was wearing plaid polyester trousers, the kind with pleats that would last, unironed, until the end of time.

She looked down and started smoothing out those pleats with her palms. "I'm planning on bringing you back home right away," she said, "before you find your wretch of a father."

"Too late," I said.

"What do you mean?" she said.

"Exactly that. Too late: I found him."

"Oh dear," she said.

"I found him at his house," I said. "He introduced me to the family."

My mom's pleats, apparently, had reached an optimum level of smoothness. Her hands froze in place. She stared at the patterned polyester. She shook her head. "You know, for years I dreamed of meeting his father and his mother," she said. "Your grandparents."

"Well," I said, "they're dead. So: That's not happening."

"How awful," she said. "Not that I'm surprised, but—how awful."

"I wasn't on the family tree," I choked. "You're not on there, either—but none of the wives are. I checked. The genealogy arises from the men. Even the daughters are only a footnote."

"I could have told you that," my mother said.

"It wouldn't have mattered," I said.

"You know, Khosi, you have no idea what it was like: being utterly solitary, left to care for a three-year-old son, all alone, in debt to my parents forever. I just don't have words." She sighed. "Here, have some *ful*. It's much better than talking about 1988."

"Mom," I said, "you really are breathtaking."

"For what?" she said. "For cooking you dinner?"

"Yes," I said. "For cooking me dinner—six thousand miles from home. I have to admit, even from you, I never expected it."

I stood and walked over and picked up the telephone receiver. The message light was blinking. I had four messages, all of them from my father, each of them apologizing for whatever had happened in those offices. As I listened to my father's anxious voice, I watched my mother stand up, walk across the room, and retrieve her carry-on suitcase. She placed it on the second mattress and began unpacking. Her pill container was the first thing she removed. She placed it prominently on the table between the two beds.

"So," I said, hanging up. "I guess you're moving in."

"Who were those messages from?" she asked.

"President Mubarak," I said. "He wants to have coffee later."

"Well," my mother said, looking at me carefully, "I'm glad you're making friends." She continued unpacking. "I just have a few things," she said. She placed a small framed photograph of the Butte skyline on the bedside table. When I stared at it, she smiled at me and said, "To remind us of home."

I went over to the window. The lights of the city glimmered in the darkened glass.

"So," my mother said, "how's your dad?"

"You know," I said after some time, "you deserved better."

She nodded. "I did," she said.

"But you didn't know that at the time," I said.

"No," she said. "No, I didn't."

I paused. "Why'd you let him hide the marriage from his family?"

My mother exhaled—a great, gray, voluminous breath. "There were a number of reasons," she said. "I was young and naive."

"So you let him trick you," I said.

"Not exactly," she said. "But I couldn't *make* him do anything."

"You agreed to it. You had to. And look what happened. You passed it on to me. And now half of my family doesn't know I exist. Not that this is the worst thing in the world, but still."

"It was supposed to be temporary," she said. "Then we got a divorce, and it just didn't seem to matter. I was young. I made a mistake."

"Apparently," I said, "one with far-reaching repercussions."

"But look at you," she said. "You're a strange and wondrous being. You're the vein of blood beneath a bird's wing. You're the sound the ocean makes when it's asleep. You're my baby, my darling baby boy. A miracle. I grew you."

I stared out the window. Cairo unfolded outside of this room, a city of seventeen million—but to me, it was suddenly vacant, a cipher. My body, too, was meaningless; unloved by its father, it was missing half of itself. It would never be whole. There could be no restoration.

"I don't feel like a vein of blood under a bird's wing," I said.

"Oh, Khosi."

"I don't feel like the sound the ocean makes when it's asleep."

"Sweetheart."

"I don't feel elaborate or special or unique or beautiful or anything but dumb."

And then I was across the room and sitting on the bed beside my mother, flattening out on the mattress, atop the newly made sheets, near the microwaveable containers of food. I hadn't cried in years, not since I could remember, but there I was, breaking down, retreating inside of myself, raw body and ribs and lungs, ragged lungs, lungs that wouldn't work to fill themselves with air. "I'm sorry," I said, though I wasn't sure if my voice was audible or even understandable. "I'm so sorry," I said again.

"Oh, Khosi," my mother said. "My sweet, darling Khosi. There's nothing to be sorry for. What on earth could you be sorry about?"

"I didn't listen to you," I said, blowing my nose in my sleeve. "I should have listened to you. I've learned something, anyway."

My mother said nothing.

"Go ahead," I said. "Ask me what I've learned."

"What have you learned, my darling?"

"Always pack your own liquor," I said.

"Very profound, sweetheart."

"It's true," I said.

From the refrigerated minibar, I took out a small plastic bottle of Glenfiddich whiskey. I snapped open the top. "Especially if you're traveling in the Middle East," I said. "This is eleven dollars." And then: "I think Dad wants to stay lost."

"That's okay with me," she said.

"To us. To you. To his past, to America. He doesn't want that to be a part of who he is. He made me use a fake name at the house."

"You're joking," my mother said.

"He made me pretend to be the son of a friend."

"And he didn't introduce you as his child," she said.

"I was the son of his friend Malik," I said. "It was a bad scene."

"Somehow," my mother said, "it just doesn't surprise me."

I continued looking out at the city. A city tells us more than anything else what our destiny and our substance is: Replicable, we build our homes in clusters—generation following sequential generation. Our urban centers are palimpsests; they carry the trace of the forgotten and the nameless in their edifices, in their streets and alleys and bright singular parkways. I turned around and told my mother about the stables—a slightly edited version, one that didn't include the weapons. That skipped the little matter of the Cairene fiancée. Even so, she was furious.

"Dammit," she said. "*You* deserved better, not just me. We *both* deserved better."

"I know," I said. I drained the rest of the liquor. I took two more bottles from the minibar—one for myself and one for her.

"It's an outrage," she said, accepting her bottle with a nod. "Just give me the go-ahead, and I'll go to his house and kill him."

"No," I said. "The plan is not to commit a murder in a foreign country."

My mother shrugged. "You have to admit," she said, "there's an upside to the murder idea. Just imagine him. Imagine your philandering, uncaring, good-for-nothing carcass of a father. Now imagine him as an actual carcass."

At that moment, sitting in my hotel room, my mother and I had a long and remarkably satisfying discussion about my father's untimely end. She proposed a variety of different scenarios. Each was more gruesome and violent than the last. Many seemed to have been stolen from the execution methods of medieval Europe. She proposed, for example, rolling him down a hill in a barrel of nails.

"Where will we get a barrel?" I said.

"That's not the real challenge," she said. "The real challenge is getting him in it."

"What about arsenic?" I said.

"Ah, yes," she said, and sighed. "From the apothecaries of the vanished past." She paused. "The son of his friend Malik," she said, finishing the liquor. "I can't believe you did it."

"It happened fast," I said.

"But still," she said. "Didn't you feel like you were compromising something important?"

"Haven't you felt that way for years?" I said.

"Oh dear," she said.

A silence inhabited my hotel room then, it rose up from the vents, perhaps, and floated out through the interior space.

"What do you mean?" I said.

"Ah, son," said the Ghost of William Andrews Clark. "I'm in a pile of trouble in the spiritual realm. I've been interfering too much on this side of things." He leaned forward on the bar stool. "Cigar?"

"Sure," I said. I reached out and took the unlit cigar. I chewed on it a bit, letting its sting numb my lips.

The ghost looked over at the bottles of liquor. "What I wouldn't give," he said, "for just one shot of that bug juice." He coughed. "Look, pardner, like I said: I'm going to take a vacation. Go play the ponies in Sarasota. I've got a great tip on a filly in the fourth race tomorrow. You know, son, always bet on the horse with the shiniest coat. It means good circulation."

"I should bring you back to Gezira," I said.

"Of course you shouldn't," he said. "But that's not why I'm here. I'm here to show you something you should know about."

He was laying a local newspaper on the counter beside me. I was astonished by what I saw when I looked at the cover. LOCAL WOMAN REPORTS ANTIQUITIES THEFT, I read. The article that accompanied the headline described a local woman—A. L. Mouri—who'd had priceless artifacts stolen from her home. The loss she'd incurred had been a large one, nearly a million Egyptian pounds. But far more interesting than this information were the photographs, prominently featured, of the items that the thieves had stolen. There, off to one side, was something I recognized. It was the bracelet that I'd found in the trash can outside my house, in the envelope marked *FOR AMY*. It glittered with a diluted brilliance on the newspaper's graying page. The caption read: *A replica of the stolen bracelet, dated to the reign of Ramesses II.*

"It's over three thousand years old," I said.

"And he's a great guy, Ramesses the Second." The ghost paused. "Everybody up there calls him Ozy."

"I guess I'm confused," I said. "Are you telling me that my father is an international smuggler of stolen pharaonic artifacts?"

"I can't help you there, son," said the Ghost of William Andrews Clark. "You have to draw your own conclusions."

"But you gave me this newspaper," I said.

"What newspaper?" the ghost said.

When I looked down, the newspaper had vanished.

"That's not fair," I said.

"All's fair in love and war," he said.

"Which one is this?" I said.

"Now, that's a better question than you might imagine," he said.

I gnawed on my lip, absorbing the information. The bracelet was stolen, then, stolen by my father from his fiancée as a kind of perverse token of goodwill for my mother. He'd smuggled it *out of* Egypt in his luggage. And now—I'd smuggled it back *into* Egypt in my luggage. I was in violation of probably a dozen international laws. Thanks, Dad.

"You've got to at least tell me what to do," I said. "Or make a recommendation."

"Didn't you listen, pardner?" the ghost said. "I'm in a heap of trouble."

"Is a heap less than a pile?" I said.

He ignored me. "You keep interfering, and you know what happens?" Here he made a sound like a burst of wind through an open window. His long, bony fingers mimed the snuffing of a candle. "Extinguished," he said. "Gone. Just like that."

"I'd imagine," I said, "that eternal rest would be an appealing option after a certain number of years."

"Nah," said the Ghost of William Andrews Clark, "the fear of death just gets bigger, the older you get. Life is all you've known, after all. Stepping forward into that open space—"

"That abyss?" I said.

"You're not helping, son," he said.

"You did it once already," I pointed out. I dredged up the biographical details. "March 2nd, 1925. You had no idea what was next."

"And look where I ended up," he said.

"This isn't so bad," I said. "Is it?"

I thought about this version of William Andrews Clark, the version I was seeing, whose life had embodied so many different things: tenacity, resolve, old American grit, courage in the face of trouble. Poor Willie Clark. Mark Twain famously slandered him. His daughter, Huguette, was still alive, at the age of 102, in a New York City hospital. It must've been lonely—even lonelier—in the afterlife for a man who'd been as powerful as he.

"It's not so bad," the ghost conceded.

"Well," I said, settling into my whiskey, "if you're not going to help me, then at least tell me an interesting story."

So we talked, and the ghost told me about the first miner who'd died in one of his mines, and how that had felt. How he'd walked in front of the horses himself, and helped bury the man in the public cemetery. The ghost clasped his hands, those haunted, pale, bony hands, propping them on the bar. "The public cemetery in those days had a triumphal arch, and I remember just standing aside and watching that hearse go under it—the groomsmen with their white coats and their black top hats, the horses wearing gray fly nets, and all my men, my miners, walking hatless beside them." He sighed. "I never forgot that, son. It's what keeps me here, I think, at least in part."

I thought of the fingers, the fingertips, turning the warm leather of the hatband, moving it almost unconsciously back and forth; thought of the feet, cold in their formal leather shoes, mud on the formal leather shoes, the stiff funeral collar, the smell of the horses.

The ghost smiled wistfully at me. "We went home," he said, "back to my little house on the hill. And I cooked up a mess of skirlie."

"For whom?"

"For his wife, Kate Stouffer."

"Wait," I said. "She was the first woman you married."

"She was indeed, pardner."

"I had no idea," I said.

"Of course not," he said. "How could you? We kept that secret close."

"In some ways," I said, "that's a terrible story."

"It felt like my responsibility," the ghost said.

"But so many men died in your mines," I said.

"And I felt every death like that one," he said. "Son, a mine is a mine is a mine. It ain't no great secret. Commerce has immutable laws. Adam Smith wrote all about them, and he's no dry gulch rattler. If I hadn't done what I did, someone else would've. Hell, Marcus Daly would have, that good-for-nothing no-'count."

What would you do if you started having full-bodied hallucinations? Go to a psychiatrist? A medical doctor? A priest? I was in Egypt—it wasn't the most convenient moment for this ghost to start appearing. Besides, whenever the Ghost of William Andrews Clark appeared, the air filled with a thousand different scents, with the odor of raw garlic, with honey, with the lingering acrid note of coal smoke. Sometimes cloves. Sometimes cardamom. It was distracting. I couldn't focus on him, on the idea, the concept, of him. I kept slipping in and out of the present; I was lost and unmoored and rudderless and lacking any navigational charts. Any maps. I had no maps. I'd just lived a week without maps, a month without maps. This next year, I was certain, would be a year without maps.

I looked over at the ghost. He was standing from his bar stool.

"I'll see you in a few days, chief," he said.

"I'm not a chief of any kind," I said. And then: "Wait. In a few days? What do you mean?"

I felt a vacancy, an absence, a cold breath of air, and then—nothing. I looked around. The Ghost of William Andrews Clark was gone.

WILLIAM ANDREWS CLARK'S ONE & ONLY SKIRLIE

Variable servings, depending on appetite

2 strips bacon
1 onion, thinly sliced
½ cup oatmeal
Salt and pepper to taste

Chop bacon into 1-inch chunks and fry. Is there a better smell than frying bacon, pardner? If there is, I ain't smelled it none.

You got to let the bacon fry nice and slow. Anything is better slow, my friend, anything you can think of. When the grease finally coats the pan, add the sliced onion. Slice it however you'd like. Cook until transparent as a window.

Add oatmeal to absorb the fat, keeping the mixture thick.

Stir for 7 to 10 minutes, till cooked. Serve with mincemeat, venison, roasted pigeon, or as a main dish if you don't got nothin' else to serve.

Eight

WHEN I GOT BACK TO the room, I took the bracelet from the bedside drawer. My mother was asleep in the other queen-size bed, a sleep mask pulled down over her eyes.

I lay down and held the thing aloft. Here it was, the jeweled object, the material substance, the incontrovertible and eternal element. It had outlasted dozens upon dozens of generations of humanity. It was streaked with oxidation. Thousands of years had worn down its luster. Still it had the power to awe. It was solid. I let it sink down and rest on my forehead. My headache was getting worse and worse and now I was shivering.

I sank gradually into a shallow, fitful sleep. I dreamed that I was sitting at the kitchen table in Butte. My mother was at the stove, cooking dinner. I stood up and went over to her and reached out and touched her face, even though that was something I'd never do in real life. I reached out and brushed my fingertips against her face, and the feel of her skin left me shuddering and cold. But I didn't want to pull my hand away. It was soothing somehow. It was peaceful. I awoke to my mother's voice: "Come on," she said, reaching underneath the covers and tickling the soles of my feet, "we have a lot to do today."

Momentarily panicked, I felt around beneath the covers for the bracelet, my hands searching until they found it. Only then did I open my eyes. "How about the Egyptian Museum?" I said.

"Not exactly the Egyptian Museum," my mother said. "I'm thinking of something a little different."

"Tea at the Mena Park Hotel," I suggested. "A trip on a ferry boat down the Nile."

"Nope," she said. "Guess. No, no, wait: You'll never guess. Which shirt do you want?"

When my mother opened my closet, she was confronted by a devastating and pure order. Spectacular. I'd arranged them by color— along the colors of the visible spectrum—carefully aligning the shirts on hangers and making sure they were positioned just so, just perfectly, tip to tip to tip.

"Whatever," I said. "I don't care."

She looked at me in mock amazement.

"Fine," I said. "Bring me the blue oxford."

"Which one?" my mother said. It was a valid question, since there were three of them.

"The lightest of the three," I said. "The light blue one. It's on the left." I cleared my throat. "Not that you asked, but I've arranged them in ascending order according to depth of blue."

"That's subjective," she said, "depth of blue."

"No, it's not," I said.

"Okay, then," she said, and brought me the wrong shirt. I put it on anyway.

Morning light had illuminated the room. It slashed across the furniture, the drapes, the bureau, the carpeting, igniting half of everything into an effulgent glow.

"Before I came here," my mother said, "I was doing a little research with Wada." She could barely contain her enthusiasm. "Well," she continued, "*research* isn't really the right word. *Snooping* is more like it."

"Okay," I said.

"Wada and I—we just got some very interesting information about your father. Very interesting, indeed. Get dressed," she added. "Get ready to go."

She was my mother, and I owed her a certain fealty. It was pleasant just to be pulled forward by the force of her personality; if she had handed me a trowel and proposed we strip the entire country of its onions, I wouldn't have objected. Also, my throat was feeling raw and the headache I'd had the previous day had not abated. And I was preoccupied by the idea of what to do with the bracelet.

"Look," I said before we left the room. "We should talk about this." I tossed the bracelet on the bedspread. "Why didn't you tell me the truth?"

My mother held her hand to her forehead. She rolled her eyes. She looked physically uncomfortable, deeply physically uncomfortable. "Khosi," she said, "think about it: What does that bracelet represent? What, exactly, does it stand for?" She sighed. "It was a gesture. And I didn't want any part of it."

"So you admit it," I said. "It was for you."

"Of course it was for me." She paused. She pinched the bridge of her nose with two fingers. "Your father said it was worth ten times what he owed me. I don't believe him. Or, I mean, I don't really care. Because even if it was worth that much money, how on earth could I possibly sell it?"

"I met some guys yesterday," I said. "I'm sure I could set you up."

My mother ignored this. "Even so," she said, "I reject the notion that he owes me anything. Because that would imply that the ledger isn't balanced. And darling, the ledger is balanced. Entirely balanced. I'm done with him completely." She shook her head. "Let's get going. Hurry up."

We went down the elevator and through the lobby and out past the security guards. The doorman requisitioned us a taxi, and without any warning, there we were in the city. My mother handed the driver a slip of paper. "Tell him to go to that address," she said to me. Then she exclaimed, "What an adventure!" and settled down in the cracked leather seat.

I should have paid a little more attention at this point. Her glee was uncharacteristic. I should have checked her medicine case. I passed along the instructions. The driver nodded. He smiled. "Yes, yes," he said in English. "Very fast. Very, very fast."

This scared me, but I had more pressing matters. "Can you share with me," I asked my mother, "where we might be going?"

"You don't want to guess?" she said.

"I don't want to guess," I said.

"Fine," she said. "If you don't want to play along." She paused. "We're going to meet your father's fiancée."

My mother turned to me, and her face was silhouetted in the

bright light of smoggy midday Cairo. The planes of her cheekbones made her face look almost oval, positioned in the window of the taxi, a round geometry set against a plane of glass. Her lips were bright red, and she seemed to be wearing lipstick—something I had no memory of her wearing on *any* occasion, formal or otherwise. This was what I realized at that moment about my mother: She had a face framed for victory. Indeed, she looked triumphant—but then I undercut her triumph.

"Agnes Mouri," I said.

She blanched. "Now, that's a surprise," she said.

"I've met her," I said.

"And you didn't tell me," she said.

I sighed. "It's a long story."

"But I *just* got the address." She paused. "Did you gouge out her eyes—you know, for your poor jilted mother?"

"That's enough murder jokes, Mom," I said. "There's a point at which they get creepy. I doubt they'll let us in the door, anyway, after my display earlier this week."

"What happened?"

"A lot of things," I said.

"What did *you* say?"

"A lot of things as well."

"Come on," she said. "Give me something."

"Okay," I said. "Let's go back to the hotel and we can discuss it there. This is a needless gesture. I've already done everything we can do."

"She knows everything?" my mother said.

"I don't know what you mean by that," I said.

205

She inhaled deeply. "I don't, either."

I began to recognize the neighborhood. The taxi had indeed brought us there very, very fast. Panic flooded me. I realized that I'd been too busy over the past couple of days to perform my morning rituals, to keep myself from utter disaster. I also knew clearly that I'd made the wrong decision—backing out of Agnes Mouri's apartment.

"We need to have a better plan," I said.

"I just want to meet her," my mother said.

"Yeah, right," I said.

"It's true!" my mother protested. "You know: Her father was a famous shipping magnate."

I turned the phrase over in my mind. It conjured images of the Suez Canal to me. There, there was a litany of facts you could really sink your teeth into. The building of the canal was, in my mind, one of the great stories of the modern world, full of intrigue, international espionage, and double and triple crosses. My brain *begged* to think about these, to sink into the comfort of the names: the Compagnie Universelle du Canal Maritime de Suez and Sa'id Pasha, the Egyptian viceroy, and the French architects fighting a duel on the steps of the parliament building over differing approaches to the blueprints. Or the Suez Crisis of 1956, which nearly led to a global nuclear war. But I was hurtling through Cairo in a taxi with my mother on the way to possibly assault my father's second wife-to-be. The air was a bit acrid through the open window of the taxi. The billboards promised *highest quality* and *most delicious* and *fastest service* and *largest coverage area.*

Everywhere I went, I imagined Evel Knievel. His spirit was in everything, in the dusty billboards, in the advertising that rose from nearly every surface and clamored for your attention. Satellite television, billboard advertising, it was a modern phenomenon, it wanted you to look, desperately wanted you to look, wanted it more than anything else. There was my imagined Knievel, soaring over the pyramids and the Nile; he was a perfect fit for a tourist-based economy.

The taxi came to a halt.

"She's going to kick your ass," I said.

"I'll think of something," my mother said. She smiled and looked intently at me. "You have to admit: I always do think of something."

"You and Dad both," I said.

We got out of the taxi. I paid the driver. He smiled and nodded and took the money and gave me no change and darted back into traffic, honking his horn to say goodbye. I'd had that headache all morning. As we approached the front door, it seemed to be getting worse and worse. Even the strange Egyptian aspirin I'd taken had done nothing to quiet the pain.

"Dad might be here," I said. "You're charging blindly into this situation because of your unresolved feelings from the past. It's dangerous."

She just said, "Hush." She knocked on the door.

Within seconds, we heard the beep of someone disarming an alarm system, and then Ibrahim appeared. He was wearing a charcoal-colored suit. "*As-salamu alaikum*," he said. "Hello again, sir. Ms. Mouri has been expecting you."

My mother, who had been standing to the left of me, sort of shrank down and partly hid behind my shoulder.

207

"Please wait in the hall," Ibrahim said in formal Arabic that almost matched mine.

Someone had added a glass bowl full of lemons to the marble-topped buffet table. My mother sat quietly on a chaise longue, glancing up at the hallway's vaulted ceiling. She was calm. She seemed almost timorous, isolated and small on the single piece of comfortable furniture in this austere but elegant room.

"I could use a cigarette," I said.

"I didn't know you smoked," she said.

"I don't," I said.

My head was pulsing with tendrils of pain; chills swept along my spine; they weakened my knees. I wobbled. We waited quite a long time there, saying nothing, looking at the plain walls. Around the corner, I knew, was an equally neutral-colored room. After my strange display three days ago, I was surprised when Ibrahim returned and ushered us in there. "She will be downstairs in a moment," he said softly. He did not offer us tea.

We waited a little longer.

"We can still go back to the hotel," I said. "There's still time."

"I'm waiting right here," my mother said.

And then Agnes Mouri appeared on the grand staircase, wearing a form-fitting black dress and, this time, no shawl.

"Oh God," my mother said. "Goddammit, she's really beautiful."

Then she was across the room and standing in front of us. My mother and I rose awkwardly to our feet.

"Please," Agnes Mouri said. "Before you say anything more, I want you to know: I do not believe you." She held up a single finger in an angry, insistent gesture. "Or rather, I trust Akram, and Akram is insisting that you are a liar and a fake." She adjusted the hem of her shirt. "But maybe that's what you came here today to tell me. Maybe that is why you left so suddenly three days ago."

"Mom," I said. "This is Agnes Mouri. Agnes, this is my mother, Amy Clark-Saqr."

My mother pointed toward me. "A liar and a fake?" she said, raising one eyebrow. "Khosi? I can assure you, madam, that my son is neither of those things."

"Oh, really," Agnes Mouri said. "Your son? Ah, I see. To extend the lie, to make the lie more believable. It's all quite clear to me."

Her accent was precise and almost English. It was also barely perceptible.

In 1835 Phineas Taylor Barnum moved to New York City. He began selling tickets to see Joice Heath, an elderly black woman whom he billed as George Washington's 161-year-old nurse. Even though Heath was a hoax, her popularity gave him the money to start the American Museum, where, over two decades, he exhibited taxidermied tigers and waxwork politicians and watery mermaids and Siamese twins and Charles S. Stratton, the twenty-five-inch-tall midget who went by the stage name of General Tom Thumb. This was the beginning of something, its genesis, the soil in which something grew—the fertilizer-rich, nitrogen-blessed topsoil for the past 150 years of lion tamers and trapeze artists and clowns in tiny cars and various and sundry swindlers like my father. He was a member of the Direct Lineage of the American Charlatan. It didn't matter where on earth he'd been born.

"And what did Akram tell you," my mother said, "about me?"

"I don't know who you are. But the woman you say you are, I've been assured, has been rotting in a coffin for twenty years."

My mother ignored this. "I'm Akram's first wife," she said. "As far as I know, his first wife. Maybe not. Maybe he had a dozen before me. Even so, I have important things to tell you."

I thought that, confronted by the same thing that had confronted me, confronted by the magnitude of my father's lies, my mother would back away, retreat, like I had. I was wrong.

"Look," she added, "I brought this with me. To show you."

She took a cardstock document from her purse and unfolded it. She smoothed the creases flat on one thigh and handed it over. I looked over Agnes Mouri's shoulder. *Certificate of Marriage*, I read. *State of Nevada, County of Clark. This is to certify that the undersigned, J. Aakre, Esq., did on the 9th day of May, A.D. 1980, join in lawful wedlock Akram Saqr of Cairo, state of Egypt, and Amy Marion Clark of Butte, state of Montana, with their mutual consent, in the presence of Rhonda Spencer and Wada Kinrabouz, who were witnesses.*

Agnes Mouri scanned the document. She swallowed once; I could tell that she was nervous. "A forgery," she said.

"Why would I do that?" my mother said.

"I don't know," Agnes Mouri said. "All I know is that I'm supposed to get married—and now the heavens have opened."

"There's a reason for that," my mother said. "It's the man you're marrying."

Agnes Mouri shook her head. *"Mishmumkin,"* she said. "Impossible. Akram has been here for the past two days. You can't imagine how upset he is."

"It's an act," my mother said.

"Wait, wait," I said. I sat down next to Agnes Mouri. "I left here the other day," I said to her, "because I couldn't imagine what you must be going through, and I felt guilty. I felt responsible. I felt like it was my fault. Now I see that it's not. It's Akram. It's my father. My mom is right. It's him."

My mother began to enumerate the ways that my father had disappointed her. The list was long and specific; I'd heard much of it before. In fact, I'd grown up with the list as the background music to my childhood, the litany of complaints about the man she'd once loved, whose life she'd carried on even after he left, in a part of her that was isolated and inaccessible and dark. What I heard was the sadness, the abandonment, the brittle sorrow. But there was something else. And I couldn't really hope to unravel the mystery of that interior space. Also, my head was pounding, and sweat had broken out on my body. I needed to find a momentary refuge so I could take a few deep, calming breaths.

"I'm sorry," I said in Arabic. "Could I use your restroom?"

Agnes Mouri nodded and pointed down the hallway. "Second door on your left," she said. She was distracted by listening to my mother. She seemed coiled, ready to leap, to attack. I wandered down the hall a little ways. I opened a door—what I thought was the second door—but I was in a different room, a room with floor-to-ceiling bookshelves, shelves containing a number of carefully spotlit items. I left the door slightly ajar and crept over to the display cases. These were the antiquities missing from the front room. I stared in wonder at it all, at the jeweled knives and shards of pottery and stone slabs with hieroglyphic writing. *It's a hell of a bathroom*, I thought.

Then I realized: *This is what I'm here to do.* This was what I had to do with the bracelet: restore it to Agnes Mouri. I took the copper object out of my pocket. I would slip it in among the other treasures.

I wavered. I couldn't quite bring myself to put it back. Everything seemed to slip in and out of focus. Everything was gauzy and distant, as if I were standing on the bank of the river in my dream. I seemed to see it in front of me, the tumbling nameless expanse of water. It shone as it moved past, glittering with a thousand individual, changeable crenellations. Beyond the river, at a certain point, the rolling dun-colored hills became a flat tapestry, a solid drape of color. Wasn't that a pine tree—*right there?*—a pine that had been devoured by a clutch of pine beetles? They can kill a tree in a year, pine beetles. They bore under its skin and lay their eggs, and then the larvae hatch and eat their way out, feasting on the soft, nutrient-rich bark. A tree usually doesn't know it's diseased until it's too late.

I scratched my arm. *Wait a minute*, I thought. *A pine tree in Cairo?*

I shook my head. The room surged back into focus, surged out of the hallucination. I looked down; I'd dropped the bracelet on the parquet floor. I heard footsteps in the hallway. I turned around in time to see Agnes Mouri batter her way into the room.

"You dirty little thief," she said, as if confirming some basic fact. "I knew I couldn't trust you." Her breath caught in her throat. She knelt on the floor. "My bracelet," she said. "My bracelet."

"What's going on?" my mother said from the hall. Now *she* was standing in the doorway. "Khosi," she said. "What are you doing?" She turned to Agnes Mouri. "I'm sure there's a perfectly rational explanation."

"He's a liar and a thief," Agnes Mouri said, brandishing the arti-fact. "And you—you are his accomplice."

"Oh dear," my mother said.

I pushed my way past her. "I don't feel so well," I said.

"I'm calling the police," Agnes Mouri said.

"I think," I called back over my shoulder, "that we should leave."

"We should leave," my mother said, and nodded.

That's pretty much all I remember. I know we left the Mouri household, dodging past Ibrahim and stumbling into the street. And then we walked, wildly and without direction, really. It was almost like I was floating above myself in some dissociative state, watching my knees fold and my equilibrium disappear entirely. At some point, I was aware of falling, of my falling body. And then I hit the ground with my shoulder, hit it hard and rolled into darkness. Voices stretched around me and wavered and disappeared. They disappeared. They disappeared.

I nearly died. I can say that now that the *nearly* is appended to the statement, now that I have a few years between myself and the illness that crashed over me on the streets of Cairo. In retrospect, it had been building for days: the persistent headache, the night sweats, the chills. I was brewing a foul and insistent pestilence inside of me.

It was the mosquito. Epidemiologists will tell you that an individual's illness is difficult to trace, that the provenance of disease is almost never a certainty, that even Patient Zero is often only a guess. But I know it was the mosquito from that first day on the Cairene street. I feel this with confidence. I can feel it in my blood. And what a mosquito it was: *Aedes aegypti*, an entire species named after Egypt. The primary transmitter of yellow fever. They live in discarded tires and oil drums and planters and any small amount of standing water. They've adapted to thrive in urban settings.

My blood was the host for the ailment, my own blood poisoning me, the yellow fever pulled through the muscle of my heavy heart, through its clench and release, funneled out into the whole of my body. I could imagine, I did imagine, that single vector of disease, that single perforation of my skin, while I was innocently walking down the street. It was probably because earlier that day, I'd eaten a plate of chicken livers. The revenge of the chicken: *You eat my liver, I will slaughter you with a vicious pathogen.*

There's a vaccine for yellow fever. It's easy to get. Any travel medicine specialist will give it to you over the course of a few months. It provides protection to 95 percent of the people who get it. I just didn't do it. I didn't have the patience.

I opened my eyes to my mother pinching my cheeks and saying my name over and over again. "Khosi? Baby boy?"

"Where am I?" I asked, opening my eyes. "It's freezing in here."

"We're outside, sweetheart. It's a hundred degrees, at least."

My mother half lifted me to my feet. Here was the strange thing: If you'd told me that she would someday end up in a foreign country, sick and in need of a doctor but unsure how to find one, I wouldn't have been surprised. It was her sort of thing, the unplanned trip, the disregard for consequences. But how had it happened to me? *To me?* I'd once labeled my underwear according to the days of the week. I liked to measure and regularize the distance between the containers in the refrigerator. I'd once parked and reparked a car fifteen times to achieve the perfect angle in the parking lot.

"A clinic," I said to my mom, even though my knees were shaking. "I need a clinic."

My mother went up to a man on the street corner and asked if he knew directions to the hospital. He didn't speak English. But as I watched, as I propped myself against the wall and held my aching stomach, shivering, he escorted her down the street to the nearest café. This was typical of Egyptians whom we met in Cairo. Almost without exception, they were kind and friendly and ready to help complete strangers.

Within two minutes, three young men were rushing toward us, three young men neither of us had ever met, and they surrounded us and helped move me down to a little wooden table at a café at the end of the street. I remember all of this quite clearly. They brought me a glass of water that I couldn't drink. And then everyone seemed to be on a cell phone at once, calling different friends or relatives or government bureaus. It was hard to focus on anything other than my body, which felt like it had been plunged in ice; and now someone was slicing out my backbone with a paring knife. There seemed to be an argument going on. One of the men, a stocky, bearded fellow, appeared to be suggesting that they take me to his house.

"It is a nice house," he said. "It is very clean."

"Take half of me to one place," I said quietly, "and half to the other."

Nobody laughed.

"Who speaks English?" my mother said. "English?" she repeated, as if stripping the sentence of everything but its noun would prompt a different response. What it did was transform our cadre of helpers into a Greek chorus, a harmony of uniform agreement.

"No English," they said, seemingly all at once. "No English, no English." Which was *some* English, after all.

I closed my eyes and leaned my head against my mother's shoulder for the second time in as many days. It felt like a revolution, an amazement, a curiosity, an impossibility. Maybe this was what I wanted so badly, what I'd dreamed of having for so many years: a reliable parent, a source of comfort in times of need. Too bad I appeared to be dying in order to get it. Then I thought about my perfect-attendance awards and scrupulously clean toiletries and persistent weekly doing of laundry. My mother had never felt like she had to be anything other than what she was: disorder, chaos, disintegration. This was it: the dream of my life when I want what I have and have what I want. All it turned out to be was my mom's shoulder, proffered at a moment of need.

"We have to call an ambulance," she said. "You can't walk." She squeezed my hand. "How do you say *ambulance?*" She turned to the half-circle of men. "Ambulance?" she suggested.

"*El is'aef,*" I said.

"*El is'aef!*" she said. "*El is'aef?*"

This prompted another chorus, this time of laughter. I slumped farther down on the tabletop. The man closest to me tapped me on the shoulder. "Tell your mother we'll carry you there more quickly," he said. "By the time the ambulance arrives, you'll already be dead."

For some reason, I didn't feel like translating this entire sentence. "They'll carry me," I said to her, and closed my eyes to rest.

Everything that happened over the next few hours happened *to* me. I was there, in that I occupied space within my body. I was unquestionably alive; my auditory nerves recorded the things going on around me; I felt the sensation of hands lifting me up, of shoulders supporting me, of the hot Cairene air against my skin. But my ability to communicate, to interact, to let my feelings be known: That dissipated. I was a slab of tissue. A butcher's delight.

The consensus was to go to the Maadi Central Franco-American Hospital in Zemalek. I was an American, so apparently this was the logical place to take me. My poor mother just nodded. She trailed along, holding the end of my pant leg, walking behind the processional. They jostled me along the city streets, up and over the Nile on the sidewalk of the Sixth of October Bridge, a spectacle for the city's drivers, many of whom showed their appreciation, or possibly wished us luck, by honking resolutely as they passed us. The sound of the horns rose and became a melody, and though it's probably not true I'd like to believe that I began, at that moment, composing this in my subconscious:

THE MAUDLIN MOSQUITO, A MEDICAL MUSICAL INTERLUDE
To a variable tune

It's too late, once you've been bit,
We crave that sweet hematocrit,
Arteries—or even veins;
We breed in tires when it rains.
Platelets, T-cells, hemoglobin,
We get you while you are disrobin'.
Our stingers, full of anesthetic,

Can be quite a nice emetic.
We'll gladly share with you our fever,
Forge in you a new believer,
In the great Culicidae,
Family of the gnat and fly.
Though you use a pesticide,
And have Homonidic pride,
We'll cut you down and make you tragic,
With our blood-borne ancient magic.

The Maadi Central Franco-American Hospital in Zemalek, despite being in the best neighborhood in the city, was a rotting hulk of a building. It had been founded in the early twentieth century by American Lutheran missionaries. Over a hundred years old, it seemed to sag beneath the weight of its own facade. The paint that had once adorned the frames of its windows had chapped and peeled to bare gray. Cracks ran through the stucco walls like air veins through a wall of ice. It was easily more terrifying than the American Motordrome Wall of Death. This was, it seemed, an actual wall of death. No Evel Knievel Days required.

They carried me—these three angelic strangers carried me—to the front door, and they managed to somehow requisition a wheelchair into which they deposited me. Then they left. One of them lingered for a few minutes, to make sure we were situated, but he, too, soon left, slipping back into the regular routine of his day. I imagined the conversation at home: *What did you do today, dear? Not much. Went to work, got some lunch, carried a feverish American across the Nile. Filed some paperwork. You know: the usual.*

As in every hospital I'd ever been to, access to the ward was guarded by a swath of sentries. Secured behind their identical desks, they triaged and admitted patients. The severely ill were funneled off immediately to some care facility. Those who looked like they were not in imminent danger of death were given paperwork and charged a bit of money up front. I did not seem like I was in imminent danger of death. Ill but not dying. Or so it seemed. At that moment.

My mother tried to find someone who spoke English. She had no luck.

"Call Agnes Mouri," I said, chills tumbling along the sides of my spine like rolling pins.

"Are you kidding me?" my mother said. "You want to go to jail in Egypt, sick as a dog?"

An admissions secretary with an enormous mole on her chin took me on as her patient. By *took me on* I mean *shook us down for a bribe.*

"Good treatment?" she said.

"Are you asking," my mother said, "if we want good treatment here at the hospital?" I was slumped in one of the two folding chairs that sat, stiff and cushionless, in front of the woman's desk. My mother scowled.

"Extra," the woman said. "You pay here. You pay me."

My mother shook her head and reached into her purse. She dug through her wallet and pulled out a plastic card. "Blue Cross?" she said, then repeated it more slowly: "Blue Cross?"

It seemed like my mother was referencing a sad religious cult.

If our administrator had ever heard of health insurance, she didn't let on. "Small gratuity," she insisted. "For me. *Bakshish.*"

"Mom?" I said.

"Khosi, hush," she said. "I've never in my life seen such an egregious violation of the Hippocratic Oath."

Our attendant continued smiling. She had not taken the Hippocratic Oath.

My mother was incensed. "I will not stoop to such a level. As recipients of medical care, we are part of an unbroken chain—a chain that extends to the ancient Greeks and Egyptians and the cradle of civilization here in the Middle East. It is a long, proud tradition."

I turned and vomited into the wastebasket.

"Okay," my mom said. "But just a few Egyptian pounds."

That became the key to my medical care over the next few days. Cash was king. Need to see a doctor? Just a few Egyptian pounds. Need IV medication? Just a few Egyptian pounds. Need some blankets or a pillow? No variation on the theme. My mother bought me a room at the back of the hospital, a room that had a view of an alleyway and a series of resolute iron bars on the windows. There was no way to escape it: It stank of urine. On the far wall, some unfortunate patient had sprayed blood in an arc across the sterile white paint. There were no paper towels. No supplies of any kind.

In short: Everything was horrendously disorganized.

The sink lacked soap or even a functioning faucet. And nothing had been changed: The sheets and the pillowcases bore broad yellow stains. *Perhaps this is the source of the odor?* I thought idly. I didn't say anything. I was busy drifting in and out of consciousness, waking up periodically to be sick. I felt like I was vomiting out my stomach lining; each breath made my insides burn.

Fever dreams are notorious for their vivid imagery and extravagant narratives. I suppose I could have dreamed anything. I could have dreamed I was a camel, wandering with a Bedouin tribe through the Arabian deserts, going from freshwater well to freshwater well, beset by febrile thirst. I could have dreamed that I was a tiny Yassir Arafat. I could have dreamed I was in the afterlife with the Ghost of William Andrews Clark and Ozymandias. But I didn't. I dreamed I was home in Montana, in the office at the museum.

It was no ordinary day at the museum. No, something was wrong. Something insidious and dastardly. I looked around me. Everything was crooked. Every picture leaned a little bit to the left or the right. Every pencil was a half inch out of alignment. All of the receipts had been shuffled so that they no longer were in chronological order. What a catastrophe. This was the obsessive-compulsive's worst fear: the world infinitesimally askew. *The horror, the horror.* I started straightening, feverishly straightening everything, but by the time I finished, all my work had been undone. Everything had returned to its state of disarray.

I would never be able to put it right.

I woke up screaming.

"Khosi," my mom said. She was at my bedside, holding my hand. "It's okay. Calm down."

"It was terrible, Mom," I said. "Do you have any water?" I was conscious of the fact that it was a hundred degrees in the room. "Why is it so hot?"

"The air conditioner's broken," my mother said. "I've been unable to talk to anyone about it."

"What time is it?" I asked. The alley outside the window was dark.

"Five in the morning," she said. "You've been asleep for almost eighteen hours."

"Eighteen hours," I said. My voice sounded flat and free of affect. I was too exhausted to express surprise.

My mother nodded. She crept closer to me. "It's disgusting in here," she said. "More important, I have to bribe everyone. For everything."

As if to illustrate the point, a nurse appeared in the doorway. She hovered. My mother automatically handed over a five-pound note. This was roughly the equivalent of a dollar.

"I think of it as a tip," my mother said in English.

"I'm here to mark your leg," the nurse said to me in Arabic.

I squinted up at her. I couldn't figure out what she meant—*mark your leg*—so I didn't translate.

"I'm almost out of cash," my mother said. "Is she asking for cash? Do you have any in your wallet?"

I didn't respond to this, either. The nurse brought out a bright red permanent marker from the pouch of her gown. She pulled down the bedsheets. Her touch was not gentle. What is the opposite of gentle? Aggressive? Belligerent? Bellicose? She seized my left leg in a bellicose manner and drew a bright red X on it, just above the knee.

"What is she doing?" my mother asked.

"Experimental treatment," I said. My mother didn't laugh. The nurse turned to go.

"Khosi," my mother said, "ask her what they're doing."

I complied. The nurse stopped in the doorway. For a moment I thought she was going to ask for more money. I saw then that she was just tired. Dense black circles looked like they were pinned beneath her eyes. "For your operation," she said. "We mark the leg so they know which one to cut."

Even in my diminished state, I must have looked alarmed, because my mother immediately stood up and clutched her chest. "What? What did she say?"

"Wait one second," I said. I turned to the nurse. "Operation? For my fever?"

The nurse squinted. "Are you not Mr. Anwas? Mr. Zahid Anwas?"

"I hate to tell you this," I said, "but I am not Mr. Zahid Anwas."

She paused on the cusp of either leaving or investigating the matter further. Then she advanced to my bed and lifted the chart that dangled from a loop of string. She flipped through the pages, tracing lines of information with the tip of her finger. She cocked her hip to one side, submerged in thought. Finally, she shook her head and looked at me. "Room Eleven, not Room Ten. My apologies." She added this quietly, as if it actually pained her to say it. Then she was gone.

"Khosi?" my mother said.

"Don't worry, Mom," I said. "They're just tagging me. Like a wild animal." And then I fell back asleep.

The second dream was more vivid than the first. I was in Montana again. In Montana, for years and years, my dreams were of the Middle East. Once I was in the Middle East, I dreamed of Montana.

In this dream I'd broken through the EPA fencing that surrounded the Berkeley Pit. I stood on the boat launch that jutted out across its toxic surface. I could smell it. The scent of the water, unmistakable and saline, a brine that hung in the air along with a faint dampness. Then the thick scent of processed coal, a smell almost like licorice, sweet and full of the odor of earth. Somewhere a smelter was firing, firing deep into the belly of the bulk of the night.

I was preparing to dive into the pool. In the late 1990s, researchers found little animals in the Berkeley Pit: strange algae, quirky protozoans, tiny fungae, multitudinous bacteria. They were extremophiles—beings that lived in conditions that killed other forms of life. I was about to dissolve myself into them, in my dream, to sacrifice my large cellular span for a smaller, more resilient one. Or was I already an extremophile—traveling on this fool's errand to Cairo, searching in this ancient city for my own link to the ancient past? I saw my body splitting into its atomic constituents. I saw my self disintegrating and diminishing and dying away.

I awoke again to find my mother pacing back and forth beside the bed. My lips were chapped. I needed, desperately needed, Chapstick.

"Mom," I said.

She turned as if pinned on an axis. "I've got a doctor," she said. "One minute." She disappeared past the ragged curtain and into the body of the hospital.

And so, after twenty-four hours, after the filthy room and the near operation and the fever dreams and the persistent vomiting of bile and the myriad miserable symptoms, the first doctor arrived. Or, rather, was led to my room by my mother, who physically held him by his coat. I was surprised she didn't lasso him by his stethoscope. He introduced himself to me, seemingly relieved that I spoke Arabic. I shivered beneath my pile of blankets. I looked to my left. I now had an IV site—that was good news. The bad news was that the site had started to itch. The IV bag itself had deflated to an empty shell.

My doctor assessed the situation. He looked at my mother and me. He glanced over my chart. He frowned. He took a moment to officiously adjust the tie that he wore beneath his white lab coat. "She is a problem," he said, to me, gesturing to my mother.

At that moment something changed for me. I felt like I'd used that exact word to describe my mom's behavior before. But to hear this doctor say it—to hear a stranger disparage her without the weight of love behind his words—I felt myself twitching, felt my muscles involuntarily clench and release with anger. It hurt me. Your parents, I had discovered, are proprietary. They might not know it, and you might not know it, but they're yours. And the things you say about them, they are balanced by a weight of equal, unsaid things, a weight of memory, that is heavy and broad and almost tactile.

"What has she done?" I said. I glanced at her. She smiled sweetly at me. The presence of the doctor had eased some of the lines of worry—lines that had etched themselves across her face.

"She has been constantly bribing the medical personnel," the doctor said.

"I see," I said. I struggled to clear my throat. "I think there's been a misunderstanding."

"It's distracting," the doctor said.

"I think she just wants the best for me."

The doctor flushed. He dropped my clipboard. It clattered against the metal frame of the bed. He turned to my mother. *"Parlez-vous français?"* he said to her. She shook her head. *"Spreken Sie Deutsche?"* Another headshake. *"¿Habla español?"* A sad, distant look.

"Just English," she said.

"Ah, English," he said to me in Arabic. "The language of colonial oppression." He turned more fully toward me. "Tell her we've tested your blood," he said, "and we've found something troubling. Have you been to Souq al-Goma'a? Or any of the *ashwaiyyat*? Maybe Moqattan Hills?"

The Souq al-Goma'a was the Friday Market, the open-air bazaar where the poorest residents of Cairo went to sell anything they could get their hands on, including their own personal possessions. I knew about it, but I'd never been there. And the *ashwaiyyat*—they were essentially the slums. Or rather, the poorer settlements, many of them squats, where over half of Cairo's seventeen million inhabitants lived. Moqattan Hills was an impoverished Coptic district. The *zabaleen*, the city's informal trash collectors, lived there by the thousands, sorting trash in their living rooms.

"No," I said. "I've never been there. I've only been in Cairo for a few days. Almost a week."

"But you are a Christian?" he said.

"What is he asking you?" my mother said.

"Hang on a second, Mom," I said. And then: "Sure. My grand-parents certainly were. But why should that matter? What did you find?" Even as I was talking to the doctor, I was starting to feel better. The headache, the awful headache that had descended upon me like a noxious fog, was starting to lessen.

"We found yellow fever antibodies. And in those places there have been yellow fever outbreaks over the past few months."

"I see," I said. I looked at my mother. "Yellow fever. They think it's yellow fever."

"Jesus Christ," she said.

"Did He get yellow fever?" I said.

"Very funny," she said.

I looked up at the doctor. "Okay, what does that mean? Will I recover? You know," I added, "I feel a little better."

"It's the initial remission phase," the doctor said. "That's com-mon with this disease."

"I see," I said. "Aren't you just the life of the party?" This collo-quial American phrase didn't translate well into Arabic. *Are you not alive at the gathering?* is what I actually said, which didn't have quite the same resonance as the original.

"I don't understand," the doctor said.

"Never mind," I said. "What can I do?"

"Nothing," the doctor said. "We wait a while here and see what happens."

We talked a little longer, my translations of my mother's ques-tions and the doctor's terse, frustrated answers. "We have to wait and see," he said, and simply walked out of the room.

We waited. We waited for five, six hours. My intellect: entirely useless. I was bored. Bored and healthy. For those few hours, those few hours in that fetid hospital room, I have to admit that I appreciated my health, my pain-free head, my ability to breathe. These were all things that I'd taken for granted my whole life. I hadn't considered how wonderful it was not to have a debilitating headache, hadn't considered the miracle that is the body, intact.

Isn't this just going splendidly? I thought. I thought of Natasha, how she'd always wanted us to travel together: Missoula, Cheyenne, Des Moines. *Wouldn't she be proud of me now?* Actually, I realized, lying there on my back, the drained IV still not replaced, hanging lifeless above me: She'd be horrified. I knew that if she could see this wreck of a hospital, this bed, this frantic wreck of a mother, Natasha would be on the next plane to Egypt. She'd be at my bedside in hours. Calvin Stuckey didn't matter. I knew that for certain. I was filled with a deep longing to be near her, to be at the Berkeley Pit Yacht Club with her, drinking Miller High Life (The Champagne of Beers™), debating whether Ernest Tubb's early records outshone those of a young Hank Williams (they did). That felt like a lost life, irredeemable in the wash of the past. I missed her, though, desperately missed her. I imagined Natasha's smile, I imagined her laughter filling the air around my filthy hospital bed.

That was when I felt it. To say that the disease rushed back would be inadequate. To say that it flattened me and butchered me and eviscerated me and seared me: That would perhaps be closer to the feeling. I felt like I was being flayed, like the tissue of my brain was liquefying and leaking out. My mother confirmed later that this was a distinct possibility. At one point during that week of hell, I bled from my eyes. When that happened, my skin was waxy yellow—a color not far from the color of a legal pad—and I cried blood tears. Blood tears? There's a point at which gallows humor breaks down and fails to raise your spirits.

And that point—that point is the gallows.

Nine

LIKE I SAID BEFORE, EGYPTIAN cooking is folk magic. Here is the perfect example: the baklava that I credit for my recovery. My aunts called it Christian-Muslim Cooperation Baklava. Each had a secret ingredient that she added to the recipe at a prearranged time. Kebi Merit orchestrated and supervised the addition of these ingredients. She was as scrupulous as a UN peacekeeper enforcing the tenets of an international treaty. Christian-Muslim Cooperation Baklava is also at the center of *The Life and Times of Akram Saqr and Amy Clark, My One and Only Parents, as Told by Me, My Mother's One and Only Son, Fruit of Her Womb, 100 Percent Maculate Conception, Part Three (Insensate Remix)*.

Acute yellow fever—15 percent of patients get it. You can bleed, as I did, from your mouth or your eyes or your ears. Your kidneys or your liver can fail. You can die. A significant portion of patients with acute yellow fever do die. It is a fatal malady. In my case, it was the luckiest thing that ever happened to me.

When confronted by a potentially dying son in a country you've never been to where you don't speak the language and you are isolated from any understanding of the culture: What do you do? My mother went outside into the street, leaving me in my hospital room, unconscious. She went to the bank. She took out two hundred Egyptian pounds. She came back to the hospital. But immediately before she did that, she bought herself a cup of tea.

It came from a tea vendor in an alley beside the hospital; Cairo is a city of alleys, of crowded alleys in which you'll find tea stalls and doctors' offices and tailors and tiny grocery stores. She bought a cup of spiced milky tea in a small plastic container. She thanked the vendor and gave him a ten-pound tip, the equivalent of a week's salary. Then she went back into the hospital, walked over to the attendant who'd admitted us, and seized the woman's phone. She handed over, wordlessly, another ten-pound note. Then she called Wada in Butte. After ten rings, Wada answered, sounding groggy.

My mother brought her up to speed. It was a worst-case scenario, she said. She told her she'd thought at first that she could handle it. She didn't want to ask anyone for help. But she needed someone, my mother confessed, who could help her deal with the doctors. "I think I might be needlessly bribing them," she said. She added, "Should I call Akram?"

"Should you call Akram?" Wada said.

"That's what I asked you," my mother said.

"I know that's what you asked me," Wada said. "Do you have his number?"

"I have his address."

"Then why on earth haven't you had someone look him up in the phone book?"

During all of this, I slept in my hospital bed. Although *slept* sounds luxurious. Actually, I rotted. I rotted slowly and with resolute feverish abandon.

Voices will move you back and forth through time. With the slightest word, the slightest intonation, you're transported to a past that you might—or might not—want to reimagine. When my mother called the number she'd secured for her ex-husband, she braced herself for a displacement of titanic proportions.

"*Aiwa meen*," he said. His voice was steely and confident and cut immediately through the sound of the ringer. "Akram Saqr."

Egyptians are well known for the way they say hello. Any encounter can begin five or six times, with variations on a greeting, with slightly different colloquialisms that alter only slightly the tone of what's being said. They will inquire about families and weather and health and almost anything else you can imagine. Often just starting a conversation can take five or ten minutes. This, however, was not one of those occasions.

"Hello, Akram," my mother said.

Another pause.

"Amy?"

"Yes," she said. "It's Amy."

A third—and final—lengthy pause.

"You know, the police are looking for you. I leave messages at Khosi's hotel, and he doesn't return them. The desk clerks say they haven't seen him. I'm concerned."

"Not as concerned as you should be," my mother said. She shifted the receiver on her shoulder. "You have no idea."

"I'm sorry?" my father said.

A word here about my father's accent when he spoke English. It was a downy accent. Soft and feathery and plush like a pillow. You sank into it, listening to him shape vowels and consonants in a way that seemed to ease toward you. The pronunciation seemed to be mostly French, though the timbre of his voice wasn't nasal. It was throaty Arabic and prep-school English. He talked like all of the characters from the cast of *Casablanca* mixed together, including Ingrid Bergman.

"I said: You have no idea," she repeated. Then she told him where I was, and what I was suffering from, and that my fever currently was 104.

Within thirty minutes, my father walked through the door of the hospital. He wore a black suit—a rich, supple fabric with a shiny weave—along with a white shirt and a maroon tie. These were the colors of the Egyptian flag. He also wore cuff links: diamond-studded cufflinks that glimmered against the woolen fabric. And he carried with him pajamas. "That was the amazing thing," my mother later told me. "The two pairs of pajamas draped over the arm of his suit."

My mother met him in the doorway. She met him under the sign, the bright white neon sign that said Franco-American Hospital, Zemalek.

"Where is he?" my father said. "We need to get him out of here immediately. Why didn't you call me earlier?"

"Calling you," she said, "is the last thing I wanted to do."

"You should have taken him to a Muslim Brotherhood hospital, at the very least," he said.

She said nothing. Wordlessly, she turned and walked him toward the ICU.

The discharge paperwork was signed within ten minutes. I was moaning, my mother told me later, moaning the whole time they wheeled me back toward the lobby and out the front door. While they were preparing the paperwork, my father was on the phone at the nurse's station. Now my mother saw why. In the hospital loading zone, we were greeted by a flotilla of cars: four identical long black sedans with mirrored windows. If she could've read Arabic, she would've translated the signs emblazoned on each of the vehicles.

PRESIDENTIAL MOTORCADE, they read. It was also written on each of the tinted windows and in looping Arabic script on each trunk.

"Impressive," my mother said.

"This," my father said, "is the fastest way to go from one point to another in Cairo."

"And you can rent it?" she said.

"For a price," he said. "It's the way Mubarak gets anywhere."

"Does it come with Mubarak?"

"For a price," he said.

"Seriously," she said, "are these his actual cars?"

"Get in," my father said.

They loaded us into the main sedan, laying me on the carpeted floor, wrapping me in blankets that they'd brought with them. My skin had started to jaundice; my liver had been taxed by the flotilla of toxins in my blood. My father had managed to procure me a new bag of IV fluids. He'd also procured—remarkably—his own doctor, a man impressively dressed in a pin-striped lab coat. My parents sat on the seat opposite me. Though I'd been given magnesium sulfate and a sedative, I do have one image, one single brief flare of a memory: opening my eyes and seeing their legs—my mother's and father's—framed against black leather upholstery. The four sedans made their way into traffic. It turned out the fake presidential motorcade *was* much faster than a taxi. Traffic parted. Roadways opened up.

"I remember holding him in my lap," my mother said as the car sped through the city. "I remember holding him when he could fit in both hands. When he was six pounds and smelled like butter."

My father looked down at me. "I held him, too," he said.

"You know, Akram," my mother said as she settled into her seat, "you really are a son of a bitch." She ran one hand over my sweaty forehead, smoothing the wet hair back and out of my eyes. The physician continued kneeling on the floor of the car, listening to my lungs, checking my pulse. "You're getting remarried. That's why you needed the papers. To cover your ass."

"There is certainly no need for vulgarity," my father said, adjusting his cuff links.

"You're not sick at all, are you?"

"Technically," he said, "I did have the flu. Not long ago. A few months ago. It was a terrible case of the flu. And there's been bird flu here, so the doctors were concerned."

My mother frowned at him.

"No," he finally said, "I'm perfectly healthy, *el hamdillah*."

"I knew it. I could always tell when you were lying."

"No, you couldn't. Jesus, Amy, could you just calm down for one moment. You have no idea the problems you've caused for me these past few days."

"Me?" my mother said. "That I've caused? How is this possibly my fault?"

My father shook his head. "Agnes is furious. I've had to make up a dozen lies. She doesn't like, as you might imagine, the idea of me stealing a bracelet from her to give to you as a bribe."

My mother sighed again. "He's going to be okay?" she said. Her voice quavered. "Isn't he?"

"Yes," my father said.

"How do you know?"

"We are going to the best hospital in the country."

And it was. The Dar Al Fouad Hospital on the outskirts of Cairo was the Mayo Clinic of Egypt: modern, sanitary, orderly, entirely free of bribes. Did my mother try? I don't know for certain, but probably not. Or at least I hope not.

The hospital, though, I can vouch for: Built in 1992, it was the first private hospital in Africa to perform a successful liver transplant. Its location in Sixth of October City, a Cairo suburb only ten miles from the pyramids, removed it a bit from the chaos of downtown's labyrinthine streets. The Sixth of October Bridge, Sixth of October City: both named by Anwar Sadat in 1979, two years before his assassination (which occurred, ironically, on the sixth of October). Both the city and the bridge (and possibly the assassination) commemorated the start of the 1973 Yom Kippur War against Israel— a grisly reminder of the violence that hovered beneath the surface of life in this part of the world.

All of that aside, there could be no greater contrast than between the two hospitals. I had a glistening, well-appointed suite. A bevy of infectious disease specialists paraded through my room, all led by my father and his personal physician—Dr. Arnyat—who was there at least sixteen hours a day. Dr. Arnyat would consult with the doctors on staff, an unusual arrangement but one that was apparently fairly common in the hospitals of Cairo. My father also flew in a tropical disease clinician from Budapest.

But I worsened.

For over a week, I lapsed in and out of consciousness. My mind has preserved some impossible images of those days: the sensation of a feeding tube in my abdomen, the raw burning pain of the infected IV site, the singing of birds through a nearby open window. It has also created the image of me submerged at the bottom of something, a body of liquid or semitransparent gas, a permeable membrane that allowed in sound. I could hear the things going on in my hospital room, but I couldn't respond to them, couldn't interact with the people I loved. Lost just beyond the edge of a vast emptiness, I was far enough to look back, to sense where I'd come from, but too far into it to communicate with the place I'd left. This place: It was a long, cold-lit sky opening out over a desiccated earth. It was a dark sky heavy with a firmament of motionless stars. It was a scouring sky moving across a barren, powdery, dust-carved desert.

My father wheeled in a portable cot. He slept there night after night, right beside my bed, a set of rosary beads in his hands, a series of bitter cups of coffee cooling on the floor between us. My mother told me that he sang to me, sang the songs that he'd sung when I was a baby in a bassinet. He would alternate between standing at my bedside and lying on the cot and ushering doctors through the room. He put cold compresses on my wan, waxy forehead. He carried my mother's meals up from the cafeteria. He and Dr. Arnyat double-checked every medication that the hospital fed into my arm. They asked a hundred questions a day, tireless.

His efforts on my part were nothing short of heroic. The nurses would cringe when they saw him coming. He supervised every single thing they did, constantly badgering them to wash their hands, to be more gentle with me, to change my clothes, which would soak through with sweat and then stick to my damp skin. He often stood at my bedside for hours, rotating the cold compresses on my forehead, keeping at least that part of me cool while the rest of me burned with fever.

And my mother? She doubted him. She fought his every suggestion. She refused to speak to Dr. Arnyat. Whenever my father talked to the nurses, she was there at his side.

"You have to translate," she said. "You can't be so high-handed about this."

"But look where he was when you were in charge," he said. "He would have died at that hospital in Zemalek."

"You still have to tell me what's happening. You aren't the governor here. Our son, my son, is not part of your imperial fiat."

My mother watched. She watched with suspicion. She practiced breathing techniques from her yoga classes. She took her medicines. She had a necklace, a necklace with a pendant of Evel Knievel, and she turned it over again and again in her hands, worrying it like her own version of the rosary. Even she had to admit that the things my father was doing on my behalf were impressive. They gave him a short respite, gave him a moment's grace, there at my side, there at her side. She struggled to keep calm while occupying a room with him. She adopted a variety of calming maneuvers. She imagined, for example, a wide, grassy field, the verdant opposite of my scouring, barren sky. A life-giving sky, a gentle rain over lush vegetation.

"I didn't know you were a praying man," she said to my father sometime in the middle of the ordeal, on the fifth or sixth or seventh day, one of the days that blended into all the other days at the hospital. The hospital with its perpetual fluorescent lights. The hospital with its never-night. The hospital with its endless vigilance and vigilant exhaustion.

"The rosaries?" he said.

"The rosaries," she said.

"Normally, I'm not," he said.

"I know," she said. "It's too gentle for you, prayer. You never prayed when you lived in Montana, anyway."

"Are you sure?" he said.

"I know you didn't want to come to church with me," she said.

"Maybe I came to church and sat in the back where you wouldn't see me."

"Why would you do that?" she said.

"Because, *habibti*," he said, "maybe I believed in the privacy of religious belief."

My mother crossed her arms. She'd bought a Cadbury Flake at the hospital cafeteria. In Sixth of October City, Egpyt—at the cafeteria of the Dar Al Fouad Hospital—the Cadbury Flake was imported directly from England and wrapped in beautiful foil packaging. She unwrapped it in a leisurely way, sniffing at the package, licking a dot of chocolate off of her fingertip. The candy bar distracted her for a moment. If my father remembered her dietary restrictions, he showed no signs.

"I very much doubt that you believe in anything, Akram," she said as she chewed.

My father frowned. "Why would you say that? You know that's painful to me."

"Painful to you? Painful to you? Are you really telling me about what's painful to you? I gave you years, years of my life. I spent years learning how to cook the food that you were raised eating—a lot of which, I'll have you know, I am not supposed to eat."

"But you always did," he said.

"Because of how I felt about you," my mother said. "Well, that and it was delicious."

My father looked at the glass panel that divided the room from the rest of the ICU. Unlike the rooms in the other wards of the hospital, the rooms here fed onto the nurse's station. The nurses needed to be able to see their patients at all times. As a result, it felt a little like the proscenium of a sadist's playhouse. The nurses sat there in judgment, an audience to your recovery or your decline.

My father lowered his voice. "I'm sorry."

My mother grimaced. "I don't care," she said. "You know, the whole reason he's here is you. The reason he's in Egypt. The reason he's sick. The responsibility's all yours."

"I really don't think that's fair," he said.

I floated. I floated far away. I floated in a dry distant space.

"You abandoned us. You left us. And this is the consequence of your actions."

Her voice—strident, vituperative, strong, clear—was marvelous in what it wasn't, in what it didn't have, in its lacks. In its lack of disconnection, its lack of gauziness, its lack of disorientation. She continued, "You've done your part, you know. You can go now."

"Go where?"

"Don't you have a wedding to attend? Don't you have another fortune to plunder? What was it this time, Akram? Blackjack? Roulette? Horses?"

Here she lost all composure. She'd been holding herself together almost literally, her palms pressed flat against her temples. Her eyes must have felt like they might fissure, like they might cave inward or shatter outward—one or the other—and then tears were sliding down her cheeks and she was wiping her mouth and her nose with the back of her hand. A kind of spasm was shaking her body. She sighed deeply, her lower lip trembling.

"Oh, Akram," she finally said. "Leave. Go get married. Disappear again. But this time don't have any kids. And don't ever come back to Montana."

He nodded. He stood. For a moment she thought he might do it. That he might just disappear again, this time at her request. But he walked back over to the bed and put his hand on my hand. I swear that I can remember the pressure of his hand, the way it felt there above mine, thick and meaty and solid. In 1858—together with his friend the illustrator Henry Vandyke Carter—Henry Gray published *Gray's Anatomy of the Human Body*. Gray was a part of the Victorian passion for quantification, for the mechanical aspects of the human form, for the easily organized part of our selves. God, I would have been an excellent Victorian. Gray's book had 363 illustrations. Here is one of them. This is, after all, my own Book of the Dead:

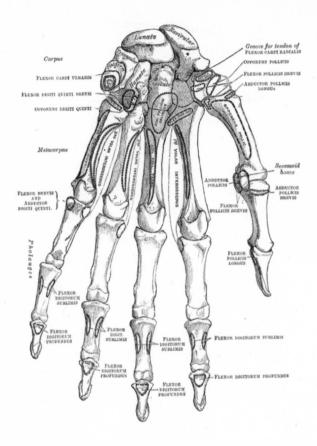

That's where my father placed his hand. Right there. Specifically there. Exactly there. Partially over the lunate bone, partly over the navicular, his fingertips brushing—the faintest pressure—against my flexor tendon, my flexor carpi radialis. I felt it. I know I felt it. I remember it.

"I don't have anywhere to be," he said. "I postponed the wedding."

My mom came to the other side of my bed. "You postponed your marriage," she said, "for the son of your friend Malik?"

"Ah," he said. "Khosi told you about that."

"He's not in the habit of concealing things, unlike you. Without you there to raise him, he only learned honesty."

"I thought maybe some things were genetic," my father said with a wry smile.

My mother took a paper towel from the dispenser over the sink. She blew her nose. "Oh, Akram," she said. "Why would you postpone the wedding?"

He put his hand to his forehead. "To be quite honest, it wasn't my decision."

My mother looked at him. "Not your decision? I see."

"I think it was probably a shock for her: After I deny everything, you show up in her house, and then—you trap me into telling the truth."

"Someone else's fault," my mother said. "As usual."

"There was no other way out," he said. "I did what I had to do. For my recovery."

My mother snorted. "Is that what you've been doing these past twenty years? Recovering?"

"You know," my father said, "it wasn't perfect. It's not like I left our perfect marriage, like I disappeared in the middle of bliss. We had our problems."

"You know what, Akram?" my mother said. "I don't remember anymore. We could have had this conversation fifteen years ago— ten years ago, even—and maybe I would have remembered. But now I don't."

My father walked back over to the chair and sat down. He brushed his hair back and into place, assembling it perfectly on his head, in gray-black alignment, in waves. "I'm sorry," he said. "For what I did to you. And to Khosi."

My mother exhaled. It was a long, deep exhalation. She breathed in deeply and out again. In and out. The sterile hospital air smelled a bit like earth, like her garden, like uprooted Egyptian walking onions.

"I'm here now," he said. "I'm here, apologizing to you. You want to know the truth? The truth is that I was an addict."

My mother uncrossed her arms. I can imagine her doing this very thing—standing at the stove, a pot of something boiling on the gas burners in front of her, the faint scent of gas in the air, along with the scents of cumin or fenugreek or clove or cardamom. Blue-lit.

"Go on," she said.

"Although, *habibti*, that word is a little bit troubling. It is a word that I find to be artificial," he said. "It is an American way of looking at a thing."

"Looking at what?" she said.

"At my gambling hobby. Problem. No, problem. That is a better word. A destructive problem."

"I have to admit," my mother said, "this is fascinating."

"Everything, you see, is so new to me. I am trying to take responsibility for my actions. I have admitted that I'm powerless before gambling—and that my life has become unmanageable. I've been going to Gamblers Anonymous meetings. This is Step Nine: 'Apologize and make amends for your mistakes, wherever possible.' I have been free of gambling for 204 days."

"Are you joking?" she said. "Because if you're not—then I'd like my hundred thousand dollars back."

"I wouldn't joke about something like this. It's a group. A lifeline. We meet on Monday nights at nine, at Kasr El Maadi Hospital."

"I didn't ask you where you meet," she said.

"I thought you were expressing disbelief," he said.

"I *am* in disbelief. I'm in Egypt. My son is terribly sick. I've just eaten a chocolate bar, and you—you are finally apologizing. What a morning. What a conversation."

I floated and floated and floated. The dunes of sound shaped themselves around me, grew into austere banks of texture and light. I was distant; I was a distant star; I was a supernova of ill health. The landscape of my darkness was an interstellar landscape. It depended on distance for its power.

"Then why did you lie to me in Butte? I've known alcoholics. Lying isn't part of the twelve-step process."

"I panicked," my father said.

"That's not like you," she said.

"*Ja'ani*, I'm not sure. Perhaps."

"You panicked," she said, "and so you told me the first thing that popped into your head: 'Amy, I'm dying, and I want to die with a clear conscience. Please sign these divorce papers to release me.'"

"In a way," my father said, "it was the truth."

"Ah," she said. "Now, there's the Akram I remember. There's the man I knew and loved. Unscrupulous to the last."

"No, no," he said.

"It was a lie."

"No, no," he said. "It was a rebirth."

"Who does that?" she said. "Even for you, it's low. What was I going to tell our son?"

"A lie is just a truth," my father said in Arabic, "that is inside out."

"What did you just say?" my mother asked.

He translated.

"That makes no sense," she said.

"It's a proverb," he said. "You can apply it loosely to many different things."

"And Agnes? How did she react to this? How did she react to your sudden understanding of the unmanageability of your life?"

"Agnes?" He seemed surprised by this question. "The only reason she's probably still talking to me after you and Khosi showed up on her doorstep is because most of this, almost all of it, was her idea. I mean: It was our idea together. That's where we met, *habibti*. At the nine o'clock meeting."

This was the ending, then, of *The Story of the Life and Times of Akram Saqr and Amy Clark, My One and Only Parents*, this was the juncture at which the narrative split apart, divorced like the elements of a frayed, flayed rope. But while the story of my parents' relationship was concluding, I was having some strange and wondrous dreams, dreams wherein I rode over sand dunes on the back of a camel, over miles and miles of sand dunes with the Ghost of William Andrews Clark. We chewed plug tobacco and drank water from tin canteens, and somewhere, in the ether of the atmosphere, a piano played the first notes of Glen Campbell's "Rhinestone Cowboy."

And that's when my fever broke.

In the room, however, my parents didn't notice. My mother was particularly energetic, coming over to my father and grabbing two handfuls of his shirt. She tried to lift him. She tried, but he didn't move. "Her idea?" my mother said.

"Yes," my father said.

"You can't be serious," she said.

"I am," he said.

She pointed to the door. "Out," she said. "I can do this alone. I can take care of Khosi on my own. I did for twenty years."

"Amy, calm down."

"Just leave," she said. "I don't trust you. Nothing you say can be trusted. It's that simple."

"Earlier," he said, "you asked me why I'm here. And I'll tell you: This is a gift from God, Khosi's presence. Before I met Agnes, before I went to Montana, I'd given up. But now he came to Cairo—my son came back for me—so that I could set things right. That's why I'm here. That's why I'm saying the rosary. I'm saying it because I am so thankful."

If my mother could have immolated him with her eyes, if she could have struck a match and set fire to my father's gas-soaked body, she wouldn't have paused for a second.

"Out of this hospital room," she said. "You had your chance. You walked out on your chance to connect with Khosi twenty years ago."

He stood up. "You can't do this. Don't forget: This is my country. This isn't Butte, Montana. I'll be right back in here in five minutes with hospital security. You're a danger to my son and a danger to yourself."

"Leave," she said. "Now."

He did leave, ultimately. My mother slammed the door. It was a hospital door, though, and hospital doors don't slam, possibly for this reason. It gently eased its way shut. Then she tried to lock it. The door was also totally unlockable. And so she hung her head. She pulled up a chair and waited. But my father didn't return in five minutes with security. Instead, he showed up in six hours. And he brought the extended family.

After he left my room, my father later told me, he was inconsolable. He wandered out of the clinic and into Sixth of October City, unsure where he was going or what he was doing. A thought occurred to him:.A little time in a casino might not be a bad thing. There's no shortage of casinos in Cairo: the Al-Andalus, the Al-Karnak, the Panorama, the Semiramis, the Cedars, and many, many more. Gambling parlors blossom like mold spores throughout the city. They will gladly separate you from your cash, hard-earned or otherwise. I've even discovered over the past three years that you can find off-track betting in a number of places near the Nile. I can place bets on American horses in Egyptian pounds with my American bank account.

My father wandered into the Al-Qat casino and found the bar, which was unmarked and located at the back of the building. All of the drinks were named for poker hands. My father ordered a Royal Flush and then a Full House. He drank them quickly. He didn't even taste them. Then he walked out onto the gaming floor. He wandered over to the blackjack table. He sat down on a plush, padded chair. "Hello, old friend," he said softly.

It was thirty minutes before my father called Mr. Ibrahim Mohammed, Agnes Mouri's butler and Akram's Gamblers Anonymous sponsor. In those thirty minutes he watched hand after hand of blackjack, politely declining the dealer's offers to join in. Eventually, the pit boss came over and suggested that my father step away from the table. My father complied. That was when he took out his cell phone.

And so it was Ibrahim—a complete stranger, a man whom I met only twice—who orchestrated my father's return to Dar Al Fouad Hospital. He shepherded him back to the family home at Talaat Harb, and just as everyone was sitting down to dinner, they staged an intervention of sorts. A surprise intervention. A surprise reverse intervention. Akram Saqr, there to unburden himself of his past of lies. Or, as my father preferred to call them, omissions. Certain omissions.

I imagined that long dining room table awash in food, surrounded by Saqrs or variations of Saqrs. My father stood there, possibly beside Ibrahim, and nervously took out a Dunhill. He lit it. He smoked it slowly, deliberately, tapping out the ash onto the tile floor. And then he disclosed the existence of my mother and me. He told his family that my mother had not, indeed, perished like he'd made them think she had, in one of the many tragic accidents that seemed to litter his early life—cars and boats and divine strikes of lightning. He told them that they—that *we*—were in fact here in Cairo and that I was terribly ill.

"I knew it!" exclaimed Aunt Banafrit.

"I suspected it all along!" echoed Aunt Fatima.

"No, you didn't," said Aunt Banafrit.

"Of course I did," said Aunt Fatima. "You're the one who's always being fooled."

"Silence," mandated Kebi Merit, and silence fell, fluttering around the mandate.

My father sat down at the table along with the rest of the family, and lit yet another Dunhill, and smoked it quietly. Everyone sat there, not speaking, the food getting cold. The minutes moved slowly by. Finally, finally, Kebi Merit stood up from the table.

"What are we waiting for?" she said. "Let's get our coats."

The return of Akram Saqr to Dar Al Fouad Hospital wasn't exactly a moment of exultant triumph.

"Amy?" he said tentatively, opening the door a few inches and poking his head around it.

My mother was still sitting in her chair. She had left it only twice in the past six hours—once to check on me and once to use the restroom. She didn't answer. Not right away. She just looked at him.

He tried a wan smile. "I bet you didn't think I was coming back," he said.

"You know," she said, "it's ten o'clock at night."

He nodded. "Please let us come in."

"Who's *us*?" she said.

"A few people," he said.

"Did you bring your fiancée?" she said.

"Not exactly," he said. He edged more fully into the room. "*Habibti*," he said. "I'm sorry again. I need to say this, just this: I didn't come on an errand for my new fiancée. I truly did not. I should have come ten years ago. Fifteen years ago, like you said. But what can I do about that now? I'm proud of my son and I brought the family and they know who he is. They want to meet him. They want to meet you. And you need my help. You need my help with the language. You can't do this alone."

"Okay," my mother said.

"Okay?"

"Okay, come in. Come in. I have nothing left. Bring whoever you want."

My father fully opened the heavy spring-loaded door. When he did, it was the destruction of the castle wall. The onslaught began. It's not that my room was small. But fourteen people wouldn't fit in almost any hospital room. And this is what he'd brought with him: fourteen people. Ibrahim, my aunts Banafrit and Fatima, their husbands, Ali and Yusef, Kebi Merit, Dr. Arnyat, and seven of my cousins. The cousins ranged in age from eight to twenty-eight. To this day I can't keep all of their names straight. And here came Aunt Banafrit, her arms opening in an ample embrace.

"My sister," she said, clasping my mother between her pillowy forearms. "My lovely ex–American sister!"

"Well, then," my mother said, because what else could she say? "Nice to meet you."

Banafrit turned to my father. "Ask your—your wife—ask her how her son is doing. Tell her—tell her I knew he was your child the moment I laid eyes on him."

My father nodded. "How is Khosi?" he asked my mother.

At that moment my eyes opened. It was involuntary. I heard my

251

name and reacted to it. Everything came slowly into focus; light coalesced into shapes, shapes coalesced into figures; figures coalesced into my entire family, crowded into my hospital room, none of them paying me the slightest bit of attention. Even my father, who'd asked the question, wasn't looking to me for an answer.

"Terrible," my mother said.

Actually, I thought, *I'm feeling a lot better.*

My father nodded and translated the answer. There was a lot of shaking of heads. *Here I am*, I thought. *Somebody look over at me.*

"I'm worried he might not make it through the night," she added.

When my father translated, I just closed my eyes. I was tired. So very tired. Let them think what they wanted, I figured. What harm could it do?

"Don't trust her," Kebi Merit was saying in Arabic, pushing Banafrit aside. She stood in the middle of the hospital room, insofar as that was possible. She pointed at my mother. "Akram, I am telling you: Do not trust that American woman. I can see that she is poisoning him. I can feel it. She's a witch."

"What is she saying?" my mother asked.

"She's saying that she's happy to meet you," my father said.

Kebi Merit spat on the ground, something that turned out to be one of her favorite gestures. "Well," she said, taking a large paper sack out of her purse and waving it in my mother's general direction, "tell this witch that we have our cure—our homemade cure—for yellow fever. It's been in the family for many generations."

"Oh God," my father said.

"What?" my mother said.

He stared at her. "You won't like this," he said. "She's brought some medicine."

"What is it?" she said.

"What is the cure?" he asked Kebi Merit in Arabic, his countenance sinking and his shoulders slumping toward the ground.

"A mustard poultice with rosemary and chicken hearts." She looked expectantly at my father, waiting for his translation. It was obvious that she was proud of what she'd assembled. There was a quiet pride in her posture.

"Oh dear," my father said in English. "It's chicken hearts."

"Chicken hearts," my mother exclaimed.

"Chicken hearts?" my father asked in Arabic.

"Yes, yes," called Dr. Arnyat from the back of the assemblage. "Certainly. The medicinal properties of chicken hearts cannot be doubted."

"It stings a little," Banafrit said.

"It stings a lot," Fatima said.

"Where's the doctor?" my mother said.

"Right here!" said Dr. Arnyat from the back of the assembled crowd.

"The other doctor," my mother said. "The real doctor. The doctor from this hospital." She went out into the hall. "I'll be right back," she said, relinquishing her position as gatekeeper of the sickroom. "Akram: Watch over them. Make sure nothing unusual goes on."

What happens to a large crowd of people when they are jammed into a small space with nothing to do but concentrate on a single, unmoving thing? They argue. My extended Egyptian family was remarkable, I now realize, for the relative harmony with which they negotiated their shared living space. It hadn't always been harmonious. "When Fatima married a Muslim," my father later told me, "your grandfather nearly had a stroke." But in he moved, and soon the family home—with its many wings and dilapidated grandeur—became a sort of experiment in religious tolerance. Icons were put up and taken down. Holy days were observed with consecration and stricture.

In the hospital, Fatima's husband looked at his watch. "I need to pray," he said. "Where can I pray?"

"There's a room down the hall," Dr. Arnyat said. "The east is marked."

Banafrit's husband immediately raised his voice. "What if I want to pray?" he said. "Maybe I'd like to pray, too. What about me?"

"What about you?" Fatima's husband said.

"I have my rights," Banafrit's husband said.

"I think they're going to fight," one of the younger cousins said.

"Quiet, all of you," Kebi Merit said. "I need silence to concentrate."

She'd approached my bed and taken the poultice out of its sack. The thing itself was bright red and carefully smeared over a wide cloth bandage. Kebi Merit pulled down the neck of my hospital gown. She plastered the bandage to my skin, just above the collarbone.

It took a moment for the odor to reach my sinuses. To say that it smelled like damp, rotting intestinal reek—damp, rotting intestinal reek with an undercurrent of spice—doesn't do it justice. The mustard burned my skin and gave off a powerful odor. Though the rosemary did add a few gentle agricultural notes, the chicken heart must have been in an advanced state of decay. It smelled very clearly like a plate of roadkill. Like the basement of a funeral home. Like the devil's favorite hot dog.

The smell was so foul that I opened my eyes and raised my right arm, placing it squarely on my cloth-covered chest. "Help," I whispered. "Take it off."

"It's a miracle!" one of the cousins shouted.

"He is cured," Kebi Merit said, leaning down over me.

"Take it off," I whispered again in English. "It's disgusting."

"He loves it!" she exclaimed, turning to everyone else. "It worked even faster than I thought it would."

Just then my mother returned to the room, another doctor in tow. "Dear God," she said. "What's going on? Akram? What did you let them do?"

My father cringed and stepped back into the assembled family. He slipped in among them and nearly disappeared.

The doctor whom my mother brought with her—an actual paid staff member—looked horrified. "I'm certain that's not sterile," he said. "You must remove that immediately."

"But it worked," Kebi Merit protested. "Look, look. He's talking. He's awake." And then my mother was at my bedside, and my father, and they were coming into focus, and I was staring up at them, and my headache was gone. Hallelujah, my headache was gone. Nobody pointed out to Kebi Merit that her poultice was probably not responsible. I didn't; I can't tell you how incredible it felt at that moment to be free of pain. I felt like I'd been bleached and wrung out and possibly rolled through the dryer. I was alive. I was alive. It was a little miraculous just to be breathing.

"Hi, Mom," I said. "How long have I been out?"

The ensuing celebration bubbled out of my room and into the rest of the ICU, encompassing even the families of the other seriously ill patients, who, more than likely, didn't have very much to celebrate. It was difficult to restrain anyone from my hospital bed. Newly returned from the land of fever dreams—I didn't mind the commotion in the actual world, in the world of Dar Al Fouad Hospital, of Sixth of October City, Egypt, of the Cairene suburbs. The doctors advised us that I needed as much rest as possible.

"That's okay," my father said. "We will celebrate quietly."

As soon as it was clear that my fever had broken, Banafrit produced a large earthenware pan from somewhere. "We weren't going to mention it yet," she said in Arabic. "But we brought our mother's famous baklava." In a stage whisper, she added, "The secret ingredient is rosewater."

I smiled wanly and was about to thank her. Before I could, Fatima pushed her sister aside. "No, no, no," Fatima said. "It's orange blossom water."

"Don't be ridiculous, Fatima," Banafrit said. "Orange blossom water makes the baklava *common*."

"Ladies," my father said. "Remember: Keep your voices down."

"What are they saying?" my mother asked me. She was standing at my bedside. Her face had relaxed a little. Her worry lines had all but disappeared.

I sighed and closed my eyes. "Dad will translate," I said.

"Akram," Fatima said, "rosewater makes the baklava taste like a garden." Then she pointed to my mother. "Tell her—tell her who's right. Tell her what the secret ingredient is."

My father frowned. "Because that's what she wants to know right now?"

"Yes," Fatima said.

"Because the thing she is concerned about most is this pastry?"

"Yes," Banafrit said.

My father turned to my mother. "They brought baklava," he said, "and they both think it's delicious."

Banafrit smiled, recognizing the English word. "Delicious," she said.

"Delicious!" her sister agreed.

In the years since that day, I've watched my aunts make the baklava many times. They can never agree, will never agree, whether it's orange blossom water or rosewater that makes it taste so good. As a result, they add a little of both. The result is a unique baklava, a baklava quite unlike any other I've ever had. More important than that—more important than the strange citric and roseate flavor of this particular pastry—is the process that goes into making it. When my aunts make the baklava, they make it together. Fatima chops the walnuts and Banafrit prepares the simple syrup. Fatima lays out the phyllo dough and Banafrit uses a brush to moisten it with butter. Their bickering comes to a halt. They work toward a single common goal.

Culture lives in cooking. People live in recipes, too. The hands that have shaped a dish continue to live as long as it continues to live. Food is an unbroken bridge, a direct bridge to the past—to the old technologies, to the old ways of eating and of harnessing fire.

A flavor repeats itself in generation after generation. It becomes part of our blood. It becomes our most elemental joy. It becomes the language of our desire. It becomes the vocabulary of our satisfaction.

Six days later, I'd recovered enough to be off the IVs and to be transferred out of the ICU. Total days in the hospital? Seventeen. I was conscious that luck actually *had* been with me. At least half of the patients who develop the acute form of yellow fever suffer organ failure and death. It's such a heinous cliché: *Life is fragile*. But in America, our entire lives seem to be set up around denying this fact, this utterly undeniable thing. We are breaking, decaying bodies; we are fallible, imperfect machines. We cannot order our lives; order fails. Order always fails. It is undone by something as tiny as *Aedes aegypti*, a creature whose body weighs a fraction of a gram.

By day seventeen, the day of my discharge, I'd postponed my flight indefinitely. The plan was for me to move into a wing of my father's house until I was well enough to go home. The plan had been developed after extensive consultation between my parents. While the United Nations hadn't appointed a diplomatic envoy to broker the negotiations, it could have. I'd spent many hours in the company of my aunts and Kebi Merit over my last week at Dar Al Fouad Hospital. During these hours, my parents had sat in the little cafeteria downstairs and eaten the cafeteria food, which was uniformly terrible (all hospitals worldwide must contract with the same lousy catering firm). They sat there and ate and drank tea and argued.

I can't speculate too much on that time, because no one has ever described it to me, unlike the time that I was unconscious, which has been mythologized by both my father and my mother, separately, as the time of their own truest heroism—and possibly, only possibly, a time of decent behavior by their former spouse. But I do know this: My mother was grateful for my father's steady presence over that terrible first week. She was grateful for the hours he spent on the cot, running the rosary beads through his fingers, translating and double-checking every medicine that arrived. She was embarrassed that she'd driven him away from the room; she felt like she'd done him a disservice that he'd only partly deserved.

This is why, upon my discharge, she made the most unusual request I could've imagined.

But more on that in a second.

On that last morning, my mother stepped out for a few hours. She'd rented a room at a bed-and-breakfast near the hospital, and she would go back there during the days to take a shower and do her laundry. Day seventeen was no exception. "I want to look good in the discharge photographs," she told me. "Maybe I'll get my hair done in an alley somewhere." She meant in one of the many alleyway hairdressers that filled the city of Cairo, though somehow it sounded wrong.

The rest of the family had retreated to the compound at Talaat Harb. They were preparing a room for me. There was a bit of argument about where the room would be, however.

"He will sleep in the room on our hallway," Banafrit said. "We have the higher ceilings."

"He will sleep in the room on our hallway," Fatima said. "We have the newer bed."

"There are no roaches in the room on my hallway," my father said. "I had them poisoned last month."

"Roaches, no roaches," Banafrit said. "You decide."

"Yes, yes," Fatima said. "You decide."

I waited for my paperwork to come through. Without my father there to streamline things, it had reverted to the usual speed at which paperwork moves, which is slightly above the speed at which moss grows but slightly below the speed of, say, a tree sloth.

For the first time since I'd been in the hospital, the phone rang. It took me a moment to locate it. It was about ten feet from the bed. I looked at the ringing phone, feeling the residue of the illness in my legs, too weak to get up and walk across to answer. It rang again. It rang and rang and wouldn't stop ringing.

I gave in. I answered in Arabic. The voice on the other end responded in English. "Khosi? Hello? Is that you? Can you hear me?"

"Natasha," I said.

"Yes!" Natasha said. Her elation at hearing my voice was unmistakable. "I'm in Montana. But—I mean—you know that. How are you? I mean, are you okay?"

"I have to admit," I said, "I've been better."

"Oh, sweetie," she said. It was strangely intoxicating to hear her voice. She sounded immediate and clear and familiar. After the hospital and the new extended family and the impending, roach-free stay in the heart of the heart of Cairo, I was longing for just this thing: a reminder of the hills of Montana, which I could close my eyes and imagine, which filled me with nostalgia. City as heart. People as the blood, as platelets, moving life from the center to the peripheries. But more important than that, Natasha, my lovely Natasha, my own Natasha, mine.

"You know," I said, "you'll never believe what I'm looking at."

"The pyramids?" she said.

"That *would* be spectacular," I said. "No, it's not the pyramids."

"The Sphinx?"

"No," I said. "It's not any kind of Egyptian antiquity at all."

"Then I give up," she said. "Jesus, the line is so clear. It's like you're here with me."

I cradled the phone in the curve of my shoulder. "You didn't guess what I'm looking at," I said. "It's an unmade bed. *My* hospital bed. And I just got out of it. And I didn't even tuck the covers in."

"You're joking," Natasha said without missing a beat.

"No," I said. "The covers are completely disorganized. I can even see the sheet. And the wrinkles. You wouldn't believe the wrinkles."

"Wrinkles!" Natasha marveled. "Maybe you should straighten it a little."

"No," I said. "Absolutely not. I will straighten nothing. Nothing at all. My bed is unmade. My bed is unmade and I'm fine with it."

She laughed. "You're a maniac," she said.

And so we talked. And it was the old familiarity, the tenderness, that had disappeared from my life, the thing among other things that I'd left behind in Montana. Outside my window, the eaves of the nearby apartment buildings sloped into each other. A few crows moved from rooftop to rooftop, floating through the air with an obsidian ease, a dark and scruffy beauty.

"Sounds like you've got something going over there, then," Natasha said.

"Now that my bed's unmade, maybe I'll start that treasure-diving business. Maybe I'll just hit the open road. Mali, Burkina Faso, Lesotho. After yellow fever, what else could possibly go wrong?"

"Yes," she said, "your luck is spectacular."

"Or maybe I'll find the exact opposite point on the globe—you know, halfway around the world from Butte. I could open a Berkeley Pit Yacht Club there."

"The pioneer spirit really is in you," Natasha said. "You know, I mailed you something today."

"I'm leaving the hospital," I said.

"I sent it to your dad's house. He gave me the address." She paused. "It's a jar of dirt from the parking lot of that very Yacht Club."

I laughed. "Good thing you didn't mail it to the ICU. I don't know if it would have been allowed past the nurses' station."

"Aren't you going to ask me why I mailed it?"

"Why did you mail it, Natasha?"

"So you don't forget Butte. There's so much waiting for you here."

"Like a jar of dirt?" I said.

"That, too," she said.

"There's very little left for me in Butte," I said.

"Your family."

"There's my mom and Wada," I said. "That's all."

"It's your city," Natasha said. "You inhabit the city more than anyone else I know."

"We inhabited it together," I said.

"Oh, Khosi," she said, "I wish I could see you. I'm not sorry for what happened."

"There must have been complications," I said.

She laughed. "You can't even imagine."

"I'm sure I can't," I said. "I guess I'm not sorry, either. I've been in love with you for a very long time, and that's just how it is." I waited a moment. "You know when all of this matters? When we're sitting in the car and driving eighty-five down the highway and listening to Al Hopkins's Original Hill Billies. But now, over a transcontinental phone line . . ." I trailed off. "Goddammit."

"God bless it," she corrected me.

Natasha laughed, a small soft low laugh, and I loved the sound of it, that soft laugh. I could have listened to it ceaselessly, in perpetuity, with no other sound, nothing besides its certain and precise music. She was there, on the line, and I was happy with that. She'd mailed me a jar of dirt. For now, anyway, that would have to be enough.

I recently read about a company that produces albums of ambient noise. They go to highways and parks and downtown city streets and record the sounds of life as it's being lived. They also do interior spaces: the office, the home, and surprisingly, the hospital. One particular album contains over an hour of sounds from an ICU: intercom pages, the distinctive sound of mechanical breathing machines, the susurration of fluorescent overhead lighting, rubber-soled footsteps moving near and far, near and far. After I talked with Natasha,

I closed my eyes and listened to the noises that I'd come to accept as a regular part of my life.

My mother returned in the late afternoon. She did indeed look composed and presentable, with a new haircut and a shirt that I didn't recognize. She edged her way into my room, flanked by yet another doctor in a white lab coat. I've always wondered why doctors wear the white coat. Why not some other color? Why not taupe or lilac or cerulean? My mother moved slowly toward me, holding me steadily in the center of her gaze. I almost felt transfixed.

"This is Dr. Mdesi," my mother said. "He has something he wants to discuss with us."

Dr. Mdesi was a straight-backed post of a man, a man with posture so perfect, he could have been the marshal of a parade. He had dense white hair and luminescent dark black skin. His English was accented with the cadence of sub-Saharan Africa. Perhaps he, too, had once been a stranger to this country, this city.

I nodded. "Okay. My schedule is wide open."

"Now, Khosi," he said, "I want you to know that we are liver specialists here at Dar Al Fouad."

"That's nice," I said, feeling the way the skin of my face was pulled taut against my cheekbones. "Do you serve it in the cafeteria as well?"

"I see that your sense of humor," the doctor said, "has survived the illness intact."

"He's always like this," my mother said. "It's a permanent condition."

"That's fine," Dr. Mdesi said, sitting on one of the chairs beside my bed. "However, I'm afraid I have something serious to discuss with you. It's about your most recent blood work."

These are never words that you want to hear a doctor say. Invariably, they don't tell you: "It's very serious. Seriously *awesome*, that is! Kick-ass numbers on the blood work, old chap. You're in great shape."

I must have blanched. I glanced over at my mother. She was as pale as the doctor's lab coat.

"There are some irregularities with your liver enzymes," Dr. Mdesi said. He listed a range of numbers, rattling off a dense vocabulary of terms that seemed oddly familiar. They'd discovered these irregularities, he told me, while doing routine tests related to the yellow fever. And then he asked me one somewhat disarming question. "Any hallucinations at all?" he said. "Seeing anything unusual that you can't explain? Any unusually strong feelings that manifest themselves in the world? A hallucination isn't always visual. That's a common misconception."

"No," I said. "No hallucinations."

"None at all?" he said.

"Nope," I said.

"Are you certain?" he said.

"Absolutely," I said. "Completely certain."

"Good," he said. "Otherwise, we'd be more concerned."

My mother was standing at my bedside and stroking my hair, pulling it out of my eyes, tucking it behind my ear. She was smiling down at me. It was a soft smile, a look of empathy, of empathetic understanding. "I'm not really here," she said.

"Very funny, Mom," I answered.

Then came the part that astonished me: Dr. Mdesi telling me that, given my family history and certain inherited propensities of the Egyptian people, it was fairly likely that I was a not yet fully symptomatic carrier of Wilson's disease.

"It's an autosomal recessive genetic disorder," he said, "caused by a mutation of the ATP7B gene."

"I know," I said, "exactly what it is. You've got to be joking. I've been tested."

"Although we're sequencing the genome," Dr. Mdesi said, "these things still aren't completely understood. They can have a rapid onset."

"It's going to be fine, darling," my mother said. "Think of it like I do: The world is just beginning to awake. It's beginning to awake, and here we are, awakening with it. Besides, I've got you covered. I brought extra pills."

She had brought me a single dose of her medication: four small brightly colored pills, pills the size of aspirin. Dr. Mdesi nodded, and she put them on the bedside table. I stared down at them. They looked like the eggs of some exotic hummingbird, nestled in a little paper cup.

"Officially," the doctor said, "I never saw this happen."

That was that. Dr. Mdesi told me that they'd like to see me on an outpatient basis while I remained in Egypt. My liver enzymes were elevated, but nothing was indicative—yet—of a full-scale, systemic collapse. That, I suppose, was the good news. The doctor left with my mother, both of them exiting through the half-pulled drapes. I could hear the murmur of their conversation as it traveled down the hall. I picked up the container of medication. I took out a Cuprimine and let it rest on my palm.

And then I heard the sound of hooves. Hooves and the neighing of a horse, disembodied and floating just outside the window. I turned toward the sound, and there he was, striding resolutely through the glass: the Ghost of William Andrews Clark. He tripped over the trash can.

"How can a ghost be clumsy?" I said.

"Khosi, my friend," he said, "you live to a hundred and sixty-six, then tell me how graceful you feel."

"Odds are against one-sixty-six," I said, raising the cup of pills.

He frowned. "Cuprimine," he said. "Cyprine. Zinc acetate. Ah, I know them well." He shifted his weight from one boot to the other. "Well, damn," he said. "I guess you'll be just fine without me, though. Yes, sir. You ain't no acorn calf."

"Acorn calf?" I said.

"Greenhorn, newbie, angel-foot, soft-hide, milkmaid, Mississippi gunboat."

"I get it," I said.

"Just offering some synonyms," he said. "You're a good egg. You'll be just fine without me."

"I guess this is goodbye, then," I said.

He reached out and ruffled my hair. His touch was soft, like you'd imagine the touch of a ghost, almost like a breath of air from some distant open doorway.

"You know," said the Ghost of William Andrews Clark, "there's nothin' funnier than a giraffe in a bow tie."

"That's not comprehensible," I said.

"I'm just happy that you're pulling through. You've got a lot to do here. I was worried about you, hoss. You're not exactly the most adaptable fellow in the entire United States of America."

"I'm not in the United States of America," I said.

"I was worried you'd have a total psychological breakdown," he continued. "You're fragile, Khosi. But you're also stubborn as hell."

"That stubbornness," I said, "is a good thing."

"It is," said the Ghost of William Andrews Clark, "and it isn't."

There was talk in the hallway of a dust storm. I overheard the scrap of conversation, the Arabic words floating back to me, and I imagined how the city might look in a haze of pulverized sand. The dust would mix evenly with the air, an emulsion. It would slip into the house, despite every door being shut, and layer over everything in a sticky covering. The hospital would have to take a series of measures to cope. I drifted into this thought, and the Ghost of William Andrews Clark drifted with me. He became a dusty wind, rising up off the surface of the desert.

"Whoa, there," he said, snapping back into focus. "You're not getting off the hook that easily. I don't know if you can tell, but pretty much everyone spends their days worrying about you."

"That can't be true," I said.

"Of course they do. You're wildly compulsive, son. You don't act right. You know that, though. You know it, and you're going to fix it."

"I give myself three-to-one odds," I said. "At best."

"You'll do fine," he said. "First of all, you stop these here hallucinations."

"I'll miss you," I said. I heard footsteps coming down the hall.

"I hitched Nugget out front," said the Ghost of William Andrews Clark. "I hope she doesn't get a ticket."

"Can they ticket a ghost horse?" I said.

He was already starting to fade away.

"Wait," I said. "Is there anything else? Anything, you know, from the Great Beyond?"

"Shucks, cowpoke," he said as he flickered and diminished into the dust of a thousand lonesome prairies. "If you feel like dancin', there ain't no need for an orchestra."

And then he disappeared.

Ten

IF YOU'RE A FOREIGN TOURIST and you happen to be in a hotel—the Mena Park, for example, or the Fairmont Nile, or even the Cairo Kewayis Marriott—and you see a wedding, ask for an invitation. You won't be turned down. Why would you be? There's food to be eaten, after all, and the band will play as long as anyone is left standing. Heaven, for an Egyptian family, is an endless marriage party. It staggers with the rhythm of the *zaffa*—the ceremonial procession—with its irresistible and hypnotic beat. How can we hope to understand love, as human beings? How can we measure the iridescent, obdurate truth, the fact that we're powerless before love's compulsions in the same way that we're powerless before the mop of the dark sky with its lashes of stars? How? With the help of Taheya Karioka, the famous Cairene belly dancer, and Um Khaltoum, singing a soft melody in her smoky operatic alto.

I am describing not only Egyptian weddings but one particular Egyptian wedding: the Egyptian wedding of my father, which happened on Sunday, September 7, 2008, just as he'd said it would. This was quite the surprise. It had taken quite a bit of apologetic maneuvering on my father's part. An even larger surprise was what my mother offered to do: the conversation that we had on the day I was released from the hospital. We were sitting together—momentarily alone together—in the kitchen at Talaat Harb, drinking cups of sweetened mint tea.

"Khosi," she said. "I have something I want to run by you before I bring it out into the world at large."

My mom floated a proposition. How would I feel, she wondered, if she offered to cook the entire wedding meal for my father and his new wife and all of the assembled wedding guests?

"I think it's a mistake," I said.

She frowned. The kitchen counter behind her, I noticed, was chipped along its rim. The tiles looked dilapidated but somehow austere. They'd worn down to a patchwork of interlaced white and yellow.

"I don't know, Mom. I do, however," and here I lifted my small glass cup, "love mint tea."

My mother shook her head. "You know," she said, "your father battled an addiction for many years."

"Come on," I said. "You can't possibly believe that. That's nonsense. He was selfish; he might still be selfish. Who knows if people can change."

"It's not nonsense," she said. "And you didn't see him at the hospital. He slept next to you for almost two weeks. If I didn't see it before, I see it now: He regrets his mistakes. I don't forgive them. But he knows they were mistakes."

"He wouldn't admit that directly," I said.

"Of course not," my mother said. She looked down into the steam from her tea. She let the steam rise up and wrap around her. "But we've been talking for days. It's all a process of negotiation."

I shook my head. Over the hum of the air conditioner, I heard the sound of the afternoon call to prayer. "I don't know," I said.

"It's probably not a good idea," my mother said quickly. "Not at all. But you know: The beauty of life is that it's yours." She cleared her throat. "And besides," she went on quietly, "this might help me deal with the part of myself that's still in love with him." She paused. "His sisters have also promised to give me all of their recipes. So it's a win-win proposition, really." When I didn't say anything more, she added, "I wish I could explain it to you. I really do."

The days passed and turned into weeks, and then it was the day of the wedding. The only objection to my mother's gesture was raised by Kebi Merit, who felt that all ex-wives wanted to murder their husbands. She felt that it was an American tradition. "I have seen the stories about it on the television program *Dynasty*," she said, and there was no amount of dissuading that would do the trick.

I was still a bit of a wreck. My arms felt leaden. They rested in my lap as I sat at the table in the kitchen and watched my mother guide the preparations. She was at the center of a foreign city that was at the center of a foreign country and a foreign culture. I thought of the hub of a wheel, which stays stationary even as the exterior turns. Even under these circumstances, she was undoubtedly the hub. She directed a fleet of vegetable choppers and lamb mincers and general, all-purpose amateur sous chefs. I remembered a damp, quiet intimacy to early mornings in the kitchens of my childhood; this was a dry, frantic, loud intimacy. An intimacy with a lot of shouting in Arabic.

At ten o'clock, my mother stepped out for an hour. When she returned, she strode dramatically into the kitchen. *Strode* was the only verb to describe the way she walked. She bore a big wicker basket in each hand. Each basket had a blanket tucked over it. The blankets were soft, fuzzy wool. She placed them in the center of the table, just a few feet from me.

"I went to the *khan*," she said, a note of triumph in her voice. "It really wasn't as hard as I'd imagined."

I translated this into Arabic for Kebi Merit.

"Was it a good price?" Kebi Merit said. I translated this. She scowled suspiciously at my mother. "Let's see them, you clever American hussy." This, I didn't translate.

My mother pulled off the blankets and revealed the contents of the baskets: pigeons. At least a hundred dead, feathery pigeons, arranged carefully in the blankets, lying atop one another, tucked under one another's wings, almost as if they were asleep. Except for the eyes. Many of their eyes were open and fixed and unblinking. They looked like the eyes of dolls. *Hamam mahshy:* Arguably the national dish of Egypt, a staple of many Egyptian weddings.

"They look," I said, "delicious."

"They're perfect," Banafrit said, offering my mother a chair.

"They're too small," Fatima said.

"She's going to poison us," Kebi Merit said, turning away and attending to a boiling pot on the stove. "The American hussy is trying to kill Akram. She bought poisoned birds for us at the market."

"What's she saying?" my mother asked me.

"She's saying that you did a great job," I said. "She's saying how much she's looking forward to cooking with you."

This dish was the centerpiece of the wedding feast. The pigeons were the important part of the meal, obviously, and they needed to be bought fresh on the day of the ceremony. There was an elaborate mythology behind the dish, one that my mother said dated back thousands of years. "The pigeon is a noble bird," my mom said as she covered up the baskets once again and the other women returned to cooking.

"It's not just a flying rat?" I said.

She frowned. "Its nobility is in its normalcy." She'd made *hamam mahshy* for me several times, but always with Cornish game hens. "You will find pigeons in every city in every country," she said. "They have a subtle flavor. Now let's pluck them clean."

"Mom," I said. "You don't have to do this. Just because he acts selflessly when I'm sick doesn't mean that you have to do him this favor."

"Who says it's a favor," she said.

"So you *are* going to poison him," I said.

"Don't be ridiculous," my mother said. But she looked warily over at my father's sisters and Kebi Merit. I knew that Banafrit, at least, spoke good English. If they were listening to our conversation, they gave no indication of it.

"I'm just thankful," my mother said, "that you have recovered. And I owe that to him, I think. Besides, I want to prove to him—and to them—that I am quite simply the best cook in the world."

Kebi Merit chose that moment to drop the lid of a pot. It hit the ground hard and spun in broad circles. "Sorry," she muttered in Arabic.

We sat down and started plucking the pigeons. The first time I did this with my mother, when I was twelve years old, I threw up in the bathroom. I locked myself in and refused to come out for hours, I was so disgusted and depressed. I didn't eat meat for months. Modern American meat comes packaged and sanitized in the supermarket. It is a flavor and a texture, nothing more. There's no sense that it was once a living creature, that it had small, creaturely dreams and enjoyed small, creaturely pleasures. Plucking a newly slaughtered bird is a different experience entirely. You get a sense that you are eating a life.

These pigeons were the real deal: They were still warm. Fatima got a huge kettle of water boiling on the stove, and we scalded each of the birds enough to loosen the feathers a bit. Then we started plucking, pulling downward with a smooth, consistent rhythm, pulling out the feathers in big handfuls. These poor birds—birds that had only recently been able to fly, to soar above the ground on their expansive, hollow-boned wings. Plucking them was nothing compared to dressing them. The pigeons were small, so it was less gruesome than dressing a chicken. I will say as little as possible about this process. Well, I'll say a bit: draining the blood, splitting the chest cavity open like a bypass surgery, cutting through the anus with a fresh knife, and removing the intestines.

I'd never been so conscious of my body as a physical thing, as something that could fail, the way a bridge fails, or a levee fails, or an

electrical circuit ceases to bear current. I was fallible. A single mosquito bite and I'd nearly been reduced to nothingness. I watched my
mother slicing into the chest cavity of a pigeon.

"Don't forget to reserve the giblets," she said.

"You're not really going to poison them, right?" I said when we
were halfway done with the pigeons. "You know that's just not an
option."

"Poison them?" my mother said. "Khosi, are you feeling okay?"
A sardonic smile haunted the margins of her lips. "You don't have a
fever, but have you taken all your pills today, darling?"

I had. The rainbow of pills that was now my inheritance. It had
crept beneath the surface of my skin, in my blood, its seeds more
prolific than an Egyptian walking onion. I had a long future of
weekly pill containers, of maintenance visits to the family doctor.
This was, I had to admit, depressing. There was a time when I would
have been overwhelmed by the news Dr. Mdesi had given me. Now
I was able to face it, like I could survive it, for sure. It was just a
fact—a medical fact. A fact like my mother's illness was a fact. A fact
like the population of Idaho (1,432,860 souls, circa 2008) was a fact.

All five of us were sitting at that big wooden table, preparing the
birds for their long, slow braise. Banafrit and Fatima were quiet and
reserved.

"It *is* a rare and blessed moment, I will admit," Kebi Merit said,
gesturing with a pigeon in her hand, "when you two aren't arguing."

The wedding started surprisingly early. People had been showing
up all day. Some of them were there to help set things up, to arrange

furniture and set up the stage for the band. In the ballroom there were some definite preparations occurring. The men, for example, were drinking heavily. They had great decanters of red wine, ornate crystal decanters that they'd filled with Syrian cabernet. All of the immediate family—that is to say, more than thirty cousins—appeared to be in attendance. It was a relief to circulate among these men and women and be essentially anonymous, overhearing pieces of Arabic dialogue, speculation about my father's reformation and his little-known but wealthy wife.

My mother had finished trussing the pigeons. I could taste them already, the sweet hazelnut flavor of the meat, the buttery texture of the wheat mixing with the acrid taste of the giblets. It was among my favorite meals that she cooked, and I was surprised that she was doing it now—and sharing the recipe with near strangers. I watched my mother constantly adjust her graying hair, tuck strands of it behind her ears as she cooked. There was the *hamam mahshy* and the *tabilch* and the *koftit roz* and the parsleyed eggs and the *koshary* and the eggplant salad. "We'll just do a simple meal," my mother had said. "Just a couple of things, a few small dishes." This didn't consider the pita bread, towers of pita bread, all of it baking in small loaves on the stone at the bottom of the main oven.

I passed out some appetizers: wedges of Christian-Muslim Co-operation Baklava, grape leaves wrapped around garlic-studded lamb and rice, spicy meat pies. I caught a few people staring at me, clearly wondering who I was: caterer? cousin? cousin who was also a caterer? Someone had a deck of cards. Someone had a laptop. By noon, people were drunk and playing pinochle and backgammon and listening to clips of Fairuz on YouTube. The dial-up connection made the wait for the download excruciating, in my opinion, but people seemed not to mind.

Kebi Merit kept a running speculation on when the first guests would start to die from the poison. "You've used something slow, I see," she said. "An American poison, I'm sure."

"What's she saying?" my mom asked me.

"She thinks your hummus is the best she's ever tasted," I said.

"I can't believe that Akram would make such a terrible error in judgment," Kebi Merit added.

"And now?" my mother asked.

"She loves the subtlety of the flavors," I said. "The way the tahini interacts with the garlic."

"Thank her," my mother said. "She's such a nice old lady."

Before the Mouris arrived, I slipped away from the commotion and went up onto the roof, which was a maze of satellite dishes. The smoggy Cairo skyline was a mix of fading sun and newly illuminated electrical lights. Big buildings sprawled outward from this point. It was hard to imagine any place in the world that wasn't part of the city. Everything felt proprietary. It felt like it was mine. Airliners banked in from the north, turning like low-skimming gulls, floating in over the continent of Africa, gliding in off the Mediterranean, heading for the distant airport. I looked at the planes and I fastened a space for myself in the Egyptian capital. To this day, the city of Cairo is the city that I call home. I have Natasha's jar of soil on the bookshelf beside my bed, next to the *Keep ridin!* Evel Knievel bookmark. These objects are the relics of my patron saint. Every night I look at the ground I left behind, the ground through which I tunneled to reach the other side of the earth. It's how I learned that inhabiting a place doesn't require being in that place, necessarily. It lives in you long after you leave it.

On the day of the wedding, the bride's family arrived in fine formal clothes, clothes that looked suspiciously like they'd been rented at a tuxedo shop in a suburban American mall. More specifically, a suburban American mall in 1994. Teal featured prominently in the cummerbunds. Nearly every dress was ornamented with lace. The bride herself, Agnes Mouri, wore an elaborately ornamented white dress. She crossed the threshold of the house holding a clutch of laurel branches.

It had been quite the process of negotiation for my father—even getting back into Agnes Mouri's house. After his initial passel of lies, the truth proved even more problematic, which was, I suppose, the fate of liars everywhere. I had no part in the talks, though I was dispatched to the Mouri household once with an overflowing platter of falafel, a special peace envoy sent with alacrity in the moment of crisis.

On the day of the wedding, as soon as she saw me, Agnes Mouri took me by the arm and led me to one side of the room. The other guests were staring at us. She looked at me seriously with her luminescent yellow-brown eyes—and then she wrapped me in her arms.

"My son," she said, laughing.

"You're suffocating me," I said.

"We will start over from today," she said.

"No," I said.

Agnes Mouri frowned. "That surprises me," she said.

"I'm worried that even with my dad's rehabilitation, you're in over your head."

"I'm sorry?" she said. "Over my head?"

"It's an English idiomatic expression," I said, "meaning that you're in great danger."

"No," she said. "I know what I'm doing. I'm getting exactly what I hoped for."

"A recovering addict," I said.

"Sure," she said. "But I've got my own past, too, *habibi*."

"It couldn't be as"—I paused here, searching for the right word—"checkered as my father's."

"No, you're probably right," Agnes Mouri said. "Look at it this way: If we have children, they will learn about family and love and forgiveness from the voice of experience."

"That seems a little extreme," I said. "It seems like a strange experimentation."

"Not at all," she said. "Think about this: What if I gave the bracelet to your father in the first place and orchestrated this entire performance."

"That *would* be impressive," I said.

"I'm an impressive woman," Agnes Mouri said.

"Wait a minute," I said. "Did you give it to my dad?"

"Of course not," she said.

She winked. At least I think it was a wink. It could have been an involuntary twitch. Maybe there was something in her eye.

"Come on," I said. "No way."

"*Mishmumkin?*" she said. "Impossible?"

"*Mishmumkin*," I said. "Impossible."

My concerns were not entirely allayed. "I keep imagining that you'll wake up, one day in three years," I said, "and you'll discover that Akram isn't actually Egyptian. He's from Mongolia. And he has fled for Ulan Bator, where he plans to retire, and in his old, old age, marry a young heiress."

Agnes Mouri laughed. She leaned in and glanced over her shoulder at the other guests in the room. "I've heard," she whispered into my ear, "that the weather is nice in Mongolia this time of year." She smiled.

Before we could say anything else, Aunt Banafrit and Aunt Fatima grabbed her—each holding an arm—and took her deeper into the apartment. I hoped they wouldn't split her like a wishbone.

There was a Coptic priest. He arrived in a hat that was at least two feet tall; it bobbed above him like the bier in a New Orleans funeral. But this was not a New Orleans funeral. This was an Egyptian wedding. There was the processional, the drumming, the exchange of vows, the dancing, the music, the food, all of it happening in the apartment, on the balcony, the balcony so big you could roller-skate on it. The Mouri family was welcoming, hospitable, warm. If they cared anymore that my father's ex-wife and son were at the wedding, they didn't show it.

All throughout the festivities, my father was a small presence. He seemed to fold into himself, to intentionally lessen himself until he was practically not there. I lost track of him again and again, despite the fact that he was the groom, and always it was while he was doing unassuming things. He was standing at the long wooden table and ladling *baba ghannouj* onto a plate; he was having a quiet conversation with Fatima's husband; he was replacing a candle in the antique silver candelabra in the hallway. Each time I looked away for a moment and then looked back, and he was gone.

At one point, I ducked into the garden behind the house, trying to find a place that might be free of people. The fountain bubbled. The mango trees were tall and leafy, offering their arboreal canopy to a hastily arranged series of benches. I sat down. All around me, vines grew from the branches, dropping to the ground by the dozens, long and bright green.

"Watch for snakes," said someone from the space behind me. "Be careful." I recognized my father's voice.

"Great," I said without turning around. "The trees have snakes. Just perfect."

He stood in front of me. "They hang from the branches and look just like the ivy," he said. "Once I reached to grab a vine, and it had teeth."

"Poisonous snakes?" I said. I flinched and drew back against the bench.

"Sure," he said. "Some. But mostly not." He reached into his shirt pocket, producing the gold and red box of cigarettes. "Dunhill?"

"You really are a walking advertisement, aren't you?" I said.

"For," he said, squinting down at the print on the side of the box, "the British American Tobacco Company?"

"Yes," I said. "I'm surprised you aren't under contract."

"You see," he said, "you're an advertisement for the brand for years, and then you die a horrific, suffocating death."

"Are you concerned at all," I said, "about that horrific, suffocating death?"

"I'll worry about it when I'm fifty," he said.

"Which happened, by my calculations, in 2006."

"Yes," he said, and sat down beside me. "That was a tough year." My father sighed deeply. He rubbed his forehead. He looked tired.

"So," I said. "You're a thief."

My father frowned. "Oh, Khosi, what does it matter? That's in the past. Agnes and I have come to an understanding."

"And what is that, exactly?"

"I understand that if I ever lie to her again," he said, "she will throw me out immediately."

"That's so romantic," I said.

My father smiled wistfully. "It doesn't really matter, does it?" he said. "A last chance is a last chance." He brushed his thick gray hair back from his forehead. "I'll take whatever I can get."

I shook my head and sighed. I reached up and grabbed one of the lowest-hanging branches from the tree. If it had been a snake, it would have been fitting, somehow. Recover from yellow fever but die of a poisonous snake bite. My hand came away with leaves. My father nodded. We sat there for a moment longer in silence.

"You know," I said, "Agnes said a funny thing when she first arrived. She made a joke about having orchestrated everything—a joke about giving the bracelet to you intentionally to bring to Butte and hide in the trash."

"She said that?"

"She did."

"Interesting," my father said.

"And?" I said.

"And what?" he said.

"It's not true, is it?" I said.

"Of course not," he said. Then he looked at me, and he winked, too. "I should really go back inside."

We made our way back through the crowded hallway, past the family tree that, in the past five weeks, had been amended with my name and the name of my mother. People smiled at my father and waved to him and tried to get him out onto the dance floor, which was a confusion of tempos and ages and styles of dress. Agnes was no-where to be seen, and my father seemed content to follow me into the kitchen, where my mother was winding down her stewardship of the meal. She'd stayed in here, not surprisingly, through the ceremony.

I marveled at how composed she looked, even as the dirty dishes built a delirious disorder around her. She stood at the stove with a dish towel flung over her shoulder. Her long, worn wooden spoon had made its way to Egypt as well. I had a momentary flash of wonder. How much of this had *she* been planning from the start?

"Khosi," my mother said. "Have you eaten? Can I make you some-thing small?"

"I'm fine, Mom," I said. "But thanks for asking."

"Thank God," she said. "Because I don't think I could feed another person."

She saw my father. She stiffened slightly, as if poised on the edge of some kind of precipice, her body taut, beads of sweat standing out on her forehead and her upper lip.

My father came over and stood across the kitchen counter from her. "Everything is delicious," he said.

"Thank you," she said. She laughed. "I am utterly exhausted."

"This is a huge effort," he said. "A monumental labor."

"Like Hercules," my mother said.

"Maybe a little more, even," he said.

If, ever in the history of pauses, there was an awkward pause, this was it. A cruel, awkward pause, a slaughtering pause, the kind of pause that physically hurts when you experience it.

"Well," I said, clearing my throat. "I've been cooking, too."

"You have?" my mother said. "When?"

"Late last night," I said. "And I've taken care of dessert."

"Really?" my father said, glancing over at my mother. "Enough for everyone?"

"Absolutely." I walked over to the big refrigerator. I took out the tray I'd placed on the bottom shelf at five the previous morning. "For dessert," I said. I looked at my mother and my father, at the family that had been so dysfunctional and fragmented and frustrating for my entire childhood, at the family that had, for the first time, come together only to be immediately and irrevocably split apart. "For dessert, I have something really special."

"What is it?" my mother asked.

"Is it a cake?" my father said.

"It's not a cake," I said, placing the tray in the center of the kitchen counter. "It's a crème brûlée. A very special crème brûlée." I pulled back the foil, revealing a hundred ramekins arranged in tidy rows.

"I love crème brûlée," my father said.

"Me, too," my mother said. "I'm so hungry, I just might eat three."

I nodded. "It has a secret ingredient," I said. "One that's especially popular in Paris."

"Let me guess," my mother said. "Cardamom pods?"

"Not exactly," I said.

"Cloves?" my father said.

"Wrong again," I said.

"Maple syrup?" my mother said. "Sometimes I put a touch of maple syrup in my crème brûlée, just to give it a little zest."

"Does Egypt have a lot of maple trees?" I said.

"Khosi's being mysterious," my father said. "We're clearly just going to have to taste it and see."

That's what he did. And so did the rest of the wedding party.

It's funny, but I haven't mentioned Evel Knievel's greatest failure—his most spectacular and catastrophic accident, one that was broadcast live to much of the world. On May 26, 1975, millions of people watched him jump a row of double-decker buses at Wembley Stadium in London. Imagine that spectacle: Knievel rocketed down the ramp at ninety miles per hour, clutching the handlebars with his leather gloves, his red, white, and blue starred jumpsuit almost blurry because of the speed. The ramp disappeared. The motorcycle rose into the air, its arc surprisingly small, its front wheel flaring and reaching for safety.

When it landed, it was inches short. The footage showed the motorcycle catching the edge of the landing pad instead of its flat surface and then bucking him up in the air like a maddened rodeo bull. "Oh my God," the announcer said, too shocked to think of anything else as he watched Knievel's body tumble, along with the Harley, through the dusty and suddenly silent stadium.

The amazing thing is this: Watch the slow-motion video from ABC's *Wide World of Sports*, and you can see that he almost made it—he almost held on despite everything, despite being perpendicular to the bike, despite his wrist breaking in half, despite the initial impact shattering his pelvis. He kept the handlebars straight. For one second, for one fragment of a second, he almost brought himself back down on the seat. But then he lost control of the throttle, and the motorcycle decelerated; that's what finally threw him to the ground.

After the accident, Evel Knievel dusted himself off. He stood up. The audience roared. Two of his trainers came to his side and walked him back up the ramp to a spot where he could see nearly everybody in the crowd. Inside Wembley Stadium, it was pandemonium; stomping feet shook the steel beams of the facility. The motorcycle lay on the ground a hundred feet away, discarded and smoking, its front wheel still spinning, turning in a gradual Ferris-wheel way. Smoke draped the air, silvery and funereal. And then Evel Knievel did something unusual. Holding the microphone in his one shaky, unbroken hand, he promised the crowd that he'd never jump again.

Did he do it? Did he keep his promise? It seemed like an unscripted moment, the manifestation of a feeling he had, of some deep interior turmoil about the role he played in the world. I think sometimes about those seconds—those airborne seconds, plunging through the air with the metal frame of the motorcycle, the engine useless, the body isolated and alone, transitory, weightless. Light everywhere, flashbulbs bursting from the bleachers, and he's done it, he's committed to the jump. It's unclear if he'll make it. And there it is, the elemental, feathering darkness, small and faint at first but then building and roaring and reaching out to consume him. I wonder something, something I'll never know.

Did he close his eyes?

Epilogue

Mammoth, grand, in flight, this fat
jetliner cruising its route. Eternity
of stars above, dark ocean below.
My teacher said, "The heavens above my head,
the earth below my feet, and I am here."
I am here. Rattle of ice in a plastic cup.
Lights dim for a newscast. People
have turned to each other to talk
of jobs, and family, and prospects, and sights.
All the shades are drawn.
A third of the earth passes by.
Voices are a strange
music; I cannot read billboards—
the hints are gone. Weeks tumble by.
Sunlight falls at a different angle.
The heavens above my head.
I do not know my way.
The earth below my feet.
In crowds, I am the other one.
And I am here.

—Stephen Toutonghi, "A New Country"

I remember the day the Berlin Wall came down in 1989. I was four years old. My mother and I watched the *NBC Nightly News* with Tom Brokaw on our thirteen-inch Sony Trinitron. Mom loved Tom Brokaw. "I'd cook his steak any way he likes it," she said to me, somewhat inappropriately. At the time I just wondered how she knew that he even wanted steak. "They all want steak," my mother said. "Trust me. You'll understand when you get older." We were sitting on the couch in the Loving Shambles, drinking hot chocolate.

"A historic moment tonight," Brokaw said, "as the Berlin Wall can no longer contain the East German people." Later that night, putting me to bed, my mother cried as she sang me a lullaby, and I remember wondering why she was crying, wondering if they were going to tear down walls in Butte as well.

"It's a different kind of wall, darling," she said to me. "There aren't walls like that over here."

Is that true? I wonder now. I had to travel all the way around the world to understand that those walls are everywhere—it's just rare that they get built in a physical form. And so in February 2011—when I camped for eighteen days in Liberation Square, in Midan Tahrir—I remembered that night, twenty-two years earlier, and our tiny television and the darkened living room a few thousand meters from the Berkeley Pit.

It had been only two decades. But in 1989 Brokaw was the only news anchor in place at the moment of crisis. Even West German news channels took hours to get their reporters to the scene. Now, in 2011, in Tahrir Square, some of us followed CNN's coverage of the protests on our smartphones. We watched Anderson Cooper film us watching Anderson Cooper film us watching Anderson Cooper film us, receding endlessly into the mirrored dark.

I can't describe those eighteen days, not really. I was shot with a rubber bullet; it left a bright lilac-colored welt on my calf, a welt that slowly became a bruise and then even more slowly disappeared. When the camels rode through the square, they nearly flattened my tent, which, after all, was nothing more than a plastic tarp thrown over a guide wire. I stood in front of the Egyptian Museum with a golf club; I slept wrapped in an Egyptian flag. My clothes were constantly dirty. I ate whatever I could find, whatever the street vendors happened to bring past the barricades. When Hosni Mubarak announced on February 10 that he would try to hold on to the presidency, I chanted, along with the rest of the crowd, "Leave! Leave! Leave!"

The protests changed everything. *Or did they really?* We don't actually know yet. There's a chance, a nagging fear, that they changed nothing at all. I do know this: I've always had a list of ten adjectives for Cairo, a list that I keep on a legal pad next to my bed. Now it reads: *flag-filled, bloody, desiccated, sweaty, petrol-scented, improvised, wired, cacophonous, hopeful, sung.*

Today I'm sitting at Cairo International Airport in the arrivals hall, waiting for a particular jet to touch down, Turkish Airlines Flight 328, a flight from Washington, D.C., to Istanbul to Egypt. I'm not sure how I will feel when I see Natasha for the first time in two and a half years, but I do know one thing: I'm going to kiss her and hold her close to me, hold her close, and I may not let go. She and Calvin have been apart for over a year now, a disentangling that began that night at Evel Knievel Days.

"Don't take too much credit for that, Khosi," Natasha said when she called to tell me she was coming, the day after Mubarak fell. "I've always said it was the American Motordrome Wall of Death that changed my life, not you."

I should say, just for the record, that the amount of hashish in the wedding reception crème brûlée was pretty minuscule. At most, the guests felt a slight buzz, a general hunger and an excited, slightly gauzy disorientation. Except, that is, in the two ramekins that I reserved for me and my mother. After everyone had gone to bed— at almost four in the morning—we took ours up onto the roof.

"You're sure I won't have a heart attack," she said.

"If you do, it's because of the heavy cream," I said, "not the hash."

We ate them. A delicate, creamy flavor, a burnt-sugar crust that dissolved on the tongue. We licked the containers clean. From that rooftop, the city argued its way into the distance, a haze of glitter— streetlamps and licorice-red brake lights and marauding taxi cabs. We leaned against the post of a big satellite dish. I could smell the Nile. Cairo was so different at night, from a rooftop. At night, copper wires brought out the structure of the grid. We sat there together, my mother and I, a little bit stoned, clothed in a diminishing dark- ness. We waited and listened to the muezzin, and then we watched as the sun rose and the sunlight erased it all.

Acknowledgments

I'd like to thank Kate Kennedy for her tireless, insightful, and patient attention to the manuscript. I also owe a significant debt to Shaye Areheart, who took a risk on a young novelist almost a decade ago, and to Skip Horack, whose comments proved tremendously useful during the revisions of *Evel Knievel Days*. My colleagues at Lewis and Clark College—in particular John Callahan and Rishona Zimring—provided support and advice throughout the four separate incarnations of this project, as did my agent, Renée Zuckerbrot. And of course, P.M.M., without whom the book could not have been written. Thank you.